W9-AFL-650

THE
REFUGEE
OCEAN

A NOVEL

PAULS TOUTONGHI

Simon & Schuster

NEW YORK   LONDON   SYDNEY
TORONTO   NEW DELHI

Simon & Schuster
1230 Avenue of the Americas
New York, NY 10020

This book is a work of fiction. Any references to historical events, real people, or real places are used fictitiously. Other names, characters, places, and events are products of the author's imagination, and any resemblance to actual events or places or persons, living or dead, is entirely coincidental.

Copyright © 2023 by P. Harijs Toutonghi

All rights reserved, including the right to reproduce this book or portions thereof in any form whatsoever. For information, address Simon & Schuster Subsidiary Rights Department, 1230 Avenue of the Americas, New York, NY 10020.

First Simon & Schuster hardcover edition November 2023

SIMON & SCHUSTER and colophon are registered trademarks of Simon & Schuster, Inc.

For information about special discounts for bulk purchases, please contact Simon & Schuster Special Sales at 1-866-506-1949 or business@simonandschuster.com.

The Simon & Schuster Speakers Bureau can bring authors to your live event. For more information or to book an event, contact the Simon & Schuster Speakers Bureau at 1-866-248-3049 or visit our website at www.simonspeakers.com.

Interior design by Paul Dippolito

Manufactured in the United States of America

1   3   5   7   9   10   8   6   4   2

Library of Congress Cataloging-in-Publication Data has been applied for.

ISBN 978-1-6680-0743-3
ISBN 978-1-6680-0745-7 (ebook)

For my cousin, Marguerite Toutoungi

MANIFEST OF IN-BOUND PASSENGERS (ALIENS)

MANIFEST NO. 24

Form approved, Budget Bureau No. 43-R019-2.

Form I-418
TREASURY DEPARTMENT
UNITED STATES CUSTOMS SERVICE

UNITED STATES DEPARTMENT OF JUSTICE
Immigration and Naturalization Service
(Rev. 1-6-48)

Class CABIN from BEIRUT JUNE 28, 19 48
(Port of embarkation)

on S. S. MARINE CARP arriving at port of NEW YORK JUL 13 1943, 19 48
(Name of vessel)

Line No.	Family Name—Given Name: Destination in United States	Age (Years)	Sex (F-M)	Married or Single	Travel Doc. No. Nationality	Number and Description of Pieces of Baggage	Head Tax Collected	This Column for Use of Master, Surgeon, and U.S. Officers
1	TOUTOUNGI, Marguerite				key 3(3) unld 7-27-48			0800-305678
	Adolfo Castillo				V 600137			1181253 EXEMPT
	Guanabacoa, Cuba	23	F	M	Syria			

Is there time left
for me to say to her
Good evening Mom
I'm back
with a bullet in my heart
and that's my pillow
I want to rest?

    —Ghassan Zaqtan, 1988
    (Trans. Fady Joudah)

O men and dogs
in times of grief
our rolling world
grows small

    —Kabir The Weaver,
    15th Century

THE
REFUGEE
OCEAN

PROLOGUE

Al-Qaterji District
Aleppo, Syria

April 2, 2014
Dawn

Naïm could smell the water before he opened his eyes. There was a bowl of it on the table next to his bed. It had a rich, loamy odor; the scent wrapped around him as he surfaced from sleep. He sat up and then drank slowly—filling his mouth and holding his throat closed, rinsing his aching gums and the parched skin of his tongue. Then a towel. He took a towel and dampened one corner of it and pressed it against his face.

He stood and collected his clothes. He wanted to drink everything in the bowl, but he didn't. The water was a luxury—and he wasn't sure how much his father had managed to bring home. His father had likely traveled to the suburbs, walking all night with the fifty-pound container on his back, slipping through a gauntlet of snipers, through the streets lined with homemade IEDs.

Naïm dressed quietly and looked at Omar, his younger brother, who was tangled up in the bedsheets. Omar had had nightmares last night. Naïm had heard him kicking and thrashing. A little bowl of water sat on Omar's nightstand, too, and Naïm saw his brother's eyes skating under their lids, moving back and forth, back and forth.

The apartment had always been small—one bedroom for the children, and one for the parents. A common room. A balcony with a sliding glass door. And one thick, orange-colored shag rug. Woven polypropylene. Bought at a bazaar in Iskenderun in 1985. Carried over the Turkish-Syrian border on a borrowed sidecar motorcycle. *In better days, khalas.* Better days, long ago—long before this day, these hours—which were its last.

Naïm walked into the main room and stooped to straighten his battery-powered Casio keyboard—which sat on the table in front of the sofa. His earphones lay beside it. And almost before he meant to, he'd flicked on the power switch and played a light sequence of notes, a little happy song for the morning. For the water in his bowl.

His mother, Fatima, looked around the door from the kitchen. "Your father's asleep," she whispered and held a finger to her lips.

"How much did he get?" Naïm said. But he kept his voice low. He hurried into the kitchen to see the container of water sitting at the foot of the sink. It was nearly full.

"I think he cut his foot," she said, "so he needs to rest."

Naïm's sister, Aysha—just nine months old—was whimpering again, squirming on their mother's lap, reaching for the plump date and the flatbread that was supposed to be Naïm's breakfast. There were only nine dates left. The last of the season—a steadily dwindling luxury.

Naïm picked up a knife and cut the date in half. He popped a bite into his mouth and began to dice the rest. "What are you doing?" his mother said. He passed the plate to Aysha. "No," Fatima said. "That's for you. You're growing, too." She tried to wrestle the plate out of the little girl's hands.

But Aysha was drooling, her eyes wide. These days, she only stopped crying when she was eating or sleeping; Naïm's mother said it was because she'd been born during the siege; Naïm knew it was because she was always hungry.

"Let her have it," he said. "Look at that face. It's like she's won a prize."

Naïm tried to imitate her, sticking his fingers in his mouth and spitting out a strand of saliva, widening his eyes.

"That's disgusting," his mother said. "Stop it." But she was smiling. She rocked her daughter back and forth. She made small soft noises close to the little girl's face. She kissed one of her cheeks and then the other, sequentially.

Outside, quite suddenly, there was the rattle of machine-gun fire—followed by the deeper boom of artillery. It wasn't close, but that could change. Naïm got up and approached the window from the side. He pulled back the curtain an inch and stared down the street. Besides the balcony, the kitchen had the best view and was safer.

"Al-Nuqtā?" his mother asked. The Shiʿa mosque was just to the west and had been a locus of fighting in recent days.

"Can't tell," Naïm said. He saw smoke in the distance. "I think it was farther than that."

They lived at 19 Tuhama Street, a five-story concrete structure near Masjid Al-Anwar Muhammadiyah. Apartment 3C. A single-level flat. Their neighborhood had swung back and forth between government and rebel control—between Assad's troops and the Free Syrian Army—in the first twenty months of this war. Fifty meters at a time. One doorway after another. The presence or absence of the pickup truck—a Toyota Hilux, painted in gray-and-green camouflage, with its rotating 12.7 mm belt-fed DShK—indicating who was in control.

"Is anyone else out?" his mother asked.

Naïm looked down at the sidewalks that ran along both sides of their street. "No," he said. "Empty."

"You should hang the laundry now, then," his mother said. "Before it gets worse." She pointed to the basket of wet clothes—which he knew she'd washed carefully, over and over, with the same small container of gray water, and a single bar of inexpensive, laurel leaf soap.

Of all the chores, Naïm disliked the laundry the most. To hang it, he had to climb the four stories to the roof, carrying the heavy basket. Then he had to return in a few hours, when the sun was hottest and everything had finally dried. It was, almost always, a daylong process.

"Can't I do it later?" he said.

"Later there are *other* things to do." But Aysha was fussing again, reaching for the bowl of dates. "Fine," his mother said, handing over the little girl. "I can hang it—if you bring it down."

The crying began less than five minutes after his mother left. Naïm grabbed his keyboard and the headphones and put them over Aysha's ears. He kept the volume low and he played a march—distracting her for a few minutes. But, ultimately, without her mother, Aysha was inconsolable. She shut her eyes and started to wail. She sounded like a siren.

"Quiet," Naïm said. He tried to make his voice gentle. "Quiet, quiet."

Her mouth was open as wide as it would go; he saw the indentations where her teeth were coming in—one on the top, two on the bottom. Tiny specks of bone, pushing through the gumline. He tried to rock her in his arms the way he'd seen his mother do it, but his sister continued crying. Naïm tried to stroke the hair on her head, which was sparse and dark and sweaty. But her face became an urgent reddish shade—almost the color of a damascene plum. He heard his father kick the wall in the next room.

"Omar," Naïm called. He walked back into their bedroom. "Wake up!"

Omar looked up at him. "What's happened?" he said, alarmed, sitting upright.

"Everything's okay," Naïm said. "Just watch her for a second."

He dropped Aysha in his brother's arms. Naïm would always remember that moment and his seven-year-old brother's look—surprised, at first, but then changing, transforming—becoming somehow more attentive. Becoming somehow custodial. "I've got her," he said.

Naïm grabbed Aysha's cotton blanket off the floor where she'd dropped it. "Here," he said, and tossed it to his brother. Omar caught it. He handed the blanket to their sister, gently kissing her temple, even though she was still crying.

In that moment, Naïm's brother lived a full life's tenderness.

Le Grand Théâtre des Mille et Une Nuits

Beirut, Lebanon
May 10, 1948

Marguerite Toutoungi sat in the fifth row at Le Grand Théâtre des Mille et Une Nuits, immediately in front of the orchestra. She was twenty-three years old. Her father sat beside her, wearing the bright red *tarbúš*, the black-tasseled formal hat that was going out of fashion. He also wore his finest suit: charcoal-colored worsted wool with narrow white pinstripes. A tailor had made it ten years before, in Damascus, in the souk at Al-Hamidiyah. A decade later, the elbows had thinned and the collar was a little ragged—its fabric worn into small crenellations, like the top of a medieval castle wall. Her father was ashamed of the suit's condition but wouldn't admit it to anyone. He was too proud for that, without question.

Marguerite's father, Édouard Toutoungi, was also going bankrupt. It was happening at this exact moment. The decline of the domestic credit market had been ongoing for decades— but it had accelerated after the Second World War. At first it was just La Banque de Syrie et du Liban asserting its power and size, but still working in parallel with the old system. But then the institutions had really taken over. European banks, yes, but also domestic banks, and Egyptian ones. And the little lending houses had to charge higher and higher interest rates to make up for their lack of volume. These rates had meant bigger payments for anyone who'd borrowed heavily to run their businesses. Like Édouard. Every night, at midnight, his interest compounded, and his loans became more and more impossible to pay off.

Of course, this wasn't what the seats in the center of the

opera house floor were supposed to demonstrate. They were supposed to demonstrate the opposite, especially from a distance. A fine suit. A beautiful daughter. An excellent view of the concert: Oum Kalthoum, the Star of the East, the most famous singer in the Arabic-speaking world. *Row C, Seats 15 and 16.* Édouard Toutoungi was supposed to seem—to his peers, to the businessmen involved in the export and sale of tobacco—like a man at the apex of his fortunes. The truth—that the bank was planning to foreclose on his trading warehouse—should be almost impossible to guess.

Ten minutes to curtain. The concert hall filled with the sound of murmuring voices. Arabic, of course, but also French and English and Italian. Marguerite closed her eyes and tried to listen. Sometimes she was able to snag a sentence or two.

"There he is," her father said. He was loud and close, his mouth almost touching her ear, his breath hot and flavored like cigarettes and anise. Marguerite didn't need to look. She knew exactly who her father meant. She didn't even have to open her eyes. *Her fiancé.* The man she was supposed to marry in three months' time. *Naguib Ghali.* The second son of the most significant shipbuilding family in Lebanon. Politically connected. Anemically thin and terrifically arrogant. His clothes always hung on his frame like garments on a hanger in a wardrobe. Ghali's voice made her particularly queasy; he was full of flattery and complimentary opinions, no matter who he was talking to. Even if some of what he said was genuine, the result was that it all seemed fake. He was obsequious. That was the word, the English word, she thought of when she thought of his image.

A single bead of sweat formed between her shoulder blades and rolled down the channels of her spine.

"Why can't you say hello?"

"I'm imagining the concert," Marguerite said. In a way it was true. Music was, to her, a meditative practice. If you created a space of quiet inside of yourself, then you allowed the song to reach backward through time and inhabit the place you'd once been, immediately before its first notes. "I need to concentrate."

"That's ridiculous," he whispered.

Marguerite ignored him. She continued looking down at her folded hands. The truth was—she was dreading the very sight of Ghali. They'd been engaged for nearly a year, but they'd only spoken a handful of times, primarily at big social gatherings. She'd managed to put off the wedding for months, but with the political climate of the region now—particularly to the south, in Palestine—time was dwindling. The UN had recognized Israel, and everything had a sense of urgency about it; now that the Second World War had just ended, almost no one wanted to be pushed back into regional—international— conflict. "Such a good man," her father added. "It hurts me to see you treat him like this."

"How," Marguerite hissed, "am I supposed to treat him?"

"With courtesy?" her father said. "With tact."

"Maybe," she said, "I should blow him a kiss?"

Anger flared in his eyes. "You know perfectly well—"

But then the lights—those distant lunar globes—began to dim. A hush moved across the room. It was almost a physical thing, that wave of quiet, so many conversations ending simultaneously. *A ripple*, Marguerite thought. The curtain rose—and there she was. Oum Kalthoum stood in place, at center stage— a regal-looking pillar of a woman, poised behind the microphone stand, hair rising from her head in a kind of tower. The orchestra, a full orchestra, began to play. One measure, then the next. Marguerite glanced to the left and the right, evaluating the dimmed palatial interior—with its curved stairways and ornamented domes and intricate archways, its Moorish revival seating, its etchings and tilework set in a series of geometric flourishes. One measure, then two. And then—the note, the first note of the love song, "Aghda'an Alga'ak"—See You Tomorrow. Oum Kalthoum began to sing, and she held the F for five, six, seven, eight, nine seconds, without wavering.

> *Will I see you tomorrow? How I fear tomorrow!*
> *How I crave and burn, here, waiting for you.*

Marguerite watched with awed silence. All these people, transfixed, listening. Attentive. Oum Kalthoum had become a hero across this crescent of the Eastern Mediterranean, appearing in films and on radio—singing about longing, about loneliness, about sorrow. Because what was desire except a lack of freedom? Her songs—were they about love or were they about democracy? Marguerite was stunned by her physical presence, the power of Oum Kalthoum's body. She stood on the stage with her head high. She commanded. Dominated. When she stepped forward to the microphone, the melody seemed to come from deep within her core.

One song after another. At first, Marguerite was intoxicated. But then, gradually, anxiety began to eat away at her. She couldn't pay attention. She was supposed to go, after the performance—with her father and Ghali—to a chaperoned coffee at Patisserie Suisse in the Place de l'Étoile. The thought made her feel ill. It overwhelmed the beauty of Kalthoum's voice, pushed it away from Marguerite, pushed it to an almost unreachable distance. And it wasn't just Ghali who was problematic. It was the very idea that she needed a chaperone. *Ridiculous.* In her mind, Marguerite saw herself as a *nisa'a mutaharrirat*—a free woman—in the tradition of modern, cosmopolitan women everywhere. And it was clear what her father thought about that.

Her father believed that delay—in all things—was dangerous. He thought that from a pragmatic point of view—it would be a mistake not to finalize the marriage immediately. *He's concerned for his business*, she thought, *not me.* How many times had she heard him say: *C'est obligatoire*. It's mandatory. *Then happiness, if there's time.*

If there's time! she thought. Anyone who knew Édouard Toutoungi knew that there was never time. He'd devoted his life to the great stacks of tobacco that came in and out of the city on the backs of mules or, before the war, on the DHP freight line from Hama. But as he'd aged—and as it had become more and more clear that her brother, Michèl, didn't have the temperament for the trading of commodities—her father had looked at Marguerite's eventual marriage as a business merger. Now, with the end of the French Mandate, and the disastrous failing economy, he saw it as a way to fight off starvation.

One song after another. The orchestra built the music around Kalthoum's soaring, plaintive voice. Marguerite's anxiety subsided and she sank into the deep rhythms of it. What did it mean to experience music like this, together—rich and poor, Muslim and Christian and Druze—all sitting together in the dark? She imagined what it would be like to be the focus of this, the creator of this, the one who orchestrated it all. Her deepest dream. To build something like this moment. Not just a single song, but each song adding to the next and the next, and the next. It was a tapestry. Notes as stitches—gold stitches—unfurling around the dimmed bodies in the hall.

And then, quicker than she anticipated, it was done. The concert ended. A roar surged up from the audience and Oum Kalthoum, the Star of the East, stood there in front of the curtain—her gold-colored dress glittering with what *did* seem like a galaxy of stars. *Could they possibly be diamonds? No.* Marguerite kept clapping, along with everyone else—with that audience that was roughly three-quarters men—men who were joyous, who were standing, whistling, screaming, waving. Throwing roses. So many white and yellow and red roses. Oum Kalthoum stood there, demure, at the center of it all. Didn't she somehow look sad?

Marguerite turned toward her father. Édouard grabbed her arm. "Let's go," he said. "Be good."

"Don't command me."

"I'm your father," he said, leaning even closer. "That's what I'm supposed to do."

There had been one other fiancé, when she'd been only sixteen—but she'd managed to drive him off with her liberal ideas, packaged in a way that she'd designed to shock him. A glimpse of a thigh. A speech about the rights of workers. Playing her hour-long piano concerto for him, in a private audience, with serious intensity. It had almost been too easy. But this one had been warned. And of course things had changed. A thigh wasn't what it once had been.

She felt her father's hand on her elbow, felt his strong fingers encircling her forearm—not in an unfriendly way, but with surety—with the power of someone who was used to command. He brought her out of their aisle and deeper into the crowd. Marguerite wondered if it would be like this when she was married.

"Wait," she said. "Wait. I have to use the restroom." Before he could respond, she shook off his grip and turned in the opposite direction, moving against the flow of the crowd. "I'll meet you in the lobby," she called back over her shoulder.

Marguerite felt like she couldn't breathe. Like Oum Kalthoum's voice was still reverberating within her. She knew obedience was a virtue, but—obedience to *what*? Sometimes she felt called to something, but she didn't know what it was, exactly. It was just a yearning, a sense that there was more out there for her. Marguerite wanted to believe in love. She wanted to believe in free will. But she also wanted to do what was right.

She made her way through the side exit and walked to the restroom. She gave a coin to the matron standing at the doorway and went inside. A few women—not many—and she was able to find a space at the sink, with its sliver of privacy. She turned the knob for cold water. She cupped it in her palms and dabbed some, carefully, at the corners of her eyes. She massaged the back of her neck, looking up into the reflection of her own face. *I look tired,* she thought.

Five minutes passed. Then ten. The other patrons filtered away. Marguerite was alone in the rectangular tiled room. She emerged into a corridor with almost no one in it. She walked toward the lobby and passed a little aperture in the wall. It was open about an inch and had been painted to look like it wasn't there. *A door in disguise.* Something no one was supposed to notice. Curious, she opened it and stepped through—stepped onto a small, dim staircase.

These stairs were not for patrons. There was no carpet, no

fine finish. She smelled grease and sweat and damp wool, all odors that were inappropriate in the *public* world of Le Grand Théâtre. The stairs turned in a tight circle and ended at the stage—just inside the heavy velvet curtain. It was moving slightly, like it was breathing. *In and out. In and out.* She could hear people all around her—could hear people in the wings on the other side of the building—ushers and patrons and staff. But the stage. The stage was dark. There were still flower petals strewn across its surface and Marguerite walked over them as if she were following a trail. And there—at the end of this trail—was Oum Kalthoum herself. She was sitting at center stage, sitting on a little wood chair. Smoking a cigarette.

This was a temple, a holy space, and there was its priestess—the woman who kept the music inside of her body. An ascetic. Unmarried, as everyone knew, at nearly fifty years old. Her eyes were closed; her skin glistened, still, with little drops of perspiration. For a moment, Marguerite watched her. They were alone onstage together. *What do I do? What do I say to her?*

"I wish," Marguerite said, her voice shaky. "I wish I could sing like that."

"No one is supposed to disturb me." Kalthoum spoke in Arabic, her voice marked by the Masri dialect, the flat intonation popularized everywhere by Radio Cairo.

"I'm sorry," Marguerite said. "I didn't know."

"Not for an hour."

"I'm so sorry, Ms. Kalthoum."

"I could hear you," the singer said, "at the top of the stairs."

Marguerite flushed. She tried to swallow, but her throat was suddenly dry. What an embarrassment. She'd disturbed this sanctified space; her presence, itself, was an offense. She wanted to flee, to weep, to run away. Suddenly, she was remembering something—a time, as a child, that she'd been scolded in church, in the Melkite Cathedral consecrated to her father's patron saint, Édouard of Enna, for staring at the image of that saint's deathbed, when he was old and frail and watched over by his friend and disciple, the monk, Daniel. What an incredible thing to have in a church, she'd thought. Here the saint was, weak and dying, a small body on a bed, a sheet over most of him, his eyes fixed on the heavens. *Me too,* Marguerite had thought. *It will happen to all of us. Me. Mother, father. Everyone.*

Don't linger, her mother had said, as if she'd understood her daughter's thoughts, and Marguerite had felt ashamed, as if her fears were written on the outside of her body, visible, exhibited for everyone to see. What a memory.

"I'm sorry," Marguerite said again, still looking at the ground.

The singer opened her eyes. She reached down and stubbed out her cigarette, an everyday act that was—in this context—glamorous. Then she looked over at Marguerite. She seemed to take her in, to consider Marguerite's form, her body waiting there—a trembling small human figure. There was something in Kalthoum's face at that moment that seemed to soften. Marguerite looked down at the floor.

"I dream of doing what you do," Marguerite said. Until that moment, she hadn't known this was true. "I want to live in music."

No, she immediately thought. *What a stupid thing to say.* She *did* feel it was true, yes—but what did it actually mean? Yes, she'd worked hard, over so many years—practicing with her teacher, her mentor, putting in hour after hour in lessons and recitals. She'd done as much, in fact, as she possibly could.

When the war had intensified, when the borders had closed and everyone had feared the end of civilization as they knew it—when the British army, through Operation Exporter, had ensured that the Nazis couldn't use Lebanon as a base from which to attack Egypt—she'd worked even harder. She'd persevered. She'd composed song after song. But how did this matter? If she was to marry Naguib Ghali, how did it matter at all?

Kalthoum smiled. "I'm wondering if," she said, "you would like a cigarette?"

The singer took a small embossed silver cigarette case from a pocket on the inside of her dress. She extended it toward Marguerite. After a moment—Marguerite nodded and accepted the case. She popped it open, selected a thin papery cylinder from its interior. She saw the inked insignia on the cigarette—the dark blue winged helmet of the Gauloises brand. She closed the case, handed it back, and leaned in for Kalthoum to light it.

She did. *A cloud of smoke.* A specific scent, a kind of sweet tobacco, so different from the broad-leaf Syrian varietals that her father loved.

Marguerite wanted to ask the singer how she might live this kind of life, how Kalthoum herself had managed it. A thousand questions pressed outward, competing for space in her mind. There were so many things to ask. *Too many.* One idea crowded out the previous idea, pushing it aside. She wondered about the singer's youth in the Nile Delta. She knew, for example, that Kalthoum's family had been conservative and religious. Muslim, not Melkite Catholic, but strict in a way that Marguerite recognized. She wondered about Kalthoum's life in Cairo during the war, in that city where so many nationalities had fled for safe harbor.

The end result was silence. Silence and, after Marguerite's first inhalation, a dry cough. Her eyes watered. She wiped the tears away and then she inhaled and exhaled, feeling a slight dizziness from the French cigarette. She smoked flavored tobacco, occasionally, from her brother's water pipe, but this was much harsher than what she was used to.

"One per day," Kalthoum said with a wry smile. "For my famous voice."

The cigarette grew smaller and smaller. It felt clumsy in Marguerite's two pinched fingers. Then it was out. The flame extinguished by saliva. After a moment, Kalthoum gathered herself together, as if she were going to stand, and that was when a dam burst inside of Marguerite—and her whole story, the story of this hour, came rushing through her, in her slightly stiff Arabic dialect, tumbling outward with the tears. Her impending marriage. Her suffocating family. Her dreams of playing music in Paris, at the Conservatoire de Paris.

The singer waited patiently. She looked at Marguerite with a quizzical expression. When the young woman had finished talking, she reached out and put her hand on her shoulder.

"My dear girl," she said softly. "Find a way to be yourself—and the world will show you the path."

By the time Marguerite found her father in the lobby, he was alone. Only the cleaning staff of the theater—suited in their gray uniforms—remained.

"Where were you?" he demanded. "How could you do this to me?"

"I wasn't feeling well."

"For thirty minutes? Do you know how stupid I looked? A man who can't control his own daughter."

"Don't yell."

"I'll yell if I want to. It's unbelievable. Stunning. *Foudroyant*."

"Papa, they're staring."

"Let them stare. They've already seen you humiliate me. At least Naguib is generous. At least he's kind."

"I was feeling—"

"I don't care," Édouard said, "how you were feeling." He paused. "We must make some changes—that's clear to me now."

The word sounded dangerous. "Changes?" Marguerite said.

The wedding, her father told her, had to be moved up. It would happen in six weeks. He'd been such a fool, he said, to have indulged her. She would stop these ridiculous music lessons. Did she—her father asked—have *any* honor? *Any*, at all? Any love for her family?

Marguerite's head felt suddenly gauzy and heavy. *Six weeks?* She reached out for the wall to brace herself but couldn't find it; she stumbled to one side slightly, trying to refocus on what her father was saying. He looked into the middle distance while he talked. He'd offered the quicker date, he told her, as a concession. Something the poor young man could take home to his family, a piece of good news. It was a miracle that Naguib hadn't simply called it all off, then and there.

He said all this with emphasis, his hand movements big and exaggerated. He spoke as if he were delivering a sermon, speaking to a vast congregation that filled the space around her, behind her, beyond her. Then, he turned and—pausing to put on his black-leather, cashmere-lined gloves—left.

Marguerite had no choice but to follow. She walked a few paces behind him down through the doors and out into the broad, open space of the plaza. There were a few of the Model A taxis there, waiting for passengers, and he walked directly toward the first in the line, his steps measured and resolute. He seemed to be channeling his anger and frustration into the way he walked. He didn't understand, Marguerite knew. *Couldn't understand.* Because he—like *his* own father, and his father's father before him—was satisfied with being a tobacco merchant. And so *she*, it followed, should be satisfied being the wife of a tobacco merchant. It was in her name, after all. *Tütün*—the Turkish word for the tobacco plant. He traded in a dozen varietals, all of them bought and sold by their family for hundreds of years. Rooted in a place, in the Belen Pass— the Syrian Gates—a conduit to the plains of western Syria and their patchwork tobacco fields. Generation after generation. And her father, at the far outpost of the business, trading the valley's products in Beirut and Damascus, which had been— successively—Ottoman, and then part of the French Mandate, and now an independent nation. Through it all, the family's profession had remained constant. A way of life that had been largely the same for four hundred years. What could be altered, for the hopes and dreams of a single insignificant girl?

Naïm

Naïm left the apartment and climbed the stairs to the roof. He hesitated as he pushed the little door open; the feeling of sunlight on his body had become a shock. Something he'd always taken for granted now felt foreign and new.

It had been almost three and a half years of war, three and a half years since that day in 2010, when a produce vendor in the Sidi Bouzid Governorate of Northern Tunisia—harassed by the police for not having a permit to sell his merchandise—had set himself on fire. *A can of gasoline and a single phosphorescent match.* Tariq al-Buazizi. Some bystanders had rushed to extinguish the flames. Others had filmed him as he burned. By the time he'd died, three agonizing weeks later, his image had traveled around the world—and the demonstrations had begun.

First Tunisia, but then Egypt, and Libya, and then—Damascus. Damascus: *Could you believe it?* Ash-sha'b yurīd isqāt an-nizām. *The people demand the fall of the regime.* Naïm had watched it all happen, live, on Barada TV. The moment had been intoxicating, a surge of oxygen deep into his lungs; it had almost made him dizzy with its enchantment. Since childhood he'd lined up every morning on the playground and shouted praise for the government: *One Arab nation / With an eternal message / Our leader forever / Immortal Comrade Hafez al-Assad.* But could that government be fallible? Could it have an end? *Qawmīya*—the nationalist ideology of the Syrian state—had taught Naïm that the government was everlasting. What if it was wrong?

But *qawmīya* was deep, ingrained in so many minds and hearts. It taught him that he should dream of sacrificing his body, his mind, his life, for the Syrian Ba'athist Party. And so it made sense, in a way, how the protests had degenerated into war. All of it made logical sense; these were clear next steps. The snipers plucking eyes from corpses; the burns scalding the flesh off a busful of children, leaving them blackened and fused to their seats, charred. Each side blaming the other for murder. No one taking responsibility—each side using the fuel of outrage to justify more attacks. It was his inheritance. Just like the Civil War of 1980 had been his father's inheritance, and the Revolution in 1963 his grandfather's. From generation to generation, a blood legacy. A nation created out of nothing by the French Mandate in 1923.

Maybe *this* was why. How could you force a nation into existence? How could you imagine, sitting in a distant office, that your pen had a power beyond the ability to write in ink? That it was more than an instrument of storytelling? That it could control lives? Could draw lines on a map of the desert and turn them into borders? That one hundred, two hundred years later these lines might be responsible for so much: for the destruction of those same demarcated nations, for the fires that consumed human cities, human bodies, human lives.

Naïm stepped fully into the sunlight. And there was his mother—clothespins in her mouth—reaching up for the long white line of a bedsheet, affixing that bedsheet to the clothes-line. He started to apologize, but faltered, aware that she might be angry with him.

She wasn't. She was singing softly to herself. And she smiled when her son appeared beside her.

And that's when he heard it—the distant, concussive sound

of helicopter rotors—the aluminum alloy blades of an Mi-17's Klimov engine, a sound that was deeper and more persistent than any other noise in the morning sky. His mother heard it, too. They both walked—carefully, slowly—toward the rooftop's edge. They stood in the shadow of a bank of satellite dishes. The rotors grew increasingly loud and—down in the street—there was a surge of noise, a desperate shouting.

Naïm glanced over at his mother. She nodded. Hesitant at first, but then gradually braver, he leaned forward and peered over the building's concrete lip. He looked down to the surface of Tuhama Street, nearly twenty meters below. He prayed that there would be no sniper.

"Incredible," he whispered, almost immediately, motioning her closer. "Come see."

There was a single Alaouite family that lived on the ground floor of the building. And now here they were, every one of them, out in the street. They were stuffing their belongings into a flatbed truck—bag after bag after bag. Fleeing.

The family's matriarch, a large old woman who walked with a cane, was herding everyone into the vehicle. *"Yalla,"* she was yelling. Hurry! *"Yalla, yalla!"*

But it was too late. If they'd been warned—alerted by someone in the government that an attack was coming—then the warning hadn't come fast enough. Because now the sound of the rotors had intensified—and it was clear that the Mi-17s were headed directly for this part of the city. For only a moment, Naïm could see them, moving impossibly fast over the rooftops, three of them in formation. They were a streak of camouflaged metal and heat and sound and then—the explosion.

The barrel bombs had been deadly: nails packed into a

barrel and set to scatter on impact—dropped on markets and public meetings and water lines. But the thermobaric aerosol bombs were worse; they reached into buildings; they seeped through any gap—no matter how small—and ignited.

Naïm's mother tried to protect him. She reached out, but couldn't quite touch him; an invisible force swept her back, swept her back and pulled her away, pulled her up and into the air.

Everything was disintegrating. Naïm felt his body twist and spin. He was light. He was almost nothing. He was twisting and spinning like a dead, dry falling leaf, and then he saw his mother beside him, and somehow—in the slowness of the frame-by-frame catastrophe—they got tangled up in the satellite dishes. They were somehow caught up in the vinyl wires and fiberglass, and, as the force of the explosion carried them onto the roof of the next building over, the fiberglass sheeting, with its polyethylene coating, acted as a heat shield. A heat shield and then—fractions of a second later—an aerodynamic sled. This was how they survived. Two in a building of ninety-six. Their lungs didn't burn because they were in the open air; they rode the shock wave of the explosion like unimportant debris. When he landed, the impact knocked Naïm unconscious. His left hand—which he'd raised to shield his face—snagged on a metal pipe and ripped in half.

MARGUERITE

The family home on the Avenue des Plumes had a wide interior balcony with a black wrought-iron railing. And every morning, their mother, Veronique, lined them up on that balcony for a tablespoon of cod-liver oil and a calcium shot. Marguerite—the oldest—and then her brother Michèl, and then the other four children—two boys, two girls.

Now! her mother called out. *Maintenant!* She stressed each syllable equally, her voice barking the vowels out in a rhythmic cadence. "Marguerite! *Vite!*" Quickly!

"I'm coming, I'm coming."

Marguerite got her breakfast from the kitchen—a single slice of toast and a café au lait—and consumed it as she waited for her mother to make her way down the line. She watched her siblings squirm as the shots went in their sides, into the knot of muscle just above the tailbone. Then they swallowed the cod liver, uniformly scowling. Michèl's expression was especially pained—a fact their mother didn't like.

"Do you want another spoonful?" she said. "I have plenty in here."

She tapped the big brown bottle with the side of the spoon. It had an image of a fish embossed on its side: SCOTT'S EMULSION—cod-liver oil, lime, and glycerin. It was supposed to keep the children healthy—to ward off disease with the strength of the sea. It was her mother's favorite medicine; no one could question its efficacy without enduring a blistering fusillade of anger. Her great-grandmother had survived the cholera epidemic in 1855 because of it. Everyone knew that.

And if they didn't know, they would soon know, because her mother would tell them.

They sat at the long rectangular table. Marguerite could still taste the saline, aquatic flavor of the cod as she ate her toast. Breakfast was a performance. The family had roles to play. Her father: Aloof, carefully dressed, wearing one of his brown work suits. Reading the newspaper. He held the newspaper up like a shield; she imagined it to be his inky, folded coat of arms. The children arrayed themselves around him: Michèl and Marguerite closest—on his right and his left, respectively. Then the others. In a constant battle to be nearest to their father.

Joseph, the youngest. Georges, his brother. Siham, the youngest girl. Katrin, the middle sister. There they were, her family. So many bodies, crashing through the space of the house just after sunrise. A rooster crowing in his rooftop enclosure; the rattle of truck engines on Bachir Boulevard.

Her father, for all of his anger the night before—he'd refused to even look at her on the taxi ride home—was now imperious and unperturbed. If he was worried about any of it, about anything that had happened, he didn't show it. Just the newspaper. He was just reading the newspaper. Even her mother was calm. If the change in plans—and the logistical chaos it would almost certainly cause—bothered her, interested her, affected her in any way, she didn't let on. Their mood seemed uniform, almost as if they'd discussed, ahead of time, how they'd behave in the dining room.

Édouard turned to Marguerite's mother as she walked past.

"Another bombing," he said. She stopped.

"Jerusalem?" She was holding an embossed glass vase, and she held it in midair. She looked poised and careful.

"Small town in the east," Édouard said, frowning. "Rift Valley."

Marguerite's mother turned and looked at her husband— at all of them, as they drank their coffee and milk. "It's a war, then?"

"Not yet," her father said.

"Monsieur Sarruf says that Palestine should be independent, and that Lebanon deserves its independence, too," Michèl said. "And I agree with him."

Monsieur Sarruf was the family's piano teacher. An instructor who'd been trained in French performance academies, he gave lessons in his second-story flat near the Place des Canons in central Beirut. For Marguerite, the sound of the piano was inextricably tied to the sound of Monsieur Sarruf's own voice. Urging her to play better, to concentrate, to build the melody with power and grace. When she wrote music—which she'd done for years—she imagined only Monsieur Sarruf, sitting at his kitchen table in his big bow tie, poring over her score, nodding his head with the rhythms of a conductor's baton.

"Monsieur Sarruf is wrong," their father said, shaking his head.

Their mother retreated as soon as he began talking. Marguerite knew, of course, that she was afraid of her father's anger, which could surge so unexpectedly. *The way that God is Our Father,* Édouard was fond of saying, *the father is the god of the family.*

But Marguerite wasn't her mother. She read the papers as well; she'd formed her own opinions about the way that the territory of Palestine—*all of it*—had been seized, taken away, to build a new state. She thought of herself as pragmatic, certainly more pragmatic than anyone in her family, and she thought that there must have been a way to establish a nation that didn't lead to rage—to fury and weaponized mobilization. She was about to say something about this to her father when—the door buzzer rang.

The morning mail. "I'll get it," Marguerite said quickly. She stood up and rushed through the curved archway to the foyer, headed out the door of their flat, and down its short flight of stairs. Her hand on the interior doorknob and then: *Here he was.* The mail carrier, holding a large bundle of envelopes tied together with a length of twine. He handed them to her.

It had arrived. She looked at the envelope with wonder. *Here it was—in her hands.* An airmail letter—PAR AVION—in a long A4 envelope. French stamps. *République Française.* Four of them. The musky red image of the basilica at Toulouse, its single ornate spire rising above a Romanesque facade. Arranged in a perfect rectangle, uncut and unbroken. Marked with a two-week-old cancellation. Paris. She held it to her chest. The document she'd been waiting for, dreading, hoping, imagining. Her admission letter—or denial—from the Conservatoire de Paris. The most prestigious music school in Europe. She could barely breathe.

Marguerite's back was turned to the stairway, though, and then she heard footsteps in the hallway above her. Quickly, she tucked the letter underneath the waistband of her skirt, pressing it taut against the skin of her stomach. She spun around and there was her mother, just a few feet away, already a step or two down the staircase. Marguerite straightened her shoulders. Hiding had become second nature to her; it was a survival tactic, no more, no less.

"A letter from the dressmaker," she said.

"Oh, darling," her mother said. Her eyes brightened; she

was clearly excited. "See? I told you. It's the most exciting time in a woman's life."

"Yes, *maman*."

"A lucky woman walks from her father's house to her husband's house."

"Yes, *maman*."

"Don't look so down," her mother said. "Get more rest. *Take care of yourself, habibti.*"

Marguerite felt her stomach clench and release, clench and release. Everywhere was a performance. Everywhere someone needed to be pleased, demanded something from her. *Yes, maman*, she said a few more times, and then she was rushing back up the stairs to her room, splitting the envelope open with her fingernail, breaking the seam, and pulling out the letter. *Pierre-Yves Malieu*, she read, *the Director of the Conservatoire de Paris certifies that M. Toutoungi, born on January 8, 1925, is admitted to the school of composition.*

Those words. Those two glorious words: *Is admitted. Été admise*. M. Toutoungi is admitted. She fell on her bed, clutching the papers to her chest. She felt the air puff around her body as she fell. What an incredible thing. Immediately, she remembered Oum Kalthoum's words the previous night. If this wasn't the world showing her the path—then she didn't know what else it might be. For one moment, Marguerite felt the joy of what she'd done. But it was brief—this satisfaction. It dissipated quickly. Because—of course—she had applied in secret.

All the work, all the fear, all the lying and forgery of documents, of recommendations, the payment of bakshish, of bribes. But—at the center of it—her writing, her sonatas, a series of them, that she'd composed over the past five years. Believing in the strength of her work but not telling anyone. Not even telling Monsieur Sarruf about the application, for fear of the news getting back to her family. A scholarship. A full waiver of fees. She had three weeks in which to notify them of her intentions and claim her spot in the fall. There was one problem, of course, other than telling her family: Marguerite had not specified her gender on her application.

She'd left the box blank, and, in the letters of recommendation that she'd forged, she'd avoided pronouns altogether. She'd worried that she'd be less likely, as a woman, to gain admission. She'd wanted her work to stand on its own. And it had. It had reached across a continent and a sea and returned to her here in Beirut, here in the city where—increasingly— she felt like a captive. *Kiss the hand you can't bite*, her father often said, but now she just imagined that hand holding her down—pressing her back against the bed, pinning her in place, making sure she couldn't move.

Outside she heard a street vendor walking by. It was the man who sold rosewater pudding. His voice rose into a trill as he moved from building to building: *Malabi! Malabi! Malabi!* She could smell the faint diesel odor of the morning air, but she could also imagine the milky sweet taste of the pudding. *The slightest scent of roses.*

Marguerite took the envelope, the letter, to her desk. She put it down on the surface of her vanity. It was an incredible thing, made more incredible by the way it looked in the context of her room. She held it up and imagined how it would be if it were framed and hanging on her wall. She imagined a diploma from the conservatory with her name on it. CONSERVATOIRE NATIONAL DES ARTS ET MÉTIERS. Just the words, themselves, were a harmonious music.

She spun around, closing her eyes and throwing her head

back with a dizzy thrill. She imagined the ink that would mark her name on the formal document of her diploma one day, bright and black and shiny.

"Are you dancing?"

Marguerite gasped. "You scared me."

It was her brother. "Your door was open. I could hear you staggering around. I didn't know you'd been drinking."

"Very funny," Marguerite said. "You know Father doesn't approve of women who drink."

"Father doesn't approve of anything," Michèl said.

Marguerite sat down at the vanity. She looked at her brother. She paused. She had something to show him, she said. It was a surprise. She was nervous. "You swear to secrecy?"

"Of course," he said.

"Absolute and total. You can't tell anyone."

He raised an eyebrow. "Of course."

She handed him the letter. Slowly, he scanned the text. She could see understanding move across his face. He was shocked, at first, but then his features settled into something different. "How long have you known?" he said.

An hour, she told him. It was her greatest dream—the same school that Monsieur Sarruf had attended. "Of *course*," Michèl said. But his tone was unexpectedly angry. He didn't seem happy for her at all.

"And what about Naguib Ghali?" he said. "Does he even know you applied?"

"What do you think?"

"I have no idea," he said. "Why do you say it like that?"

"Because he's the last person in the world I'd tell anything," she said. "And you know that."

"Do I?"

"You do."

She stared at her brother. He looked, more and more, like their father. He already had his mannerisms—the rough hand gestures, evidence of his heritage in the Turkish countryside, a legacy of his family that living in a city, a city like Beirut, couldn't erase. These were physical mannerisms passed down unconsciously from generation to generation; his body was a replica of some long-forgotten ancestor in the tobacco fields of Latakia. She loved this about him, sure, but it also frightened her.

"Never mind," she said. "I thought you'd be happy for me."

"Ghali is a businessman," Michèl said. "The family needs him. *We* need him. All of us."

"Some more than others," Marguerite said.

It was a painful thing to say. It was calibrated to hurt her brother. Because the truth was—in some ways the engagement was a direct result of her father's lack of faith in Michèl. Though no one would say it explicitly, their father had already given up on his oldest son. Michèl went to piano lessons with his sister. He loved the opera and the ballet. His priorities were not the right priorities for the family business. And she was aware that her brother carried this failure with him, in the same way that she carried the fear of her father's anger.

"I need help," Michèl said. "That's all."

"Why is that my responsibility?" Marguerite said. "Neither of us want to be father. It's wrong for them—both of them—to expect that."

But Michèl wouldn't relent. Had she been to the warehouse lately? he asked. It was in terrible shape. Falling apart. What if Édouard lost the ability to support them? What then? What would happen to their mother? To their brothers and sisters?

All of them so young? So vulnerable? "It's getting bad out there," Michèl said.

"Where?"

"The world. Look at it. Just look. Atom bombs. Armies that scour the land clean, wipe everything away. It doesn't matter who you are."

"That won't affect us here."

"It will affect *everyone*." The city was getting wilder, too, he told her. Hadn't she noticed? They needed Ghali, now more than ever. Needed his money and connections. "You have to be careful, Marguerite. Don't just throw away what we have— because you want something that you can never get."

Naïm

Naïm awoke in a hospital bed. There was wailing in the corridor—*God, my God*—someone crying, a woman's voice, saying the phrase over and over. *God, my God. God, my God.* Naïm's head was wrapped in a bandage, a strip of gauze that was tightly wound and surprisingly heavy. The balance of his head was all wrong; it felt unsupported by the muscles of his neck.

Someone else was sobbing, too, and he tried to prop himself up on his elbow, but he couldn't quite manage it. He lay on his side instead and looked out into the hallway. He could see a swatch of the far wall and there was a smear of blood on the white tile floor. No windows, of course. *Zarzous*, he immediately knew. The infamous underground hospital; the one that had replaced *al-Shifa* after the government had bombed it. His father had told him about this—only last week—about the way the government kept bombing the hospitals, one after another, and how they'd had to go underground, how they were running out of basic supplies, running out of blood and oxygen and amoxicillin and lidocaine. Naïm had watched the interview with the pediatric surgeon on the news; the man had described debriding soft tissue without local anesthesia, putting a tube into a boy's chest to evacuate fluid and remove shrapnel from his lung—while he wailed with pain.

In the hall, Naïm could see a child's foot, a foot and a part of a leg. No sandal. It was connected to a body, at least, a living body, because the foot seemed to twitch, to raise itself off the ground and then settle back down. People rushed by. A nurse.

45

Another nurse. Everyone was yelling. Then two women in black abayas. *Help*, he wanted to say. But it felt like there was a gulf between his mind and his voice, like the distance was vast and unbridgeable. He tried to speak but his mouth was dry and his tongue felt swollen and everything smelled and tasted like blood.

There was an IV in his right arm. This was the next thing that Naïm noticed. The line of the IV snaked up and around the sides of his bed and into a translucent plastic pouch of some kind. His left hand was wrapped in a ball of gauze. It seemed to not exist at all. *I've lost my hand*. The thought of it seemed to cut him in half, pushed him backward, off some internal precipice, and he plunged back into the darkness where, with a meager kind of mercy, he could not feel. This darkness, he would later think, where was it? It was inside of us, but also somewhere else.

His eyes opened again. There was a hand on his face. His mother's hand. Fatima's hand. Where had she come from? She filled his field of vision. Her forehead, creased with lines—the long horizontal ones, but small vertical ones, too. Signifiers of anxiety, worry, fear. She had a *misbaha* in her hand, a long brown chain of prayer beads, and she'd placed it on his chest. She'd placed it there and she was praying. *Subḥān-allāh*, she said, again and again. And then: *Al-hamdu lillāh*.

He thought about this image, the image of his mother praying, the image of her holding the prayer beads in her hands. He didn't need to glance down to know what it looked like; he could easily envision her wrists, her fingers—with their freckled and loose skin, their thin bones—a skeletal secret, a disclosure. The chain looped around her arm, the beads moving one after another through her fingertips. He could see his father's

46

hands, too, parceling out their religious devotion. His father had purchased these *misbahas* on his pilgrimage to Mecca, many years before.

With that thought, Naïm was spiraling away, into a dream or a memory. Playing soccer with Omar in the street; they'd stuffed a plastic grocery bag with hand towels and tied it off to make a soccer ball. It was late at night. The final prayer call filled Tuhama with its melody. He ran toward the doorway they'd been using as a goal. In his mind, Naïm was Lionel Messi, he was Zinedine Zidane, he was Didier Drogba, spinning near the top of the eighteen-yard box, keeping his head over the ball, striking it with the inside edge of his right foot. *I'm unstoppable*, he called. *Invincible!*

Maggot! Omar yelled back. *You make it too easy!* Naïm's brother was there in front of him, suddenly a fierce defender. He deflected the ball as it rocketed forward, and Naïm watched the shot rise up and up and up. It became something else as it rose, Naïm himself rose with it, rose through the wall of their apartment, like a wind, like a shock wave. Naïm was small and he was circular and he became a bead on the prayer chain, moving through his mother's hands, counting out the ninety-nine names of God.

Awake again. Immediately, he saw Fatima's eyes, saw the bright worried color of her eyes; eyes that he felt momentarily ashamed to look into. It was his fault, he immediately thought, it was his fault she'd been on the roof. That this had happened to her. That she was standing over her injured child, looking at his bloody body framed by white hospital sheets. He'd made a mistake. He should have done the task that she'd asked of him. Her neck had a blood-darkened bandage on it.

"Thank God," she said.

He tried to summon words. "My back hurts," he said, because it was true, and it was the first thing he thought of to tell her. "And my shoulder."

"It's not safe here," she said. She glanced into the hall. It was loud and chaotic; more people rushed back and forth, some nurses, some doctors, some civilians.

"Where's Dad?" he asked.

Fatima's gaze seemed to harden. She started to speak, then shook her head, cleared her throat, looked away. Her implication was clear.

"Anyone?" he asked.

She shook her head slightly.

"Nobody?" Naïm felt panic surge up and surround him; it was the inverse of what he felt when he settled into a piece of music—playing a sonata on his Casio. Instead of comfort washing up and around him, instead of the soothing sound of the melody, he felt his palms start to sweat, his heart seized by a fist of anxiety. "No one?"

She didn't answer. Instead, she reached for his arm—the undamaged arm—and she had his IV tube in one hand, and she braced her other palm on his body. She pulled. One quick pull, like taking off an adhesive bandage, and it was done. Blood flowed from the site, a quick rush of it. One pulse of the heart and then another and then it was just oozing. She covered the wound with the sleeve of her abaya and she reached behind him and then he was standing and walking, but he didn't know where they were going. They went through one set of doors and another, and then up a long flight of stairs and through a checkpoint with armed guards—older teenagers, mostly— teenagers with Kalashnikovs.

He was cold. So cold, and shaking. He staggered, stumbled

beside his mother, up a set of stairs and then onto a narrow street. *Danger,* he thought immediately. *Sunlight is danger.* "Are we meeting Father?" he said, but his mother didn't reply. But then it seemed that they *had* met up with him, because he was walking alongside them. He was floating, almost, along with Omar and Aysha; his father and his brother were taking over-large steps, they pressed down against the ground with each footfall and then seemed to soar. Naïm couldn't keep up. "Slow down," he said to his father, "you're going too fast."

"No," his father called back over his shoulder, "we're not going fast enough." Naïm heard his father's voice in his ear then. "Darling," he was whispering, "I know you can go faster than that." He could feel his father's coarse beard against his skin, smell the scent of his Drakkar Noir aftershave. "Let your mother help you."

His mother was there then, and she hooked her hand under his armpit and supported him as best she could. But Naïm could see that his father and brother and sister were getting farther and farther away. "We're losing them," he told her. "We're losing them."

"Quiet, *habibi,*" she said. "Don't worry. Keep walking."

And then they were in a little open-air bazaar, one of the impromptu markets where the residents of the city sold anything: parts of appliances, used clothes, blankets, canned food, candles, plastic Coke bottles filled with cooking oil or gasoline. *The sick and the damned,* his father had said just last week, *selling to the sick and the damned.* Or was it last month that he'd said that? Or last year? Everything in this market was arranged on blankets, so it could be quickly picked up and hauled to safety, in case a rebel group, or a federal army unit, appeared.

Someone had a tiny flat-screen television—and had hooked

it up to a portable generator, and some kind of satellite modem. A group of men crouched around the monitor, totally silent, watching what Naïm recognized as Al Jazeera news. Incredibly, Aleppo was the lead story. And not only Aleppo but East Aleppo; Naïm heard the name of his neighborhood, his tiny swatch of land, spoken by a news anchor in Qatar. He stopped walking. The war was escalating, the reporters said. The Free Syrian Army was smuggling weapons across the Turkish border. There was no sign of a cease-fire.

Naïm lost track of his mother. He lost track of everything: his wound, his feverish body, his ghostly family. He listened to an editorial discussion of his life, listened to complete strangers who had opinions about his city, the city in which he'd always lived, the city that felt like a part of him, like his heart or his lungs or his spine. And then—the program ended. *Assalamu alaikum*, the news anchor said. He signed off.

For a moment, the screen went blank. The men who'd gathered around the set—about ten of them—seemed to be released from an enchantment. They had nothing to say, though. One of them reached in his pocket and took out a pack of cigarettes. He lit three, holding all of them in his mouth at once, and then passed two to the men on either side of him. And then the satellite feed blinked to life. It was halfway through an advertisement for candy. *Deemah Caramels*, the voice-over narrator said. *For decades and generations, the favorite of families around the world.*

Naïm turned away from the television. *It was true.* His brother loved caramels, Naïm remembered. They should stop and get him caramels. But Naïm couldn't find a candy vendor among the old men and women selling household goods. He stopped to rest in a doorway. His wounded hand throbbed with pain, a pain that felt like a burning net, one that opened and swallowed him. He braced himself against the doorway with his other hand. There was an old woman nearby looking at him, staring at him, and so he tried to explain that he was looking for caramels for his brother, who'd been killed in a helicopter attack, because his brother loved caramels and maybe Naïm could bring him some. "I left him downstairs," Naïm said, "and he's probably tired of waiting for me." He waved his bandaged hand and saw that the gauze had soaked through with a dark liquid. He pointed to the ground, but immediately felt ridiculous doing it; of course downstairs wasn't underground. Or was it? He'd just been in an underground hospital, after all. So many of his friends now lived in basements and underground bunkers.

Then they were in a different part of the city. He asked his mother, again, where they were going.

"Don't worry," she said. "Keep walking."

But it was so cold. Why was it so cold in April? Wouldn't their father be cold in his grave? They needed to ensure he was warm. They should ask him, so he knew that they were still concerned about him, that they were worried. The cold was getting worse. Naïm shook uncontrollably. And then there was a sound that—after all these months of war—Naïm knew well: the clatter of automatic-weapons fire, which meant that the street fighting wasn't far away. Fatima was there next to him and he told her he wanted to find a place to sleep. *To sleep. Please. Right now.* There were young men on either side of him then, too; his mother was talking with these men—soldiers— and they brought both Naïm and Fatima into a courtyard.

The courtyard was rubble. It had once been the interior space of a large home, a multistory house that had opened inward on this private area. There was a burnt stump of a tree. Maybe it had been a lemon tree? A mango? An apricot? Naïm remembered his cousin's house near Homs. Visiting him when he'd been a boy. They'd had two apricot trees in a little court-yard that they'd used to make jars of apricot jam. Maybe *that* was where the family should go—now that their apartment building had been destroyed. He tried to suggest this to his mother, but she only put her arm around him and held the top of his head against the curve of her chest.

An explosion had destroyed one wall of this building. It was just a pile of broken concrete, with ghostly strands of rebar poking out of the rubble. This group of soldiers had been using it as a redoubt from which to shoot out across the city. Not much was visible beyond the ruins. The corner of an abandoned apartment building. No glass in the windows. The gray sky. And then another familiar sound: the low-toned rush of a mortar. And then an explosion nearby, and the ground shook with the force of it, and Naïm lost his ability to stand; he pitched downward to the cracked asphalt. He crumpled. Naïm lay there and closed his eyes. *Caramels.* Omar loved caramels. *I'll buy him some as soon as we get home.*

"Concussion," Naïm heard someone say. "And a fever. That's more troubling."

"What can we do?"

"Wait."

Aunt Maheen? He opened his eyes only slightly. He recog-nized that voice. It was a voice that he'd know anywhere; its accent was so particular, so specific to Aleppo, to this part of the city, to *his* family, to *his* part of the world. He said her name and she was there—standing next to his mother, and the two of them were looking down at him. He'd seen them before, standing next to each other, of course. They were sisters. But he'd never had them watch him so intently—both looking and not looking, preoccupied.

Dear one, Aunt Maheen said. Her eyes were full of tears. *I should stand up,* he thought. He looked around. He saw that they were in another underground space. He was lying on an air mattress in a windowless, concrete-walled room. It was a cellar of some kind. *I should stand up,* he thought again. But his legs were too weak. He couldn't move.

"Just rest," his aunt said.

She put her hand on his forehead, feeling the temperature of his skin. Her palm felt so cold, almost unbelievably cold, like the first touch of ice from the freezer, so cold that it's sticky and dry. He listened to Maheen and Fatima have a conversation then, about him. About antibiotics. About the front, which was swinging back and forth across the city, sweeping everything away, scrubbing it from the face of the earth with an evil vigor. As neighborhoods changed hands, the soldiers stripped every abandoned apartment. They took anything valuable, of course, but they also took the infrastructure of the building itself, its metal pipes and copper wiring. This is what his mother and his aunt discussed as Naïm lay there, opening and closing his eyes periodically, shivering, feverish.

"We can't," his mother said. "Not like this. Not anymore."

"It's not forever," Naïm's aunt said. "Just until someone wins."

"Wins? *Habibti,* how? How is there winning?"

"Kill them all. One side kills the other side completely."

"*Tamaam,*" his mother said. *Okay. Fine.* As she said this

word, *tamaam*, she dipped her head slightly and opened her hands. She frowned. *Enough,* her body language said. *Don't say any more.*

Panic moved through Naïm. *"Umi?"* he began. His mother silenced him with a look. "We'll be safe here, darling," she told him. "Don't worry."

But already Naïm could hear the air-raid siren, hear it gathering intensity in the building above him. It echoed down through the ground—a shock of noise, a bitter sound, raw and loud and suffocating.

"Make it stop!" he yelled.

"I'm here." And his mother was indeed there, holding him close to her body. She rocked back and forth, back and forth, cradling him. Her headscarf sat back on her head, tucked accidentally behind one ear. He could see a lock of her hair, black hair streaked with gray, curling out from beneath the fabric. The siren continued echoing. It seemed to be building in intensity.

"Make it stop!" he yelled. "It hurts!" Even as he howled he felt pathetic. Full of self-loathing. What fourteen-year-old cried like this—in his mother's arms? He was cowardly. *A coward. A pathetic coward.* His brother wasn't crying now, despite being dead. His father wasn't crying. No self-respecting man would cry like this because he'd heard a siren. How could he be so weak?

Is it my *fault, though?* Naïm thought. Or was it someone else's? His mother's? Was *she* the one to blame for all of this— for their survival, for the fact that they were cowering underneath the city? She'd stubbornly insisted on continuing the ritual of the laundry. Despite no electricity. Despite no water. What a terrible decision. What a mistake. He looked at her face and felt a sense of revulsion. Her concern was guilt, wasn't it? Nothing more than guilt. That was the truth of it. *Wait,* he thought. *No*. That was crazy. Why was he thinking like that? She wasn't responsible. She'd lost everything, too.

An explosion. The walls shook. The lights—bare lightbulbs screwed into a series of sockets on the ceiling—flickered. A moment later there was the sound of something collapsing. A wall, most likely. Nearby. But not on top of them. Not the wall of *their* building. That was when he understood where they were. They were still in the city. The cellar was his aunt's cellar, but in the southwest, in Hamdaniya, near the M5 highway, the road that led to Homs, and then—farther south—to Damascus. He understood the room differently, knowing this information. It was more recognizable. Familiar. But did that make anything better, he quickly wondered, or was it worse?

"God is good," Aunt Maheen said. "It missed us."

"It hit *someone*," his mother said.

Yes, Naïm thought, too weak to add his voice to the conversation. When the army fired an SA-3 into a city, it never missed. If your target was *any* target, then your weapons were always effective.

There was a second explosion then, but this one was farther off. Much farther. Maybe half a kilometer, he thought, silently calibrating the distance. What Naïm had learned about explosions was that if you heard them—if you got to think about them, to register them in your mind as *happening*, either nearby or far away, if God granted you that luxury—then you were likely safe. Because the missile that killed you wasn't the one you heard. It just killed you, from one breath to the next. Inward, one breath. Outward, a second breath. And then eternally inward—like a child's lost balloon. Released into the air, you rose and rose until you couldn't rise anymore.

MARGUERITE

A reception and a formal dance. All of it happening at Prime Minister Riad Solh's offices—Le Grand Serail—the block-long art deco edifice in the center of Beirut.

Marguerite had spent the week in an agonizing between-space, unable to make plans. The five prayer calls, which usually brought her a feeling of quietude and grace, now made her feel more and more frantic, as each hour brought her further into the future. She'd found herself losing track of her present moment, standing at her writing desk for twenty minutes at a time, immobilized, somehow incapable of movement. What was the name of this feeling? It was a breathless agony. She wanted to do so many things at once, things that were impossible to reconcile. She wanted to please her family. To please her father and mother. To feel their pride in her. But then again, she realized, they didn't want to have pride in who she actually was. They wanted her to be a particular thing: a dutiful, proper daughter.

And maybe this was appropriate? Maybe it was what her family, her society, needed. Her family couldn't have chaos. They were precarious enough. *Everyone* was precarious. Her city—which was, from time to time, gripped by sectarian war—needed its citizens to support the social order. There were few places in the world as intricate as Beirut. Here, where a single block harbored a half-dozen languages—either in the present, or in the recent, lost past, just one or two generations before. Turks, Armenian Maronites, Greek Melkites, Arabic-speaking Muslims, the Italians, the French, the English. Everything here was a matter of balance. *Languages organized around religions*. Or was it the opposite? she thought. Religions organized around languages? Or could you even separate them? Even the Hamidiye Tower—which rose twenty-five meters over Le Grand Serail—married several traditions: the architecture of Europe and the needs of the Islamic faithful, marking time from sunset to sunset and ringing out those invitations to prayer.

This was what Marguerite was thinking as she walked into the prime minister's palace. The foyer had been converted into a ballroom. An orchestra played softly in one corner—fifteen instruments at least. It was a cold night. A bank of polished copper heat lamps gleamed along one side of the room. Tuxedos and formal wear. Fewer tarboosh than she was used to seeing; the hats were slowly disappearing, it seemed, going out of fashion. Marguerite wore a modest black ball gown. She'd accented it with a peridot brooch, one that had belonged to her grandmother.

"Stay close to me," her father said. "Don't disappear again."

A few couples waltzed on a raised, square, parquet dance floor. The occasion—ostensibly a celebration of the end of the British Mandate over Palestine—wasn't being commemorated in any official way. *No politics*, her father had sternly commanded, and this *did* seem to be the rule of the evening. Everyone somehow looked lighthearted. The other women's dresses didn't match Marguerite's. Hers was funereal in its color. They wore apricot and pink and aquamarine. She felt like a crow by comparison.

She thought about the image of the world that her brother had painted for her just last week. Beyond the capital, Marguerite knew, the entire country was in crisis. The French had completely withdrawn. Thirty thousand French citizens had just left Lebanon, left in a flotilla of boats, taking their money with them. There was talk of war—imminent, widespread war to the south—as the United Nations prepared to recognize Israel. Protests had turned violent. Strikes. Inflation and food shortages. Bread, in particular—the hot flat loaves that Marguerite bought on the street each morning—had grown scarce.

In this room, though, it was as if nothing had changed. Marguerite's father made his way to the champagne. He got himself a glass, but nothing for his daughter. She was looking at the table, trying to find the appropriate beverage, when her father's voice boomed through the space just behind her back.

"There he is," he said. "Just the man I was looking for."

She didn't even have to look. She knew who it was. *This* was the real reason, Marguerite knew, that her father had requested she come. Naguib Ghali was the prime minister's nephew. *Of course* he'd be here. There was no way to escape it.

She turned, and there he was, standing much too close. *"Enchanté,"* Ghali said, taking her hand and bringing it to his lips. They felt like rubber against her skin.

Marguerite murmured a greeting. She felt the desire to flee, to scale the walls, to use the chandelier as a swing and propel herself up and through the long stained-glass windows, crashing out into the night. "I trust you've been well," she said.

"I missed you at the concert last Saturday," Ghali said. If he was flirting with her, his eyes didn't betray it. They were cold and flat and serious. They lacked joy.

"I fell ill," she said. Maybe his lack of joy was contagious? After a moment she said: "What did you think?"

"Terrible."

"How so?"

"I don't care for her voice," he said. "In general, I don't approve of women who sing."

"Now, now," Marguerite's father said, reappearing from wherever he'd disappeared to. "There's no need to make sweeping judgments."

"It's not a sweeping judgment," Ghali said. "It's a fact. A woman who's singing might as well be a prostitute. She's putting herself onstage for everyone to stare at. It's immodest."

Contain it, Marguerite thought. *Push it down.*

"I thought she was rather beautiful, actually," she said.

Ghali frowned. "Nothing about that night was beautiful," he said. "Nothing at all." Marguerite could smell—even from some distance away—the odor of his breath. It had the odor of water in a vase of week-old flowers. An element of decay. An element of rot.

"I thought she was brave," Marguerite said.

Her father shifted his weight slightly, taking up more space beside his daughter. *Certainement,* he said, *certainly different people have different opinions.*

"Monsieur Toutoungi," Ghali said. "With all due respect, sir. No wife of mine, no daughter of mine, will be performing music. She'll be too busy running the house and raising children. Those are tasks that require a maximum of dedication."

"Well," her father said. "Certainly."

"It's no small task," Ghali said, "educating the next generation of leaders."

Marguerite stared at him. "And who do you imagine those leaders will be?"

Ghali looked at her. "Who do you think?" he said.

"Your sons?" Marguerite said.

"All ten of them," Ghali said, nodding, his face so expressionless that it took Marguerite a moment to decide that he was joking.

"No," she said. "All fifteen."

And then everyone—relieved—was laughing, and the conversation moved onward. Marguerite felt herself sinking underneath an enormous weight. *That suffocation.* That almost unbearable feeling of being pressed down. Crushed. But she couldn't let it defeat her. She was an *admitted student*—after all—at the Conservatoire de Paris. The most prestigious of all European music schools. *Fauré. Berlioz. Debussy. Saint-Saëns.* They were all alumni. Her name would stand among theirs someday. There was a space, beside them, for her voice. For the melodies that she put down on paper, marking the notes one at a time, slowly slowly slowly, using a fountain pen and ink. Even as she stood there, Marguerite turned her imagination inward. She imagined that ink, cool and black and watery, staining the tips of her fingers, collecting in the seams of her fingernails.

"No daughters?" she said. "Don't you need at least two—so you can have a dozen?"

The laughter eased. "Yes, yes," Ghali said. "Quite right. A dozen."

Marguerite looked at him. Her lungs felt like they had no air in them at all. "I'm glad you agree," she said. "If you'll excuse me." *Desolé.* Her voice trailed off. *Friendly*, she thought. *Look friendly and solicitous.* She tried to smile. There was a staircase that led to the building's second floor; as she reached those stairs she snatched a flute of champagne off a tray.

No wife of mine. The phrase echoed and echoed in her mind. *Mine.* The clarity behind this word, the ease of possession—it nearly took her breath away. But why should it surprise her?

She saw it in her father, of course, in the submissive way her mother accepted his arguments when he was angry, when he became loud and aggressive. She even saw it in her brother, in the passionate way he mimicked her father's tone, learning from him to be assertive at the breakfast table, in school.

Marguerite gulped the champagne. She placed the empty flute on the ground near the top of the stairs. She walked down a hallway and then another hallway. She walked until she could just barely hear the sound of the orchestra, until she could hear only the suggestion of music, its distant arpeggios and minor chords, its swells and diminutions. There was a bench to one side of the hall. Plush leather. Cushiony. She sat down, and, for just a moment, rested.

Marguerite had been reading a novel in English—*The Heart Is a Lonely Hunter*—by a writer she admired, a woman barely older than she was. She'd brought the book along, hoping for a solitary moment like this. She took it out of her purse now and began to read. The writing was beautiful. She loved the sound of it, but what she really loved was the challenge of reading in English. It was a language with a strange music, English, with its wild admixture of German and Latin and French roots, with its unpredictable spellings and dozens of irregular verbs.

The novel followed the fate of two deaf protagonists, one of whom went mad, and a girl—Mick Kelly—who dreamed of owning a piano and of building a violin from scratch. Marguerite felt the rhythms of the language as soon as she started reading; every sentence built into the next, adding up to, she felt, a fugue. She'd just sunk into the story when she heard a voice from nearby.

"A wonderful book."

Marguerite looked up and there he was—a tall, thin young

man with large round glasses. He was wearing a three-piece suit. His pocket handkerchief, she noticed, was bright red.

"You know it?"

"I do," the young man said. "I bought it because of the title."

"It's *charming*," Marguerite said, looking for the right word, scrambling to translate from the French, *charmant*.

They began to talk then, discussing the way the story built slowly—the way that it seemed to follow one set of characters, but then followed another, and another. As she talked, Marguerite became conscious of how surprised she was. How unexpected this was. *Is he flirting?* He was so earnest. So bright-eyed. He'd been looking for a place to hide from the party, he told her. He had a book of his own, he said. He reached into his lapel pocket and pulled out a thin volume in Spanish. He handed it to her. It was a lightweight paperback—published in Argentina by Editorial Losada—*The Eighteenth Brumaire of Louis Bonaparte*. A novel was one thing, Marguerite thought. But who carried a book like *that* in his pocket?

"Karl Marx?" she said, handing it back.

"The traditions of all dead generations," the young man said, "weigh like an Alp upon the brains of the living."

It would be, then, an unusual kind of courtship.

The young man's name was Adolfo Jorge Castillo. He was Cuban. His father was part owner, together with some American men, of Francisco Tobacco, a corporation that controlled two tobacco plantations—and a number of factories—in his home province, Pinar del Rio.

He'd been sent by his father to explore investment opportunities in Turkey. Francisco Tobacco wanted to diversify their holdings; the board was hoping to develop contacts in a variety of industries around the world. He was supposed to be, right now, in Cairo. But Palestine roiled with war. Four Arab nations—the newspapers said—were planning to invade. And so they'd sent Adolfo north—with the assignment to investigate tobacco farms in Lebanon and Syria.

"Tobacco," Marguerite said. "It's a filthy business."

"Is it?" Adolfo said, smiling. "Why do you say that?"

"It just is," she said, though in truth she didn't know if she actually meant it. "What would Marx say?" she added quickly. "You. A wealthy landowner—hoping to exploit people all around the world?"

"The *son* of a wealthy landowner," Adolfo said after a moment. "We don't choose our class at birth." And then he switched languages. *Pardon*, he said. *Peut-être nous pouvons converser en Francais?* And so their conversation moved back and forth. It became clear to her that he hated his role—but was trapped in it, an emissary for the family business, forced to work far from home, doing things that he didn't believe in.

"I know what that's like," she said.

"You do?"

"I do," she said. "Trust me."

"I *don't* trust you," Adolfo said with an intensity that surprised her. "I doubt you understand it. The pressure of the family. Of our position."

Marguerite laughed. She began to argue with him, asking him to enumerate the ways in which he felt his situation was unique. She listened patiently and, when he was done, told him that he was wrong. *Her* life, she told him, had more pressure. Pressure of the same kind that he felt. Exerted by the chain of familial history, by the place in her society that her family occupied. Even as she said this, she anticipated it would make him angry.

"Can I make a confession?" Adolfo said. "I've lost track of what we're arguing about because you're so beautiful."

But ideas were flowing through Marguerite; the hours spent reading and studying and thinking were suddenly coming alive. And now—in her native language—she felt at ease and confident. "I was pointing out," she said, "your lack of belief in the power of my experience. I was pointing out your narcissism. You empathize with your own plight, but not the plight of others. That's what *I* was doing. But you—you were just making noises with your mouth."

"That's all?"

"That's all," she said. "But when you changed languages . . . that was quite nice."

They continued talking. Marguerite looked at Adolfo. He was beautiful; his skin was rough and stubbly across his jaw, the strong line of his jaw, which tapered to an elegant point. He was tall. She looked at the sweep of his bone structure, the way his cheekbones feathered upward toward his pale gray eyes. He was talking now about the way the pressure of capital—combined with religion and the patriarchy—served to subjugate the working class. He was talking about Catholic superstition and how it was manipulated by the local priests, manipulated to enforce social control. She felt a sudden surge of excitement. She wanted to tell him that she'd been going to meetings, Communist meetings, right off the Corniche, meetings where editors and professors discussed ways to remake society. She wanted to tell him how suspicious she was of the religious registry in Lebanon—the one begun by the French Colonial Mandate in order to build a power-sharing agreement in the country. But then she pulled back. She didn't say any of this; she'd known Adolfo for hours, after all, not weeks or months or years. Instead, she told him the meaning of her name—*tobacco*, combined with the suffix for merchant, *gi*.

"Marguerite Tobacco," Adolfo said, using the French word *le Tabac*. "Lovely and delicate, like a tobacco flower."

Adolfo's main responsibility here, he eventually told her, had been to make a connection—for his family—to the prime minister. But he'd failed to do this, too. He hadn't *wanted* to do it; he worried that he'd want to engage the prime minister in debate, for example, about the troubles in Palestine, about the looming conflict with the Syrian Social Nationalist Party, and not simply make a connection on behalf of his family's interests. "I'm a failure," he concluded. "One simple task and I've failed."

Marguerite smiled and took his hand. It was the first time they'd touched, and the warmth and softness of his skin startled her slightly.

"I don't think you have," she said. "I can make you a success right now."

The next morning, Marguerite awoke before the sun rose. She was unconscious and then she was staring at the wall of her bedroom, eyes open, unaware that she'd made the transition from sleep to wakefulness. What a day. What a *night*. She *had* introduced Adolfo Castillo to the prime minister. They'd all had a conversation; despite some awkwardness, Adolfo had managed to give Riad Solh his business card. Then Marguerite and Adolfo had slipped out of the party and spent the next few hours talking on a balcony above the city.

She'd never met anyone like him. He wanted to remake the world in the image of equality. He understood the ways it was unequal, but this understanding created *ambition* inside of him. He was so different from her father, she'd reflected as she'd gone home in the taxi, who understood the same things, but then used them to his advantage. *Find the power in the room*, her father had often told Michèl, *and then make it your ally.* She'd mentioned this to Adolfo—once she'd told him more about her family. He'd frowned. *Find the power in the room and dismantle it*, he'd said. *That's the right thing to do.*

But by the end of the night, nothing had changed. *Not really.* As she was leaving with her father, they'd talked with Naguib Ghali. Her father had invited him to dinner in a few days' time. She'd stood there beside him and smiled and nodded and Ghali had avoided eye contact. It made her realize something from her time talking with Adolfo: he'd looked unrelentingly into her eyes. It was the thing she thought of immediately when she thought of him. His gaze, fixed on hers, almost luminous.

But now she couldn't sleep. Soon, sleep would be irrelevant. The house would be awake and full of noise. *It's hopeless.* She got up out of bed. She walked over to the desk where she kept her work. She allowed herself a moment—one brief moment—of thinking about Paris, of fantasizing about her life there, about the flat she would have in the nineteenth arrondissement, near the conservatory. She would walk to her classes each morning, bundled up against the cold, her head full of music. She'd be surrounded by it.

Marguerite had been writing a sonata for months now, using a 1 mm pencil and filling page after page of her small leather-bound notebook—the notebook with blank paper on the left and five rows of staffs on the right. What had begun as the "Beirut" Sonata had now lost its name. She thought of it as a nameless piece, an orphan piece, the "Orphan" Sonata in C Minor—the key in which Chopin had composed the Revolutionary Étude, the three-minute piano study he'd written after the bombardment of Warsaw, during the failed November Uprising in 1831. It was, without question, the piece of piano music she loved most, with its wild-feeling, right-hand chords that built into a terrifying, sorrowful melody, one that hung behind the constant demands of the left-hand semiquavers rolling up and down the keyboard. She thought of those chords like the flowers of a climbing vine—bright, blood-colored bougainvillea that hung on a trellis. They blossomed within the melody, within the leaves, both a part of—and something outside—the body of the plant, the structure of the song.

Marguerite loved these chords. Four of them. She would hear them, sometimes, when she was walking down the street, going to Souk El Franj for her mother—or meeting one of her younger sisters at La Collège de la Sainte Famille. They'd wander into her mind. But not in just any form. Because, Marguerite felt, pianists would often play them wrong, play them without the slight hitch, the *smallest* hesitation between the initial and the subsequent pair of chords. And this missing quarter-second would destroy the song. Transform it. Change it. Without the hesitation, the étude was different. It didn't say, she knew, what Chopin had meant it to say.

She sat at her desk in the quiet, looking down at her composition book. The music, of course, only lived in her imagination. Because she couldn't just go to the living room and play the piano. It was forbidden. She'd be reprimanded as soon as the notes moved out through the house. *Why was she waking everyone up?* So she'd simply done what was necessary. She'd memorized the keyboard with crystalline precision. And now it lived in her imagination, as powerfully as if she were playing it, her music echoing out through the living room of the apartment on Avenue des Plumes.

She looked at the sonata. She was happy with her first subject and her second. But its development—the section where she wanted to elaborate on her first two themes—kept sliding further and further away. She could imagine a coda. She could imagine the quiet, reflective way that she wanted to finish the piece. But the middle was elusive. It was elusive because it could be anything. The melody could develop in nearly any way. And this always bewildered her.

A few weeks ago, she'd thought the piece should express one thing. But now—now everything felt different. A single conversation and everything felt transformed. *Why should it be that way?* Marguerite wondered if this was proof of madness. She'd always wondered if her love of music was crazy, if it was an illness, and now it seemed, to her, like that was possible. She hummed a strand of notes, remembering Adolfo's eyes, remembering his melodic, passionate voice. And it seemed suddenly that her sonata didn't express *enough* of what she was feeling. It failed. It failed completely. Because what part of the music was music? And what part of the music was love?

She imagined Monsieur Sarruf's voice: *Again. Play it, again,* he'd say. The thought of this steadied her. She looked at the page and situated herself in the melody. She concentrated now, her mind focusing with care and precision. She felt a bead of sweat trickle down her back, traveling from the nape of her neck down along her backbone. She added a few bars to the score—an elaborate flourish. She imagined what it would be like to play it, play it in a theater of the size of Le Grand Théâtre des Mille et Une Nuits. She'd do that, someday, she vowed. She'd play her work there and finish to a soaring round of applause.

But now—sitting in her bedroom—there was of course

nothing. Only silence. And she was trapped, pinned in place by her own hesitation. She hated it. *Hated it!* Why couldn't she just march out to the piano, take ownership of it, stand up to her father's frustration, her mother's disapproval? Why was she so afraid? Her work had been validated. She *had* value, according to the most prestigious music academy in the world. But then she looked down at the composition book. *Eight notes.* She'd added eight notes. It was pathetic. She hoped to be a composer one day—for her work to be read and performed by orchestras around the world—and the most she could manage was eight notes? She had to do more. She was about to put her pen back down on the paper when she heard her mother's voice, close to her bedroom door.

"Dear one?" her mother was saying. "Darling?"

Marguerite stashed the sonata beneath her pillow right as her mother stepped into the room. *Calm,* Marguerite thought. *Project an air of calm. Demure. You are demure.*

"I need you to buy roach poison," her mother said. Her mother couldn't do it because she was getting breakfast ready. The *baqqala* on Rue de la Égalité would have some. Her father had left early for the office; there was a big shipment, apparently, coming in from the valley.

"What about Michèl?" Marguerite said. "Can't he go?"

"I don't want to bother him," her mother said.

I see. But you do *want to bother* me. "Yes, *maman.*" Marguerite bowed her head, and her mother handed her a little stack of coins.

It was a cool morning, with the wind coming in off the Mediterranean. The roosters were out in full force, arguing from courtyard to courtyard about the arrival of the day. She walked to the little corner store—no more than a window in the wall of Madame Shirzat's kitchen—and stood in line. Teenagers, all of them, some on their way to school. Some buying candy. Others buying the flatbread that Madame Shirzat heated, to order, on her gas-burning hot plate. Marguerite, of course, was buying roach poison. That was how her life went, it seemed.

She watched the students, only a few years younger than her but still so different. They wore school uniforms—Hama was a neighborhood where the majority of the children went to school. Marguerite, herself, had worn this uniform, with its too-hot long-sleeved blouse and modest skirt. Even as a girl she'd hated it. It had never been comfortable. Her body had never felt at ease within its strictures. Buttons that were too tight. Zippers that never seemed to work properly. But she'd been reminded constantly by everyone—her father, her mother, her brother—how lucky she was to even attend school. For her brothers, of course, there was no question. *They'd* attended the prestigious Mission Laïque Française in West Beirut, like the last three generations of the family. But for Marguerite, for a girl, everyone said, it was a privilege to walk through *any* schoolhouse doors.

But it was something else, too. *A cage!* It was a cage. Yes, she knew she'd been lucky to get an education. But music had taught her more than she'd ever learned in school. She'd never learned enjoyment, pleasure, in her classes. Even the languages—French, English, Arabic. The text was read for grammar. It was a formal, unchanging, fixed thing. All of her education, *all my life!* she thought, had been this way. Everything taught for the certification exams conducted by the state. Music, though, was freedom. It could take you anywhere at all.

Standing there, considering all of this, watching the schoolchildren lining up obediently to buy their sweets, Marguerite remembered Madame Perpignani, the Italian widow who lived a few blocks to the east, near the tracks for the tram. She was a fallen woman. Everyone called her a widow, but then they whispered the truth: she'd had an affair with a younger man, a Lebanese guest worker in Sicily, and she'd left her husband to follow him here to Beirut, nearly forty years ago, before the Great War. Of course he'd left her. Now she lived in a single room on the ground floor of a crumbling apartment building, drinking plum-skin brandy from a little wooden cup all day long, gradually wasting away, selling what she could from her stoop.

Marguerite felt a sudden surge of emotion. Something she couldn't quite recognize. She wandered away from the line at the *baqqala* and walked the eight blocks over to the tramway. It was chaos. Motorbikes, donkey carts, a single round-fendered municipal bus making its agonizingly slow way along the street that was much too small for its size. She'd worn a loose-fitting housedress and a gust of wind pulled it briefly up past her thigh. Someone whistled. She hurried on, conscious of the coins in her purse. They were freedom. Limited, sure, but freedom nonetheless. Marguerite came around a corner and, sure enough, there she was—Madame Perpignani—wrapped in a knit shawl, leaning on the doorway.

Al Mutallaqa, everyone called her, the Divorcée. But this is how it was in the city. A weakness was transformed into a permanent identity. It became the thing you were known by. *What if that was me? If that was me—what name would I have?* What would they call Marguerite if she married Ghali? The woman who surrendered her dreams? Or was that even a category? Was that simply every woman's identity, the thing that was expected?

"*Bon matin,*" Madame Perpignani said. *Good morning.*

"Glow-Rite paste?" Marguerite asked. The items arranged on the blanket to one side of the doorway did not include anything remotely similar to the poison.

A moment passed. Madame Perpignani stared at her. She was unreadable. *No,* Marguerite thought. This was a stupid impulse. But then the old woman smiled. *Bien sûr,* she said. *Certainly.* And with great effort, she stood and went into her house. Marguerite could hear the sound of cabinets opening and closing, a foreground melody to the rest of the sounds of the neighborhood—the insistent chirping of sparrows, the swirl of shouted voices here and there as various households came awake. The street vendors, more and more numerous, pushing their carts through the city, each with a different call.

The old woman returned. She was smiling. "Half a tube," she said. And handed it to Marguerite. It was, indeed, half a tube.

"*Combien?*"

"Nothing," the old woman said. "It's yours."

Marguerite shook her head. "I have to pay for it," she said.

Madame Perpignani smiled sadly. "Happy to help," she said.

It was difficult for Marguerite to understand, at that moment, what she was supposed to do. On the one hand, this was a kind gesture. Paying for the roach poison might offend Madame Perpignani. But then again, *not* paying might be offensive as well. She took a coin from her pocket—the twenty-five piastres embossed with the image of the Lebanon cedar. It was a fraction of what she'd been expecting to pay.

Madame Perpignani nodded. She took the coin. But she seemed sad—so sad—to take it, and Marguerite realized that she'd made a mistake. There was nothing to do then but leave, and she did, clutching the tube of roach poison in her hand, her cheeks fiery with embarrassment.

As Marguerite walked, she looked down at the little tube's label. The pale yellow, glow-in-the-dark phosphorous paste had been one of the great joys of her childhood. She and her brothers and sisters had spread it on their faces at night, pretending to be tigers in the jungle, sneaking from room to room in the dark, their skin itchy and glowing. It was a radioactive isotope that made the poison glow; Marguerite had always felt a little light-headed when she'd inhaled it for too long. Now she slipped it into her purse.

She walked one more block and then stopped at a street corner, hesitating. She realized that, if she turned there, she'd be heading down toward the waterfront. *Have you been to the warehouse lately?* Michèl had said, and this sentence echoed through her mind. *Lately?* It was a loaded word, a word that implied a lack of diligence, a lack of understanding. Why not see for herself? It couldn't be as bad as Michèl had described. Could it? Was it really endangered? About to collapse? Her father, who hid all of himself away from them, concealing his life behind a facade of officiousness and formality—was he losing control? Was he losing his grip on his financial life, and putting all of them—his family—in danger?

After another moment she turned and began walking west, the scent of the sea getting stronger and stronger. *One kilometer. Two.* She'd be late for breakfast, of course, and her mother would be angry. She'd be a disappointment again. *As always.*

She reached the wharf. The district was old, one of the oldest in Beirut, and even the commercial buildings had sandstone walls. The neighborhood had deteriorated during the war, Marguerite saw. Every painted doorway was chipped; every metal pipe seemed to be corroded. There was a ruined building—an old colonial mansion that had somehow collapsed—and the bricks had never been cleared. They'd simply spilled into the street, creating a hazard for anyone walking, or driving, by. The streets of Beirut were, at their best, a kind of splendor. The architectural styles of a hundred years colliding and creating a pastiche, a visual landscape unlike any other. But *here* the main thing she felt was destitution. This was the embodiment of five years of conflict and the depression before it—this last decade that had been so difficult. That had brought challenge after challenge, year after year.

She had to work to find the address. She thought she remembered it, but that memory was wrong. She ended up finding it on a side street, up a steep hill. When she *did* find it, it was smaller than she remembered, and the doorway—a massive metal rectangle—had rusted badly. The rust had eaten a hole in the space around the door handle, so it was dangerous to open, to try and roll it aside without cutting her hand. But she did. She took a few blind steps inside, her eyes adjusting to the difference in the light between the street and the warehouse.

It was from here, Marguerite knew, that Édouard directed the rolling arrivals from their network of farms. The Compagnie Internationale des Wagons-Lits brought the pallets of leaves from Eskişehir and Aleppo, along the tracks of the Taurus line. Her father organized the separation of the Burley strains from the Latakia strains, the flue-cured from the fire-cured leaves. He collected and dispatched, collected and dispatched, sending pallets back out to cigarette factories throughout the region. Some of the leaves he blended at the warehouse itself, manufacturing a variety of products that were later stamped with brand insignias elsewhere.

Immediately, she saw the workers. They were hunched over the pallets of burlap-bound tobacco leaves, removing sheafs of them from the bales and feeding these sheafs into the shredder. They were tall, these shredding machines—seven feet tall at least—with mechanized wheels and fusillades of rotating blades. They minced the dried, yellow-brown leaves and sent them through a hydraulic tube up into the ceiling, to the next level of the factory. Everything reeked of tobacco. The life span of a factory worker, Marguerite knew, was twenty years; the tobacco dust, alone, was as dangerous as the coal dust in the mines at Ereğli.

The workers looked up—a line of them—as she passed. She felt like an exhibit as she crossed the floor. Even though she was wearing that formless housedress, she felt as if she were wearing nothing at all. She could almost *feel* the heads swivel to watch her move. It was the thing she could never accustom herself to; men watching her body as she was simply doing daily tasks. *They want to destroy me*, she thought. Or, *no*, that wasn't correct. They wanted to possess and control her. The way her father did—by right of his position in the family. The way Naguib Ghali would, through a contractual arrangement, blessed and certified by the state.

She took the stairs up to the women's floor. This was how the factory operated; men worked the shredding stations, positioned anywhere that the tobacco arrived, anywhere it had to be hefted or sorted with brute strength. Women worked the upper floors, at the rolling machines, where the shredded product was folded into cigarettes and sorted into boxes. Marguerite tried not to think of her father as a spider—an overseer of a great web, in which he'd snared the bodies of hundreds of workers.

But something was wrong. Something significant. The women's stations were mostly abandoned. Five women were working here, where there had easily once been a hundred. Marguerite remembered them. They'd ignored her presence, glancing up when she'd entered, but then turning back to their work. Their machines should have given off a steady buzz, a drone that would be accompanied by a dozen other drones— all of them combing to form a hive, a constant surge of activity. But now? Almost nothing.

She made her way to the third floor, where her father had his offices. The stairs gave way to a vestibule, where his secretary, Renée Ayrout, sat at a long desk in front of a door that said, in big letters on frosted glass: ÉDOUARD TOUTOUNGI, TOUTOUNGI, LTD. Marguerite nodded. At least Ms. Ayrout was where she expected her to be.

It had been a risk for Édouard to employ Renée Ayrout, Marguerite remembered, many years ago; she was the orphaned daughter of a friend of his—a woman whose life, quite literally, had depended on him, when he'd hired her at nineteen. His plan to employ her at the warehouse had caused a flurry of concern across the whole of his family—among all of Marguerite's aunts and uncles. There had been an extensive web of whispered conversations, many of which had happened in the kitchen of their flat on the Avenue des Plumes, with her mother offering comfort and reassurance. No, nothing was suspicious. No, she herself wasn't worried.

"*Habibti,*" Ms. Ayrout said as soon as she saw Marguerite. "*Mon cheri. Quelle surprise!*" *What a surprise!*

Renée walked across the room and embraced her, kissing

Marguerite on each cheek, left and then right, *faire la bise.* She held her at arm's length—her hands strong on Marguerite's shoulders.

"Are you alone?"

"I walked," Marguerite said.

"By yourself?"

Marguerite laughed. "How else?"

"With your brother? Someone else?"

"I'm not a baby," Marguerite said.

"But what about a taxi?" Renée asked, her voice trailing off. It was true; the taxis were plentiful and cheap. Ever since automobiles had replaced the horse-drawn carriages that had once lined the boundaries of the Place des Cannons, there'd been a proliferation of them. But Marguerite felt like she was being interrogated.

"I was happy to walk," she said. She sat down. Renée looked at her with what was—at best—skepticism. This was part of an ongoing dialogue between her father and his secretary, Marguerite suddenly realized, a dialogue about her, and her desires, her choices. Marguerite wasn't sure exactly *how* she knew this, but she did. It was clear to her, simply because of that single look.

"Anyhow," Ms. Ayrout said. "I'll see if he's available."

See if he's available? For his daughter? The first time she'd been here—in years? As she waited in the office with its twenty-foot ceilings, waited for her father to come to the door, she understood the lack that had driven her here. She needed something. *Important, it was important.* It had taken her to Madame Perpignani's and now to the warehouse. She needed, she sensed, her father's approval. Because inside of her there was a bright desire—a coiled, bright desire—to be understood.

For her hopes, for her imagined future, to be seen by someone. Someone she loved and respected. It was a tautness in her abdomen, a feeling like a rubber band tightening, a feeling of gathering force, a breathlessness. *Al Mutallaqa*, she thought. *The Divorced Woman*. How would Madame Perpignani's life have been transformed if she'd been understood—by even one person who was close to her? What kind of refuge would *that* have provided?

For some reason, at that moment, Marguerite thought of the fact that she—a woman of twenty-three—was still getting calcium injections from her mother, along with all of her teenage siblings. There was no differentiation, in her parents' mind, between their children. They were all just boys and girls—different from each other, to be sure, but forever juvenile.

There was a surge of noise behind the frosted-glass door. Marguerite could hear the back-and-forth of two voices, one of them clearly her father's. What seemed to at first be a discussion quickly escalated. She could hear her father's familiar voice with its familiar anger, something that she'd endured all her life. When he was angry, his voice surged upward in intensity and volume; it became almost otherworldly in its power. It was an orchestral flourish. In the German composers, especially, Marguerite recognized the texture of her father's moods.

She heard Ms. Ayrout scream. And then: a crash. Something shattered. And then a complete silence. Marguerite stood from her chair and rushed to the office door. She turned the knob and pushed it open and saw Ms. Ayrout standing to one side of the room, clutching her head, bracing herself against the wall. Marguerite's father was lying on the floor. His coat was off—another surprise—and his tie seemed to be loosened. There was a vast pool of liquid spreading out across the floor.

Blood? No. With a pulse of shock, Marguerite realized it was alcohol. She could smell it from the doorway.

Édouard tried to roll over and talk, but his body seemed somehow disorganized, as if he couldn't quite put his limbs together in a coordinated way. He said something unintelligible. Glancing down at the floor, Marguerite saw the shattered remnants of a bottle of some kind. Ms. Ayrout seemed to sway; she took a step toward Marguerite and nearly folded at the knees. *She* was bleeding from a gash in her head.

"Are you all right?" Marguerite asked, but the woman didn't answer. She steadied herself on the wall, straightened her back, and walked to the office door. Without looking at Édouard, she pushed Marguerite back out into the vestibule. She closed the frosted-glass door behind her.

Marguerite shook her head. "Are you all right?" she repeated.

"Your father is unavailable," Renée said in reply. "But if you come back in a few hours—he might be ready to see you."

Naïm

Za'atari Refugee Camp
Jordan

Za'atari. A word that had moved like an electric cur-
rent through their lives for months now. *Maybe if we could get across the border—maybe if we could get to Za'atari— we could start over?* But as soon as the smugglers dropped them at the front gate, they were overwhelmed by the sight of it, a sight that they'd been *theoretically* prepared for. Tents. On all sides—north and south, east and west, a sprawl that seemed completely unplanned. Tents everywhere. Many of them stamped with the light blue UN seal. But many just built from tarps. Sand and dust covering everything; a silver-white miasma hanging in the air, making it hard to see into the distance.

Naïm stood there, mute. Fatima stood beside him. They both read the same sign: WELCOME TO ZA'ATARI REFUGEE CAMP, MAFRAQ GOVERNORATE. The Jordanian flag was stamped there, and even that was strange to Naïm, who was so used to the Syrian flag, which the government displayed everywhere at home—with its red, white, and black bars, its two green stars. He looked over at his mother.

"What's wrong?" he said.

"Nothing, *habibi*, nothing. Don't worry."

She tried to reassure him. Everything would be fine, she told him. They'd be safe here. She took his hand in hers. But her palm was cold and sweaty, and he could hear the low rasp in her breathing as she forced herself to try and retain her composure.

"Are you sure you're fine?" he said.

"I've just never traveled without your father," she said after a moment. "That's all."

The main building was a generic rectangle—but at first glance it was different from the rest of the structures that surrounded it. Its walls were solid, constructed from a permanent-looking, stucco-like material, and this alone made it unique.

Fatima went haltingly through the main door, step by single step, hesitating on the threshold. There was a line of people in front of her, and she and Naïm joined it. After a time, they sat down. It was a strange thing to suddenly be sitting on a concrete floor, in a line, after being smuggled over the border in the back of a dark, hot van. Naïm leaned over toward his mother. "What if they send us back?" he said.

Her eyes widened. *"Zhkor el dhiib,"* she said. *Mention the wolf.* This shut him up; she didn't need to say anything else. The full saying hung in the air between them. *Mention the wolf—and have your club ready. Zhkor el dhiib hayye el adiib.* If you talk about danger, prepare yourself to face it.

Twenty minutes later they were sitting at a small table in an air-conditioned office. Across from them was an official in a light blue polo shirt.

"My name is Ihab Siddiqi," he said, "and I'm a community services officer here with the United Nations High Commission for Refugees." The man's voice was soft. He spoke in colloquial Syrian Arabic. He looked directly at Fatima, and then at Naïm, making eye contact with each of them in turn. "Are either of you injured today?"

It was a surreal question to answer.

"No," Naïm's mother said. "I am not."

"Of course I've been injured," Naïm said. He held up his bandaged hand. "What do you think this is?" The skin over his wound—the amputation—hadn't fully healed. It still oozed fluid in places. The bandage needed to be changed constantly, in an environment where there were almost never any clean bandages.

"I'm sorry," Siddiqi said. "It's a form I have to fill out."

And, in fact, the community services officer did have a form on a clipboard. He continued asking questions. Had they had enough to eat and drink in the last seven days? Did they have any chronic medical conditions? Could they share details regarding their religious affiliation? He asked about their *hawiyyat*, their ID cards. Did they have them? He used the informal term, rather than the official name, *bitaqa shakhsiya*. But, like almost everything else, the cards had been destroyed in the blast. They had nothing that proved—on paper—who they were.

Without your father. That's who they needed, of course. It was bad luck that he couldn't be here, Naïm thought. *That he was in transit.* He imagined his father being processed by the United Nations in his own camp, holding the rest of Naïm's family close, the way his mother was doing now for him. *Feigning bravery.* Naïm was so proud of his mother for this. She just needed to be strong until his father arrived. Then things would return to normal.

But as the questions continued, Fatima grew more and more reticent. She repeated the single word, *hawiyyat,* a few times. Then she grew very still. Quiet. Then a single shiver moved through her body. Naïm watched it shake her, watched it make her legs and arms tremble. And then, for the first time since the attack—even through the attack and the hospital stay, even through the second and third bombing while they were sleeping on the floor at a cousin's house, the helicopter attack that hit a nearby apartment building but not theirs, even through the agony of birthdays, of Eid with a room full of strangers, even through making his father's favorite breakfast, vermicelli noodles in sweetened milk, and letting it sit on the table all day on their wedding anniversary, untouched, as an offering to him, to his memory and his immortal soul—even through all of that and so much more, so much more almost unimaginable horror—for the first time, she broke. She began to sob.

Siddiqi disappeared through a sliding panel door. In a moment he was back, carrying three small bottles of water. He handed one to Naïm. The other two were for Fatima. But now he stood there, his face impassive, neutral. Naïm looked up at him. That question, *hawiyyat*—Naïm wondered—had it been purposeful? So many families must have lost their family books. And it was such a clear embodiment of loss. How many times each day did that question elicit this response? Five? Ten? More? There were tens of thousands just like them. A litany of grief.

Siddiqi gave them a space in the infirmary for the night. Two beds adjacent to one another in a room that was right off the reception hall. The infirmary had the feeling of a field hospital; on this night, there were two dozen people, several families, crowded into sequential cots, one after another. Naïm glanced up and down the ward. All of these cots—waiting for their daily influx of tragedy. It was astonishing to imagine the ghosts of the people who'd come before him, animating this room with their broken lives. He'd leave himself here, too, some part of himself. Some molecules. Something so small it was almost invisible.

There were clean bandages. His mother changed the dressing for him, singing the whole time she did it, an old Arabic lullaby that she'd sung to him as a child, a song about a family on a farm, a family that kept bees and picked berries. The images were some of the oldest things he'd remembered. He remembered thinking about the father of the family in this song, the father who went out into the orchard to tend to the beehives, and the mother, who collected berries in her apron. These were deep mysteries to him, as a small boy, especially since he hadn't seen his parents do either of these things.

Naïm couldn't bear to look at it, to look at his damaged hand. It had a terrible odor, a smell that was foreign and repugnant to him. The hand was just a round, meaty lump. His surviving fingers had been blistered almost beyond recognition. They itched all the time; it took his full attention not to unravel the wrapping, not to scratch at its constant discomfort.

He brushed his teeth and got ready to sleep. Naïm was wary of sleep, but so very tired. His body ached for rest even as his mind feared it. His thoughts became confused. Before long, he'd crossed the boundary between his conscious and unconscious mind. He was dreaming. In his dream, he was sitting at the little yellow table in his family's kitchen on Tuhama Street. His mother was at the stove, cooking dinner. His brother was there, too. His brother was standing at the window, turned away from Naïm, looking out the glass into the indeterminate distance. Naïm reached out and touched Omar's face—even though this was something he'd never do in real life. He reached out and brushed his fingertips against Omar's face and the touch of his brother's skin left Naïm shuddering and cold. There was a coldness inside of his brother, he felt, that was bigger than the coldness inside even the Damascene mountains.

He bolted awake. *Bombs*. Bombs falling. A distant sound, but not so distant as to be unrecognizable. It was far away, but clear. He looked to his left. His mother was gone. He sat up. He scanned the room, saw half a dozen anxious faces illuminated by the distant light of the nurses' station, a station where his mother was already standing, having a heated conversation with the nurse.

His mother glanced toward him, noticed he was awake, and started to come back over. *No*, the nurse was saying, *it's not necessary*. But his mother was standing over him and taking him by the hand again, and they walked through the infirmary door to a little stairway, one that went down into the ground, into a rough-hewn, concrete basement. Immediately, Fatima sat down, crawling under the shelter of the stairs. She motioned to her son and he came and sat beside her. Instinctively, Naïm put his head in her lap. She began to pet him, to stroke his hair, her hands heavy and familiar against the sides of his forehead, soothing.

After some time, the sound of the bombs faded away. Eventually, his mother's hands grew still. She leaned back against the wall and he could hear her breathing become steady—a metronomic, regular noise. *In, out*. A noise that fit into the darkness. But Naïm's eyes wouldn't close again. He couldn't close them. He waited. He organized the elements he was hearing into a musical piece. Everything sounded, to him, like a fugue. There was the rattle of the wind—a strong wind—moving through the camp, clattering along the tops of buildings, fluttering through unsecured tarps. There was the sound of his mother's breathing. There was the hum of an air-conditioning unit one floor up. A damp rattle. There was also something else: a silence that surprised him with its weight, hanging there behind everything.

In the morning, the nurse came and got them. She was solicitous and kind; she led them back to the cots they'd left in the middle of the night. Ihab Siddiqi was there as well. He smiled and said good morning. "The first step," he told them, "is to get you registered." Nothing was unusual, he seemed to imply. Any sort of suffering was expected.

He took their photographs and printed them each a small plastic ID card. Then he gave them something that he called a welcome kit. The welcome kit was a Mylar tarp wrapped around blankets, sleeping mats, canned food, and some tough plastic cutlery. "Fully biodegradable," he said.

Fatima looked through the food and sorted it—within the box—into several categories.

"Oil," she said.

"You can buy it on the Shams-Élysées," Siddiqi said. The Shams-Élysées, he explained, was the main road in the camp—the central arterial that began just outside the reception center. This was a pun, of course, a joke that referenced Bilad al-Sham—the name for the Syrian region in early Islamic times—and combined it with the grandest boulevard in Paris, the Champs-Élysées, the arterial that bisected the French capital and led to the Arc de Triomphe.

Siddiqi told them that in the past three years, everyone had forgotten the official name of Al Souq Street—that its name had been replaced by this new, informal designation. The Shams-Élysées was a paved marketplace, Siddiqi told them. "Maybe three, four hundred stores," he said. You could buy almost anything there. Clothes, school supplies, a SIM card. This last one was important, he said. FRiENDLi Mobile was the only service provider that got reception at the camp, and any camp-wide messages would be sent over their network.

"What kind of messages?" Naïm asked.

"Well," Siddiqi said after a moment's pause. "We've never had to evacuate. Because of . . . weather, for example. But, in that eventuality, we'd send a message to your mobile."

It was an ugly word, *evacuate*. Naïm hated it. It was part of the vocabulary of war. *Artillery, siege, barricade, air strike, insurgent, regime, rebel, captive, faction, massacre.* Those words were its brothers. Words that he'd never heard as frequently as over the past thirty-six months. And this even-tempered United Nations official was hiding something. What he was really saying—Naïm knew—was that if the Syrian army struck across the border, rolling over the invisible, imaginary line in the desert that separated the two countries, then all the refugees would have to flee.

So, Naïm thought, his mother had been right. They *hadn't* been safe the previous night. They'd been in danger still. Because death was a binary proposition—a one or a zero—there was no intermediary space.

Siddiqi looked down at his clipboard. "Did you work?" he asked, looking at Fatima. "In Aleppo?"

She shook her head. "But my husband is—was—a civil engineer."

Siddiqi nodded. He continued to explain the rules and regulations of the camp, to outline some of the available facilities.

There were seventy-one mosques, he said, roughly five or six in each of the twelve settlement zones. Naïm would attend a school in their district. "You're in District 12, Block 2, Shelter 22381. So that's . . ." He consulted the monitor and used the trackpad to toggle through something. "School 7. It has a view."

Naïm frowned. *School 7,* he thought. It didn't sound promising. "A view of what?" he asked.

"The desert," Siddiqi said, and shrugged. He tapped his pencil against the form. "Do you speak any additional languages?"

"No."

"Do you have any special talents?"

"No."

"That's not true," Fatima interjected. "He's an incredible musician."

"I am not," Naïm said. "Please," he added, "don't write that down."

"Why?" his mother asked.

"*La!*" Naïm said, perhaps too loudly. "*No!*" He hid his maimed hand behind his back. "Do not—*please*—please do not write that down." His throat hurt from how loud he'd yelled.

Siddiqi's face remained neutral. He nodded. "Because there is a school for children with special talents," he said.

"No," Naïm said again. "No, no, no."

"Of course," Siddiqi said. "Don't worry." He told them that nothing on the form was permanent, that they could make additions or changes, as was necessary. They could do it at any formal UNHCR point-of-contact. For example, he said, they'd need to go to the Office of Nutrition and Food Security—the one for their district—to pick up their bread ration cards.

ONFS would have the ability to make any changes to his intake paperwork that he wanted to make. Naïm nodded, his breathing becoming more regular. Whatever terror had briefly held him in its grasp began to relent.

The last thing they discussed was money. For this, Siddiqi wheeled the cart closer. They were implementing a pilot program, he told them. Payment at the main stores was now happening through an iris scan. He took a small handheld device and showed it to Naïm. "We make a map of your eye," he said. "It's like a fingerprint. And we tie it to your UN bank account."

Of everything Naïm had seen, this was the most surprising. "You mean," he asked, "there's that much difference? From person to person?"

"Oh," Siddiqi said. "Without doubt. The differences are almost infinite."

Naïm and his mother labored through the heat. Sure enough, there was the mobile phone store—with the FRIENDLI logo spray-stenciled on its plywood wall. There was a store with racks of colorful dresses, solid colors and prints, all draped on hangers that jutted out into the street. There was a tiny barbershop. Inside, a man sat in an actual barber's chair, talking with the barber, who was trimming his sideburns. Whatever Naïm had anticipated Za'atari would be, it wasn't this.

It took a few repetitions of their street name for Naïm to realize what it meant. Al-Ghafūr. One of the ninety-nine names of God. The All-Forgiving. He thought of his father, sitting with him at the kitchen table, holding the beads of his *misbaha*, moving through all the names of the divine, explaining each one to his eldest son. Naïm closed his eyes. Had he forgotten the sound of his father's voice? He tried to replicate it in his imagination. He strained, reaching deep into the sounds of his past. The world fell away. *There it was.* It came back to him through the sound of prayer. Clear and bright, his father praying beside him. *Al-Ghafūr*, Naïm heard his father say. *It speaks to the worst thing ever done to us. It touches this place deep in our heart. It carries the quality of forgiveness inside of you. That's al-Ghafūr.*

Sure, sure, Naïm said. *But where are you?*

Not far, his father replied.

But where?

I said, not far. Why are you so impatient?

We need you—that's why. I know you're dead, but could you hurry up and come back to us?

Of course, my love, his father said. *Of course, dear one. Whenever you pray like that, I'm here in the sound of your prayer.*

No offense, Naïm said. *But that's not good enough.*

"Naïm?" It was Fatima's voice. "Where are you going?"

She was standing at the entrance to a little dirt lane—a narrow pathway between two sets of provisional structures. Naïm shook his head.

"Sorry, sorry." He joined her as she turned and walked down their street.

The UNHCR had a team waiting at the site. While Fatima met them there and watched them assemble the tent, Naïm had to go and pick up their ration cards at the Office of Nutrition and Food Security. He followed the directions that Siddiqi had written on a sheet of lined paper.

Negotiating the streets of the camp felt like making his way through a warren. Everything was tightly built—with tents on both sides of the street—until it wasn't. There were occasional, sudden gaps of open space, when the sky, and the broader desert landscape, were both visible.

The ONFS building was busy. The agency had been preparing to move its offices, and no one seemed to know where anything was. People scurried back and forth carrying cardboard boxes. The official who greeted Naïm spent ten minutes logging into his network. The internet failed several times before he was able to make it work. He finally located Naïm's record and pulled the ration cards out of a big stack. The official apologized again and again for the disorder. Handing Naïm the two cards, he said: "Sorry it's so chaotic. We can barely keep track of what's coming and going."

Allāhu Akbar. God is Great. *I bear witness that none is worthy of worship but God.* The sound of the fifth call to prayer filled the air. The *asr* rose from the mosque on the farthest perimeter of the tent city, and, for one moment, only one voice was singing—strong and persistent, reed-thin and alone. Then a second mu'adhin began singing, and then a third, and then many others. The call was timed to the second, and so it rolled across the camp in a regular pattern—following the movement of the sun. Walking back to the tent, Naïm yearned to pray— longed for it like he'd never longed before. He wanted to reach down and touch the ground, touch holy dirt, place his palms and forehead against it, darken them with it.

His mother wasn't alone at 22381, as he'd expected. Sitting with her—wearing bright red argyle socks, crossing his skinny legs, and letting his ample gut hang down over his belt—was a middle-aged, self-satisfied-looking man. He was smoking a cigarette but, since they had no ashtray, he was tapping his ash into one of the two little metal cups that the UN had issued them.

His name was Zayit Abbas. Fatima had just removed her black headscarf before Naïm had left; now she'd clearly rushed to put it back on—a laborious process, one loop and then a second, fixing it in place with a safety pin, straightening the line of fabric on her forehead, making sure it was straight. This was the more formal aspect of his mother, something he wasn't used to seeing, and it made Naïm somehow feel uncomfortable. Off-balance.

Naïm sat down on the floor. He looked over at Abbas. The man's eyes had a glassy surface to them, almost as if they were actual glass eyes—taken from the drawer of some nineteenth-century chemist. There were many artificial eyes in Aleppo; it was an industry that had been booming since the start of the war. The eye, after all, was one of the most vulnerable parts of the body. A common target for wayward shrapnel. Or, Naïm had always thought, not wayward. Doing exactly what it was intended to do. What it was *designed*—by other human beings—to do.

Zayit Abbas was fifty-three years old, Naïm would learn. He had a head of thick silver hair. Originally from Dara'a Governorate, he'd owned a chain of electronics stores, but had offended the Assad regime—he wasn't clear on how. He'd barely escaped, fleeing across the border fence in a hail of gunfire.

"It's not true what you'll hear, though," Abbas said.

"Oh?" Naïm asked. "What will I hear?"

"That I rode a horse across the desert. That I stole a Jeep from the Syrian army and drove it over. That I flew across on the back of a drone."

Both Abbas and Fatima laughed. He was sitting close to her and—as they were laughing—he reached out and put his hand on Naïm's mother's knee. Naïm saw her startle, flinch away from the unexpected, unfamiliar touch—but continue smiling. It made him furious.

"Why are you here?" he asked.

"Ah," Abbas said, "so this is the boy I've heard so much about over the last hour."

"I wish that weren't true," Naïm said. "But I guess it is."

"Naïm!" Fatima said. *"Sakker temmak."* Shut your mouth. It was his mother's harshest admonition. Once, Naïm had said it back to her. He'd never seen her more furious, her eyes glowing with a wild indignation.

"No," Mr. Abbas said, narrowing his eyes. "It's fine. He's a young man. He's going to have opinions."

"My opinion is that I don't like you," Naïm said.

Mr. Abbas laughed. "I'm doing something kind for you, *boy*," he said, lingering on the word, as if to emphasize its diminutive nature. "That's all I do. I bring kindness wherever I go." But Abbas hadn't moved his hand off of Naïm's mother's leg. "I like to pay a visit to every new family as they arrive. Especially if they don't have a man to . . . take care of them in the camp."

"We don't need any kindness," Naïm said.

"Khrass," his mother said. *Hush.* "Mr. Abbas brought us a pizza." She pointed to the small cardboard box that rested on her cot. "It was very generous of him."

Naïm looked over. It was somehow incongruous, this object, in its surrounding circumstance—red and green slices of pizza silhouetted against a white-bleached cardboard background. He was hungry, he realized, very hungry. He hadn't eaten anything since they'd left the welcome center. Neither of them had.

In his peripheral vision, Naïm suddenly noticed his father.

He was sitting there, playing *banakil*, but on his own, playing both sides of the two-person game, picking up each hand of cards and battling against himself. It was a game Naïm had played with him so many times—too many to count—and he could hear, at that moment, his father's voice, his lovely tenor, singing "Sawaah (Vagabond)," by Abdel Halim. He only sang, of course, when he was winning. The winning would animate his whole body; his movements would become more frenetic; he would smile and play his cards at the key emotional moments in the song.

What do I do? Naïm said.

What can you do, habibi? his father said. *Just help her.*

And then he was gone. Naïm shook his head and sighed. He looked at Abbas. "They have pizza here?"

"Of course!" Abbas said. "They have anything you want."

Naïm nodded. "So I've heard." After a moment, he looked Mr. Abbas in the eye. "What if I want safety?" he asked. "What if I want to be the person I was—before *this*?" He lifted his bandaged hand and waved it in front of him. He brandished it like a weapon. Because that—that was the truth. That was what he wanted. And, of course, it could never happen. Of course, it was impossible.

Naïm's school—School 7—was segregated by gender. The girls attended in the morning and the boys in the afternoon. The classrooms were big, nearly eighty students per homeroom. There was a single meal served in the middle of the day, fruit and milk and bread in a World Food Program paper bag. The students ate in a big group in the common room.

Off to one side of it, next to a window box full of reddish-purple geraniums, there was a tiny table—one that had only two chairs. Naïm sat there each day, next to the flowers. There were two particularly robust geraniums and one small plant that was struggling to thrive. Its leaves had yellow spots and its blossoms had started to wilt and turn brown around their edges. He named the little plant Naïm. "Hello, Naïm," he whispered quietly to it each afternoon, when he sat down with his bag of food. One day, he noticed that Naïm's soil was dry. He had a small box of milk and, after searching—*Milk for plants?*—on his phone, he poured it carefully over the geranium's roots.

One afternoon, leaving the school building, Naïm noticed a series of bright yellow flyers among the numerous advertisements on the school bulletin boards. PIANO CONCERT, they advertised. STUDENTS OF SCHOOL 7. The posters seemed to invite him forward, to pull him deeper into the halls, deeper into the school's interior. Instead of walking through the front door with the stream of students, as he had the previous few days, Naïm turned to the left and went into a little hallway between two conjoined portable buildings. That's when he heard it: the sound of a keyboard being played haltingly—but loudly—echoing through a large, empty space.

He followed it. He reached the last portable before the exterior fence with its loops of razor wire. Beyond this there was only desert. Stand at this point and look out, and you could imagine that you were the only person in this camp, that you—alone—had survived the war's violence.

In that last portable there was an open room—a practice space, he later understood—with an open door. He walked up to it. Inside, there was a boy, a teenager, playing a Yamaha on a folding stand. An instructor sat on a bench beside the boy, coaxing him to repeat the same scale, C major. He was following him through the major scale formula, but the boy couldn't get it. He kept missing the third whole step on the back end of the scale.

After a while, the boy started to play a song. It was, Naïm could quickly tell, the very beginning of the first book of Bach's *Well-Tempered Clavier,* a piece that he knew well. This knowledge felt somehow illicit to him; maybe it was standing in secret just outside the classroom door, maybe it was how removed he felt from any part of his life from before he'd awakened in that hospital bed. But now he listened, and the emotion inside the music seemed to be twisted by ineptitude.

Naïm stood still. His right hand followed along. Then his left. And, as he moved his left index finger, the web of his hand began to pulse with the familiar pain. He felt the ache of the missing digits, the absence of his fingers. His whole hand twitched as he imagined reaching for the new C, one octave higher. The boy getting the piano lesson missed that note—which added, somehow, to Naïm's pain. Accentuated it.

He almost fled. He did start to leave, but then the student made another mistake and—annoyed—Naïm turned back. He stepped inside the portable. His appearance startled both the boy and his teacher. The boy broke off playing immediately.

"You can't play it like a funeral march!" Naïm said, realizing too late that he was yelling.

The sound of his own voice shocked him—and he fled the scene as quickly as he'd arrived. His first steps were backward, and he stumbled into a waste bin, one of the large cardboard recycling bins that were installed at intervals throughout the camp. It made a loud crash—much louder than Naïm could have imagined was possible.

"Hello?" the piano teacher called from inside the little rectangular building. But Naïm had already made it out through the doors. He was running home.

Shaken, Naïm made it back to Shelter 22381. He took his shoes off, stepped inside, and scanned the little space. The UNHCR had given them numerous blankets—that seemed to be something the camp had an excess of—and Fatima was curled beneath them, despite the sweltering heat. She was rocking back and forth, back and forth, moaning.

"Umi?" Naïm said. But she didn't answer him or acknowledge that he was there. He reached out, carefully, and touched her shoulder. She shrank away from him. *"Umi,"* he repeated. He sat beside her on the ground. "You're scaring me."

They'd kept their bottles of water near the back of the tent. He retrieved one of these and carried it over to her. "Water?" he asked in a small voice, almost a whisper, close to her ear. "You're sweating."

"Can you hear it?" she said.

Naïm narrowed his eyes. He glanced around the room. "Hear it?"

"There it is," she said. Suddenly, she sat up. "It's coming closer." Her eyes were wide and terrified. "Listen."

Naïm did listen then, and gradually he began to hear something. It was a sound like a puff of air, sporadic at first, but then getting a little louder. Then, a low rumble, and—unmistakably—the sound of impact.

Shelling. He couldn't believe he hadn't noticed. He'd been so deeply involved in what had happened to him at school that he'd lost track of even his physical environment. He looked at his mother. "For hours now," she said. "Just like that."

He felt it, too, then, a version of the panic she was feeling. He put the water bottle down on the canvas floor and went back to the doorway. He stepped carefully out into the street. It was empty. Or, at first, it was empty. Then a man bicycled along—carrying a bag of onions in his front basket. He seemed unconcerned. Naïm thought about flagging him down, but decided against it. Then two older women came walking by. One of them was wearing a bright red abaya with floral ornamentation around the waist.

"*Afwan*," he called, aware that he was being informal. *Excuse me.* He approached the women, who seemed startled. *That fighting*, he asked. *The artillery.* Could they hear it? They stopped and listened. *Yes, of course.* The woman in the bright red abaya shrugged. Of course they could hear it, she said.

"That's the war," she said. "As usual."

As usual, Naïm repeated. As usual. He asked them if they were worried. Before they even answered, though, he anticipated what they were going to say. "What can we do?" the first woman asked. She turned to her friend. "Every few weeks . . . ," she said. She trailed off.

Her friend shrugged. "Every few weeks," she repeated, nodding in agreement. The fighting ebbed and flowed, she told Naïm. It moved along the border. It came nearer, then it retreated. "Are you new?"

He nodded. "New," he said, wondering what the word even meant.

Naïm thanked them and turned back to Shelter 22381. He was surprised to see his mother standing on the threshold now, peering out at him.

"Let's go inside," he said.

She didn't move.

"Come on. *Yalla.*"

Nothing.

"*Umi—*"

"We can't stay," Fatima said.

"Let's lie down," he said.

"We just can't stay," she said. "They're coming for us."

"Nobody's coming."

"They are. I know it. I can feel it."

But she did turn and step back inside. She waited for him to come all the way through and then she zipped the tent closed. It was a sound, Naïm briefly thought, like the rustling of bones. A thousand sequential vertebrae—stacked in a row, crackling.

Fatima walked over and got back under her pile of blankets. Naïm lay down beside her. "We're safe now," he said, even though he didn't—in his heart—believe it. "Don't worry," he said. "It's fine. We're safe."

"Safe," she repeated.

"That's right," he said. "Safe."

"Safe." She shook her head. It looked like she was trying to shake something away.

They lay like that for a long time. "I went back to the reception center today," his mother finally said. They'd been quiet for so long that the sound of her voice startled him. He sat up, propped himself on one elbow. The panic seemed to have left her somewhat. She was almost breathing normally.

"And?" Naïm asked.

She'd wanted to ask them how to file an asylum application, she said. She'd stood in line for two hours simply to ask that question. When she'd gotten to the counter, she'd given them her name, registration number, and identification, and they'd taken it somewhere for fifteen minutes. "It felt like ten hours," she said.

"They came back, though," Naïm said. "So it wasn't ten hours."

"They came back," Fatima agreed. They'd taken her to an office where an official—*How many of them were there anyhow, an infinite supply?*—had explained how it all worked, and what to expect at the various stages of application. There wasn't any way to pick a country, the man had told her. And applications were almost at a standstill.

"That's not good," Naïm said.

His mother nodded. She recounted the rest of her conversation. She'd asked the official if there was anything—*anything*—that she could do. She'd told him that she needed the asylum application not just for her, but on behalf of her son, who'd been wounded in the war. The official had told her then that she could—for a fee—apply for the expedited process. The amount he'd quoted her, though, was astonishing.

"How much?"

"I won't tell you."

"*Umi*, how much?"

His mother refused to answer. Anyway, she told Naïm, she'd filled out the initial paperwork and filed it in the usual way. It could take years.

"I think that he *can* expedite the process if he wants," his mother said, smiling sadly. "But there's no extra fee. That's just for his wallet."

"There's always a price for everything," Naïm said, unhappy with the way it made him sound.

He lay on his back and looked up at the ceiling, trying to keep the tears from his eyes. His mother was lying on her cot as well; he didn't know, though, if her eyes were open.

For some reason, Naïm remembered now a story his grandfather used to tell—one of his grandfather's favorite stories for family gatherings on Saturday nights. He'd been a child in Damascus during the Second World War, and his building had been used as a munitions depository by the Vichy French. But when the Free French and the Allies had taken back the city, in 1941, the Vichy army had to abandon its weapons. On the roof of Naïm's grandfather's apartment building were boxes of carbines, artillery shells, grenades—both live and defective. His grandfather and his friends would pry open the shells, cracking them in half and playing with the gunpowder—setting up long trails of it in geometric patterns, and then lighting the patterns on fire. Then they'd drop some of the shells from the top of the building, aiming for the cats in the alleys.

Nothing had ever exploded. But thinking about the bomb that had ripped his own body apart, Naïm wondered: Had that moment folded in on itself, somehow, during his grandfather's childhood? Had the explosions flowered sideways through time? Had they simply opened, vicious and fiery, into 2014, all those decades later—claiming the life that they'd been denied, two generations before?

Naïm arrived early the next morning to School 7. He was silent in his classes, taking notes and being as unobtrusive as possible. At lunch he found his customary seat—next to the little geranium. Naïm realized—after a few minutes—that he'd been clutching the paper lunch bag in his hands, squeezing it as tight as he could. He relaxed his grip. His hands had cramped. Loosening them alleviated the pain that he hadn't even noticed.

He turned to the window, looking at his little plant. *Hello, Naïm,* he whispered. Its leaves were shaped like a club. They had fine white hairs that were visible in direct sunlight. Its flowers were a bright purple-red color. A red lavender, almost. They looked so fragile. He counted them. *Thirteen blossoms.* Thirteen blossoms; thirteen artillery shells; thirteen corrupt officials, hoping to turn human suffering into profit.

He reached out his right, undamaged hand, and traced the soft skin of the bloom. Traced down along the anther, the filament, the stamen. He circled it with his index finger, then moved his touch out along the body of the petal. One petal after another. And then he felt a wild pulse of anger, anger without a clear antecedent, and he grabbed the blossom between his finger and his thumb—and snapped it off. He dropped the flower on top of the table.

Naïm looked around. No one seemed to have noticed. There was a teacher at the far end of the room, and about thirty kids, clustered in groups of four or five. But no one wanted to even look at him. And so he was filled with a sudden greediness. He wanted to destroy them all. One after another, he snapped the heads off the blossoming flowers, off of Naïm the geranium, denuding it entirely of its blooms, of the things that had made it beautiful. He tossed them onto the floor, beneath the lunch table, deep into the darkened space, where only a broom would eventually pull them out, rotted and wilted and dead.

Next, he thought, he'd pull off the leaves. Then he'd see if the plant could survive that way—just stem and stalk, just dirt and pot and roots.

After lunch—instead of afternoon classes—there was a surprise announcement. Everyone would be gathering in the courtyard for a ceremony. Confusion rippled through the student body. Nobody knew what to expect. Naïm joined the boys filing through the halls. They went back to the building's anterior courtyard. There was a big tarp back there—stretched from pole to pole—a tarp that provided shelter from the sun and created an auditorium. At one end of the tarp, he could see, the administration had set up a series of risers, with a podium and a microphone. They'd hung the UNHCR logo behind the risers and closed off that end of the space to make a pavilion. It wasn't until Naïm sat down that he saw—off to one side of the assembly hall—that same Yamaha keyboard, the one he'd heard being played so badly on the other side of the school compound.

Once everyone was seated in a folding chair, the principal appeared. He wore a gray suit made from a shimmering fabric. It almost seemed to undulate as he moved. He walked with purpose and authority up to the lectern; Naïm considered how different his own life would have to feel for him to be able to walk that way.

"We've gathered here today," the principal said, "ahead of next week's concert, to celebrate a significant achievement for School 7." He was ebullient. He spoke with grand, sweeping gestures. "We have a student among us whose perseverance and dedication have achieved great things. As it is written in the hadiths: 'Indeed, I have rewarded them this day for their patient endurance.'"

The principal droned on and on. He thanked various individuals and foundations. Then he shared a story from his childhood, something about taking violin lessons. This snagged Naïm's attention; he shook his head and tried to concentrate.

"And so it is with great pleasure that I announce," the principal said, "an award for one of our students, Salsat Daeifa." There was a round of applause. The principal looked out at the assembled students and said that this boy—this one sitting in the first row—had been granted a full scholarship to the National Music Conservatory in Amman. It was only through the generosity of Queen Noor al-Hussein herself that this was possible. "We should all be grateful for her attention and on-going support. It's only because of her efforts—and, *of course*, Salsat's talent as a pianist—that he has received this scholar-ship and will be leaving us."

It was raucous. More yelling and cheering. Verging on bed-lam. Because Amman meant something—it was a path beyond the razor wire, a path to the future. And he was one of them, Salsat, a fellow prisoner in this particular purgatory, and now he, and his family, had a clear trajectory beyond the camp, be-yond Za'atari. And then Salsat stood up. He smiled and waved and walked up to the stage. The principal helped carry the Ya-maha out to the center of the riser. Salsat sat down, cracked his knuckles, and—after a moment's pause—began to play *The Well-Tempered Clavier.*

Immediately, Naïm could hear the errors. It was worse, in fact, than the day before. The music wasn't doing anything close to what it was supposed to do. But when he finished, the crowd roared. The applause felt like a constricting sea. Naïm had the surreal experience of being the only still point in a moving mass of humans. He listened as the principal came back onstage and announced that Salsat would play one more song—the second piece in the first book of *The Well-Tempered Clavier.*

That piece—even more than the first—was a composition that Naïm loved. It was both unexpected but also simple, a beautiful study in the shape that music could take. Sad and real. The boy prepared to play. Everyone was poised in antici-pation. And that's when Naïm broke.

"No," he said. He stood up in the middle of the entirely silent audience. "Wait." He was speaking loudly. "You really can't tell how bad this is?" The boys who'd been sitting around him edged away—almost as if he were on fire. "It's bad," he said. "I don't know why we're all pretending." He looked around him, making eye contact with a few confused students. His voice became almost conversational. "Why are you all pretending?"

The teachers were standing up then, making their way toward Naïm through the crowd. "I mean," Naïm said, "what are we rewarding here? Effort? Because we all make the effort. Don't we? Every day we make the effort."

The teachers had almost reached him. He didn't want them to touch him, to put their disgusting hands on him—and so he pushed his way down the row, shoving people aside. He was shoving people aside and then he was running out toward the street, looking for a space, any space, where he could breathe. His hand was throbbing. He clutched his damaged wrist and held it up in the air. He was pulling at his wrist, at his ugly ruined hand, and if only he could just cut it—cut it off entirely— he would. Why retain an unfunctioning part of a functioning body? Why retain memory without possibility?

The teachers caught up to him. One of them reached him near the exit and wrapped him in his arms. He was detained. If they'd had handcuffs, he was sure, they would have put him in handcuffs. As Naïm submitted to their authority, as he stilled his body and fell to his knees on the ground, he could hear the Yamaha piano rising up and out through the afternoon air.

They escorted him to the office. Someone called his mother and—within fifteen minutes—she was there. *We'll have to decide a punishment,* the principal told her. But for now, he added, it was important to just get Naïm home.

They walked back quietly to their shelter. Naïm couldn't find the words to talk to her about any of it. He didn't know if anything he said would make sense. Maybe it would make things worse?

She'd cleaned their tent during the day—scrubbed the seams of the canvas with a sponge and a small bowl of soapy water, swept the bare floor that had accumulated a significant amount of sand and dust over just the last few days. For their dinner, Fatima had cooked a large pot of rice on the two-burner electric hot plate. She'd flavored the rice with salt and onion and put cheap food coloring in it—red, orange, and yellow— as a substitute for spices. Yellow instead of turmeric. Orange instead of cumin. Red instead of sumac. She'd cut up cucumbers and tomatoes and made a salad with dried mint and fresh parsley. Seeing all of this made Naïm feel even more guilty.

They sat down on the floor and began to eat in silence. After a while, Fatima said: "Did you play that game you like today? Candy Cross." She said the name of the game in English.

"Crush."

"What?"

"Candy Crush," Naïm said. "The game is called Candy Crush."

"Yes," she said. "Candy Crush."

Naïm looked at his mother. She'd put down her plate. She was drinking from a bottle of water. She seemed to be worrying the bottle in her hands, running her fingers along the label. "What happened?" she said. "*Habibi*, what happened?"

Naïm shook his head.

She made a clicking noise with her tongue. The silence settled around them. "You don't want to talk about it, then," she said.

He nodded. She looked away and sighed. *Well*, she said, she had some good news to tell him. When he didn't answer, she said: "I've been to see Mr. Abbas."

Naïm's throat tightened. "And?" he asked.

"He can help us," she said.

"Oh," Naïm said, trying to retain his composure. "How?"

"He didn't say exactly."

"Sounds promising," Naïm said.

"He told me to come back tomorrow," his mother said. *"Bukra, inshallah."* Tomorrow, God willing.

"Are you going?"

"Of course," she said. "Who else is there?" She paused. *"Habibi,"* she said, "what happened?"

But he couldn't answer her.

She sighed. *"O you who believe!"* she said. *"Fear God and be with those who are true."*

Her voice fell in register—the serious, deep tone that she used, always, to quote from the Qur'an. She was formidable in those moments. She seemed to expand; her already stout body becoming even more solid, solid like a pillar.

Naïm nodded. "I'll try to fear him," he said. "I'm doing my best."

They called him into the UNHCR offices during the following school day. Some bureaucratic process had occurred in the off-hours; the story of what he'd done had moved—probably through WhatsApp—from place to place within the camp. It was a long walk back to the front gate, and a long wait in front of the wire mesh of the fence that separated the rest of the camp from the UN's office modules.

There was a guard stationed there, and a dozen boys pressed against the chain-link barrier, reaching their arms through the gaps, holding their mobile phones as far beyond the fence as they could. The UNHCR wireless passcode changed constantly, and it was supposed to be secret—but in effect it was just another item on the black market, something that could be bought and sold for a dinar, if you knew where to look. These teenagers came to the edge of the office compound to try and snag the signal; once they had it, they could get online with the stolen passcode and access Facebook, talk with anyone they'd left behind in the Dara'a Governorate, in Homs, in Aleppo. FRiENDLi Mobile, though it was ubiquitous, was also expensive; Naïm himself had just run out of gigabytes on his current plan, after only four days of Candy Crush.

The guard let him through. He waited, again, in a sweltering little hallway. After fifteen minutes, Ihab Siddiqi appeared and ushered him into an office that was—mercifully—air-conditioned. They sat down on opposite sides of a desk.

"In my official capacity," Siddiqi said, "I'm concerned."

"I understand."

"And in my personal capacity, I'm even more concerned. This isn't a good sign. For you, Naïm. Acting out like this."

Naïm nodded. "I know," he said. "I understand."

They waited there in Siddiqi's office—which was just a tiny, walled-off section of the caravan module—for quite some time. The space had the desk and almost nothing else. There was a calendar tacked onto the wall, but it showed the wrong month and year—November 2013—and seemed unused anyhow. The smell of factory-new plastic, a smell that took months and months to fade, permeated the air.

Siddiqi had outlined a variety of potential consequences for disrupting the awards ceremony. He wanted to keep this unofficial, he said. Because any official notation on Naïm's record could have an outsized effect on his ability to gain resettle-ment. "What were you thinking?" he finally asked.

It wasn't a friendly question. There was no response Naïm could imagine to *What were you thinking?* that would be satis-factory. Even if he could explain his thought process—which was complex and intricate and full of things that he couldn't totally understand himself—it wouldn't matter. The explana-tion would be unsatisfactory. What Siddiqi really wanted was an apology—an apology from a boy he barely knew. And Naïm felt stubbornly unwilling to say those words. He looked at the floor. "I wasn't thinking."

"Of course you were," Siddiqi said. "You can't just do some-thing like that—without thinking about it."

"Yes you can," Naïm said. "I did. So I know you can."

There was a long silence. The plastic scent seemed to in-tensify. "Listen," Siddiqi said. "I'm on your side." But his positivity—the cheerful demeanor of the day of their arrival—seemed to have disappeared.

Naïm waited. It was silent. Completely silent. He looked at the ground, counting his heartbeats. It seemed like he might be able to leave, and so—after another moment—Naïm tried to stand. He was going to step out of this silent office and rejoin the day in progress. But as he stood, Siddiqi also got up. "Wait," he said, and motioned for Naïm to stay where he was. Siddiqi came around the desk then and stood directly in front of him. "I want you to remember this," the man said, and then—with a motion so quick that Naïm could barely track it—Siddiqi slapped him, hard, across the face. "It only gets worse from here," he said.

Pain exploded through Naïm's lower jaw. The room spun as he took a step back and stabilized himself on the frame of the doorway. *Why?* he wanted to say. *Why would you do that?* But his vision was unsteady, and he couldn't summon the words, and then Siddiqi just turned around and went back to his desk.

Naïm stood there—barely able to breathe. The sadness of it, the sorrow of being treated like this: it was just something that he was supposed to absorb.

"Go," Siddiqi finally said, and pointed to the door.

When Naïm returned to the tent that night, his mother was gone. She'd left him a two-word note with a plate of rice and a few tablespoons of chickpea stew. *Dinner,* the note said. *Love.*

Naïm sat on his cot and—despite the heat—gathered his blankets around him in a nest. He was sweating slightly and reading Ahmed Tawfik's *Utopia*. It was a science fiction novel about the near future and the divide between the richest Egyptians and the poorest. In some ways, Tawfik's world was a mirror for the actual world—in other ways it wasn't. Though there was suffering and poverty in *Utopia,* it wasn't the kind of suffering that Naïm had to endure. It was a stylized suffering, and for him, that was a relief.

After a few hours, though, he started to get nervous. The sun was setting, and his mother wasn't back. Naïm got his shoes on and stepped outside of the tent. He paced nervously, paced beneath the night sky—the sky full of stars, with only a fragment of moon. But he saw something in the globe of the streetlight nearest the UNHCR tent. It was a faint gray fog, iridescent—a shimmering cloud. Dust? It seemed to almost be—*No, it couldn't be*—swirling and organizing itself into a shape. He felt his breath telescope outward. There was something in that darkness: fecund and feral and almost formless.

Restless ghosts, he thought, and he smelled it then—the rot of death. Raw blood, the artery of the lost past.

His mother returned just before sunrise. She didn't say anything. She simply arranged her body on her mattress—still wearing her clothes—and went to sleep. Naïm could barely see her outline as she was lying there, covered in a thin sheet. He listened to her breathing. It was ragged at first, but then it evened out. It became slow and even—as slow and even as the rhythm of a metronome.

Instead of going back to school like he was supposed to, Naïm went in a different direction. He went toward the edge of his district, the streets that bordered the Shams-Élysées, and asked where he could find the home of Zayit Abbas.

When he did find it—a large, modular unit on Al Andalus, one that Abbas had made by welding two shipping containers together—it looked something like an apartment in the city, the vanished city, with a stand-alone electric stove, a kitchen sink, and two maroon couches surrounding a little rug. It was more furniture than Naïm had seen in any other place in Za'atari. *Come in, come in,* Abbas had said when he'd answered the door. He'd made Naïm a glass of mint tea, and they'd sat together in the main room. As they sat and talked, Naïm had to continually suppress the urge to attack Abbas, to seize some improvised weapon and plunge it deep into the man's throat.

On one wall, the wall closest to Naïm, was a set of photographs. They were old—five of them—two in black and white and the rest in color. Most of them featured horses, racehorses, although one photo was of a younger version of Abbas, sitting at a roulette wheel, wearing a tuxedo.

"What are those?" Naïm asked.

"Bludan Casino," Abbas said, "and the al-Dimas racetrack. But, of course, that was long ago."

Naïm had never heard of Bludan Casino or the al-Dimas racetrack. "In Damascus?"

"Where else?" Abbas said. "On the moon?"

Listen, Abbas said, and then he started to tell Naïm a story—a story about the way the races used to be attended—at al-Dimas—by the biggest stars, the wealthiest businessmen in the Arab world, before they'd banned it all in the 1960s. There were Egyptian soap opera stars. European heads of state. Many thousands would change hands on every race. The jockeys were celebrities.

Imagine being at one of these races, he said. Imagine a cool day in February. It was six o'clock in the morning. The prayer call had just sounded in the distance. There was dew on the grandstand. Trucks delivered the morning newspapers, bundled in stacks of a hundred and bound with twine. A dozen boys were out on the track, harrowing and watering the dirt. Here came the track superintendent, wearing a shirt and tie, with his sleeves rolled up. He was carrying a cane. He put his cane in each harrow, gauging its depth. *Look at him,* Abbas said, *what a joy. A grown man who spent his life playing in the dirt.* "Do you see him?"

Naïm shifted on the couch. "Sure," he said.

"Can you *really* see him, though?"

"Yes, I can."

"That was my father. And that's the photograph I wish I had."

Getting young people to learn anything about the past, Abbas said, was nearly impossible. Why do you think we have this war? he asked. No sense of history. No understanding of the *range* of it. We were one thing, sure. But we were also another before that. Nothing is as simple or as straightforward as governments make it seem. It was like this camp. If you understood how it worked, if you had the right perspective, there were many ways to earn money—and you could buy almost anything you wanted.

"We don't want to buy things," Naïm said. "We want to leave."

"So does everyone else," Abbas said.

"I don't want to stay here," Naïm said. "I'd rather die." And with a start he realized that what he'd said was true.

Abbas took a sip of tea. He shook his head. He looked at Naïm with a condescending expression, as if he were deeply weary and the boy was making elementary errors of perception. "Of course, I can help you," he said. "But not because of anything you do. Not because of anything you steal." He paused. "Your mother is a charming woman," he said. "She'll find a way to repay me, I'm sure."

It would take almost nineteen months for the letter to arrive. Fatima handed it to him one night, after they'd sat down to dinner. He unfolded it, confused. He scanned the text. *Congratulations*, he read. *You've been selected to enter the affirmative asylum process with United States Citizenship and Immigration Services, via Form I-589.*

As soon as he saw that sentence—translated into Arabic in the space immediately below the English—Naïm looked up. Fatima was smiling at him sadly.

"But how?" he said. And because he couldn't think of any other words, he repeated himself: "How?"

"Let's just eat," Fatima said, shaking her head. "Please."

He nodded. He dipped his bread in the zhoug, the cilantro dip that was laced with cardamom. Earlier, he'd helped her crush the cardamom pods carefully, using the rounded wooden mortar, then brushing the dusty spice from the pestle and into the bright green sauce.

Fatima reached across the food and brushed back the hair at the side of his temple. It had grown long. It had a curl to it, a natural curl, and its length accentuated that. Naïm closed his eyes. He could feel the gentle pressure of his mother's hand on his skin, her thumb smoothing and organizing the strands of his hair, combing them into place, arranging them in a kind of order.

"How can I raise you without help?" she asked. He didn't answer. "Without anyone. How can I teach you what's right and wrong?"

But he felt—right then—like he understood already that crucial difference. Or, rather, that lack of difference. Because there *wasn't* a clear distinction between one state and the other. And, as Naïm moved forward—as he moved through time, transitioning from one country to the next, from one culture to the next, from Za'atari to the United States—he would only feel this more strongly, feel that this understanding grew deeper and more complex.

That night, though, Naïm wanted to comfort his mother.

"You *have* taught me," he said. "*Of course* you have." But even as he said it, he was thinking, *Because there is no right and wrong. There is only power.*

MARGUERITE

Marguerite rushed home from the warehouse. On the balcony next door, Madame Wafa—a politician's widow who spent most of her days perched above the street, smoking cigarettes—was singing a song. Oum Kalthoum. "Raq el Habeeb"—Delight the Beloved. It was the most recognizable single floating around Beirut at this moment in time; it played on the Société Radio-Orient channel, on Victrola 78s in the streetside cafés, everywhere. Right now it was echoing out of Madame Wafa's apartment—and the familiar voice of the singer was a surreal accompaniment to the old woman's somewhat raspy voice. A background singer.

"Hello, Marguerite!" Madame Wafa called, breaking from the chorus to call out and wave, cigarette pinned between two of her fingers.

"Bonjour, Madame Wafa," Marguerite replied, as always. She paused beneath the balcony, squinting up into the sunlight. *"Ça va?"*

"Ça va bien," Madame Wafa said.

And that was the end of the ritualized exchange. Marguerite opened the unlocked front door. She was thinking of Oum Kalthoum—and the plaintive melody of that particular song, which was about lost love. It was somehow even more beautiful sung together with Madame Wafa—in a duet.

Though she went to her bedroom initially, Marguerite eventually came back downstairs. She wanted to be there with her mother when Édouard failed to come home. If her mother showed any anger at all, any frustration—if she exposed that vulnerability, that humanness, to her daughter—then she'd say something. Then she'd share the story. She'd tell her what she'd witnessed, how troubled it had made her feel.

How Marguerite yearned for closeness with her mother! But time after time, year after year, she was shut down, refused, turned away. Maybe this would be the chance? The opportunity for her to reach out? Or maybe it would only make her angry? She would kill the messenger because of the message. Whether or not that would have happened, Marguerite never discovered. Because her father came home within thirty minutes, walking through the door—steady on his feet—as if nothing had happened.

Angry. That was how he looked when he came in. *Furious.* His coat was buttoned, his suit properly adjusted. Why, *why* would she come to visit him at work? he wanted to know immediately, even before he sat down at the table and had a demitasse of coffee, as was his custom. Shouldn't she be preparing for the wedding? *That* was what she was supposed to do in her free time. Not run around the city, going anywhere she pleased. What if she'd disrupted important business of some kind? What if he'd lost a contract because of her? "What would you think then?" he said, his voice rising and rising.

Normally, Marguerite deferred to his moods. Normally, he was free—in the world of the family—to get as angry as he wanted to get, to soar through their midst untethered, turning his fury into volume, terrifying in his elevation. It was an unspoken agreement. No one pushed back. Everyone just got out of the way. But today Marguerite was angry, too. She was sick of it.

"Preparing for the wedding," she said. "What about you? Is your business in trouble? Are we going to lose everything?"

He was stunned. He looked at her, his mouth opening and closing, as if he didn't know how to respond. Her mother, who'd been standing nearby, pretending to dust the sideboard, now left the room, walking through the revolving panel door and into the kitchen.

"Of course not," her father said.

"Have you been drinking?"

"Never!" he said. "Absolutely not."

"Are you sure?"

"What kind of insulting question is that?" he said.

But she knew it was a lie. She could tell. He wouldn't make eye contact anymore, whereas normally when he was angry he would demand it, trying to find her gaze and scald her with the intensity of his eyes. "I think," Marguerite said, "you aren't being honest."

"I don't have time for this," her father said suddenly, and he stood up, pushing himself back a little too violently from the table. And then—without another word—he was gone.

One morning, a few days later—a Thursday—Marguerite's father announced that he had big news. "Children! Children!" he said, using the voice he only used in his happiest, most ebullient moments. It was a side of him that Marguerite only remembered from her deep childhood, a part that had disappeared over the last decade. "I have a surprise for you!" It was an astonishing stroke of luck, he told them, practically floating up out of his chair at the head of the table.

The prime minister, their father said, *is coming to dinner.*

"When?" their mother asked. Clearly it was the first she'd heard of this.

"Tonight!" he said. He told them that he'd just found out—by morning post.

He delivered the news as if Christ himself were consenting to bless their home. The prime minister was eager to discuss an agricultural irrigation project in the Beqaa Valley. It would be mixed use, their father told them—as if this were a critical detail—but with an extensive focus on tobacco. They were to all be on their *best* behavior. No tantrums. Only polite conversation. Marguerite, however, knew what the secondary agenda was. The prime minister was pulling a lever of power on behalf of his nephew. Naguib Ghali would be accompanying him, her father said, with a look that made her body grow immediately cold, a wave of coolness passing from one part of her to another.

The day passed slowly. Marguerite spent the morning and afternoon in silence; she was surrounded by a cloud of frustration. She read in her room, a novel by Zola, but she couldn't concentrate. She followed one paragraph and lost its thread. Her attention wandered. Twice, she fell asleep. Finally, she relented and went to the kitchen to see if she could help her mother.

"Perfect," a voice said, even before she came into the room, when she was still walking down the stairs. "You're here to chop onions."

"Hello, *maman*," Marguerite said. Her mother was a broad-shouldered, broad-hipped woman. She'd given birth to seven children, six of whom had survived. She wore practical dresses, often accented by an apron. Now she was standing at the stove, stirring a pot of red lentils.

"Poor man's rosary," her mother said. It was a common

dish—but one that depended on the seasonal price of mutton. Marguerite's mother used a paring knife to make small incisions in the viscous pink flesh of the leg of lamb. Then she inserted half-cloves of garlic. The garlic-studded lamb would roast slowly in a bed of potatoes and onions and tomatoes and salt. "There's lots to chop."

Marguerite took the bowl of onions and the cutting board and sat down at the little table in the corner of the kitchen.

She wished she could somehow express—in a single image—what she was feeling, an image through which her mother might be able to comprehend the magnitude of it. But what would that image be? A sky full of locusts? A burning forest? A gallows? *I could just leave*, she thought. *Get on a train and disappear. Seek my fortune in Baghdad.* Why marry Ghali? I could leave and the fact of the leaving would be just that: A fact. A beautiful, unemotional fact. *When someone left, they were just gone.* There was nothing complex about it.

Her mother was standing at the stove. She wasn't talking. She seemingly had nothing to say.

Marguerite looked down. *Pinch the knife at the intersection of blade and handle. Keep your fingertips folded underneath your knuckles when you chop.* This was just one technique her mother had taught her. There were so many others. *Tilt the bowl when beating an egg with a fork—so the air spreads through it more quickly and it foams. Sear the meat for ten seconds in a hot pan on both sides before roasting it in the oven. Add rosewater to the honey in the baklava.* No end to these instructions. But what about her emotions? Why had there been no discussion of those? Except the implicit rules: Ignore desire. Feelings are immaterial. These are both a distraction.

"You haven't eaten," her mother finally said, after Marguerite had been working for a while. "I'll make you an omelet."

Marguerite didn't answer—which was a gesture of acceptance. Her mother began to cook, ladling a spoonful of butter onto the surface of the frying pan. Marguerite watched as the milk fat melted; she could smell the briny scent of its disintegrating lipids.

"Are you excited for tonight?" her mother asked.

"Yes."

But her voice was flat, monotone. "You know," her mother said, "I met your father when I was fourteen. We were married the next year." *Yes,* Marguerite thought. *I know the story.* You were riding in a bicycle taxi when your hat blew off. He almost caught it. Almost, but not quite. It landed at his feet.

"*Maman,*" Marguerite said, "that was a different time."

"Of course it was, darling. What are you going to wear?"

She began to offer her daughter suggestions. She needed to have her hair up—because her neck was so long and beautiful. Be sure to ask questions. Ask as many questions as she could possibly think of. And wear perfume. Did she have anything summery? Veronique had something that Marguerite's aunt had brought back from Paris. It smelled like orange blossoms. Marguerite should put it on ten minutes before they arrived. But only on her neck and the backs of her wrists.

"Isn't this all irrelevant?" Marguerite said. "You know why he's here. It's not like I matter at all."

Marguerite's mother stopped what she was doing. The omelet was finished; she'd just transferred it to a plate. It sat on the counter beside the stove, steaming. She straightened her back ever so slightly. In that slight adjustment, the slight straightening of the vertebrae and the concomitant shift in posture, there was something that Marguerite recognized, a certain subtle disappointment.

"Maybe it's better to say less," her mother said.

As a girl, Marguerite had learned that, in ballet, there were five true and five false positions. The false positions differed from the good—or true—positions, because they were of little use in subsequent steps. Not being able to achieve the true positions—or achieving instead the false positions, which often looked so similar—meant failing to properly align yourself. Even the simplest moves would fail—or they would lack a certain intensity, a certain beauty. But it wasn't always clear, as a dancer, where you were. Were you in a false position? Or had your body landed correctly, the muscles conforming to their muscle memory, and guiding you safely into the proper form?

The truth was, all of this was supposed to be invisible. Purposefully. To the audience, to the dancers. For the form to work, for it to attain its deepest beauty, the raw power had to be obscured. Otherwise, everything would be too clear. When everything was clear, there wouldn't be anything mysterious left to dazzle you.

Waiting in the entryway to greet their illustrious guest: this was not a vantage point from which she could understand anything. He was ten minutes late. The entire family had lined up there, all her brothers in their Easter shirts—even Michèl, who chafed at his collar, constantly trying to readjust it.

Finally, the car arrived. It was a long black limousine with massive chrome bumpers at the front and back, chrome detailing all along its side panels. Her mother was the first to see it, spotting it as it pulled up at the sidewalk of Avenue des Plumes. She'd been looking through the window, holding the curtain back, and now she let it fall. "They're here!" she said, her voice much too loud, since everyone was right there, sweating in their formal clothes, only a few feet away.

Marguerite's mother opened the door. Sure enough, there on the steps were the two men—the prime minister and Ghali. The politician smiled broadly as soon as the door opened. "So nice to be here," he said, "in your lovely house."

"We are so glad to have you," Édouard said, stepping forward. He held his arm out to one side, welcoming them into the foyer. "Can I introduce you to the rest of my family?"

The prime minister hesitated. It was less than a second, but long enough for Marguerite, who was watching the exchange closely, to notice. He smiled. He had to apologize, he said, because he'd brought along an uninvited guest.

"A promising young man," the prime minister said, "who told me he was quite interested in our tobacco. I said," he added, "that you were the one to talk to."

The two men parted, and there—standing on the stairs, wearing a shimmering gray suit that reflected the cloudlike color of his eyes—was Adolfo Castillo.

The seating arrangements had been an intricate puzzle. Marguerite was sure that her mother had spent hours agonizing over how to best arrange things. This was, then, a calamity. A new place had to be set. Marguerite's mother would have to hurry into the kitchen to get the requisite place setting. But if she felt any annoyance, she didn't show it. Her face retained its cheerful mask. It could be cast with plaster, Marguerite thought, with awe.

Of course, *of course* she sat next to her fiancé. But also—in a surprise that must have been accidental—directly across from Adolfo. It was easy to catch his gaze, especially when the conversation slowed. She caught him looking at her several times. And each time she did, he didn't look away. It was the opposite. He seemed glad to be caught, seemed to hope that she'd catch him. His eyes filled with pleasure, a slight crease at their edges and a sense that they were opening inward, that there was something much larger behind them, in the interior mechanisms of his thoughts.

Naguib Ghali was, himself, just as thin—and charming—as a suit on a hanger. His laugh was short and sharp, like the bray of a donkey, and in the company of his uncle he wanted to seem—if not amusing, then at least amused. So he laughed. He laughed at moments when laughter wasn't called for—something that put everyone on edge. He also held forth on various topics, including the nature of war, since that was currently preoccupying the country. The army had moved hesitantly, largely unsuccessfully, across the border of northern Palestine. "Or Israel, as they're calling it now," Ghali said, and—there it was—the braying, inappropriate laughter.

"Yes," the prime minister said. "I worry about our soldiers."

"Of course," Marguerite's father said. "They're in great danger."

"It won't affect us, though," Ghali said.

There was a pause in the conversation. Marguerite looked at Adolfo with wonder.

"I'm sorry," Adolfo said. "*Je ne comprends pas.* I didn't understand. My French is not perfect."

Ghali straightened in his chair. "Here in the city," he said, "we won't have any problems." He took a bite of his lamb. Still chewing, he said: "So I'm not very concerned." He laughed.

The pattern continued. He said something terrible or offensive or ignorant, and Marguerite and Adolfo would look at each other. After a while, this became a game. It was a secret communication between the two of them. After a few rounds, Marguerite realized something surprising: this made dinner not just bearable—but fun.

Everyone was poised. Even the young children—who were quickly fed and dismissed to the attic floor with a nanny—behaved themselves. It was all very courtly and—Marguerite thought—European. This was so different, she knew, than the way her family had eaten for generations and generations. When her aunts and uncles came to visit from the countryside, her mother would send her to the attic to retrieve the three copper sinis—the thirty-inch inlaid trays that she'd pile high with main dishes and rice and grains and warm, flat loaves of bread. Everyone would sit on the floor in the main living room. They'd move the couches aside, ignoring the table. There were no individual plates; the forks and knives also stayed, washed and stacked, in the kitchen cabinets. Everyone used their hands—or the bread—to take food from the communal trays. Not forks. Turkish—not Arabic, not French—became the primary language of the meal. *Ellerine sağlık*, everyone said to the cook. *Health to your hands.*

Suddenly, looking at the prime minister in his suit—at his equally formal nephew sitting there beside him—Marguerite understood something that she hadn't understood before: the distance her father had traveled, the changes he'd made to his life, to his language and his customs. Everything that she'd assumed was natural—her very way of life—had been partly his creation. And her mother's. The two of them building a culture in a cosmopolitan city, a city on the edge of an empire. It was a new awareness. But it didn't fill her with tenderness, only sorrow. *What a missed opportunity.* To create your own world, in some sense. What a gift that could have been.

After dinner, Édouard asked his son to play the piano for their guests.

"You've been taking those lessons with Monsieur Sarruf," he said. "Let's see if they're worth the money."

Michèl blanched. "Of course, Papa," he said. There was strain in the word *Papa*, as if it were a challenge for him to keep his voice even, to put the proper stress on each syllable. This had been a common occurrence when they were small: sing for the guests at dinner. Say no and the punishment would be extreme. Once, when Michèl refused to sing, their father had beat him with a belt in front of the entire party. Marguerite was sure this wouldn't happen now because of the lack of power their father was probably feeling, but also because—after that day—none of the children had ever refused again.

They left the dining room and went to the big main room that held the piano. Michèl sat down and, into an expectant silence, began to play the piece of music that was open on the stand, Chopin's Étude Op. 25, no. 11. "Winter Wind." Marguerite could see the sweat collecting at his temples; could see the broad streak of it down the length of his spine. He started out well, and she exhaled with relief. But then he stumbled. He missed a note; there was a clear dissonance in the piece, loud and unintentional. Then he misread a progression. He hesitated, stopped altogether, started the section again, and finally found his footing, moving forward with a certain shakiness. The tempo was slightly rushed, but not enough that anyone other than Marguerite noticed. Then he was done.

The room filled with polite applause. Édouard cleared his throat. "Shall we go have a drink on the balcony?"

People started to gather themselves. But then Adolfo said, in his careful French: "Marguerite, you play as well, am I correct? Why don't you play for all of us, too?"

Marguerite breathed in with surprise. It was a shocking thing to say—revolutionary, within the world of that dinner party. And there would be consequences. She looked over at her father. He glanced away, ignoring her, staring at the wall. His message was clear. She hesitated. "I can't," she finally said.

"Why not?" Adolfo asked.

"If she doesn't want to play," Naguib Ghali said, "she doesn't need to play."

"Exactly," her father said.

"But that's not what she said," Adolfo protested. "She said: *I can't.* What does that mean?"

"It's not allowed," Marguerite said.

"Not allowed?" Adolfo said. His voice wasn't neutral.

"She understands," Naguib Ghali said, "that it would be inappropriate to play for an audience of men."

"Actually," Marguerite said, standing up immediately, "I've changed my mind. I will play. Right now."

There was a murmur in the room, and Michèl ceded the bench. She walked over, and the whole time she could feel Adolfo watching her, watching as she sat on the bench, as she arranged her pages on the music desk, as she brushed the tips of her fingers over the keys, then rested them lightly on the bar of the key slip in front of her. In her peripheral vision, she could tell that Adolfo was continually following her movements. She could see him observing her hands as they negotiated this intricate process.

She didn't want to play the same thing as her brother. So she turned through the pages until she found something short, something that she'd memorized—the third movement of the Suite Bergamasque by Debussy. "Clair de Lune." She'd played it many times during the day, when the house was mostly empty, the only audience a bank of ferns that grew in the window. She'd sometimes imagine the plants as her audience. She thought of them affectionately as *her ferns*, a personal retinue that she cultivated and cared for—at least in part—with her practicing.

Music was, in Marguerite's mind, the space *between* the notes. It was in the intricate pauses that hung in the air. Their resonance. It was *time*, really, that everyone was listening for. Time and decay—as the amplitude of each wave disappeared, or sometimes lingered—especially with the augmentation of the pedals. The beginning of this song was simple and slow and delicate. But still—there were a few critical pauses. It couldn't be played straight through, or the mystery of it, the magic of it, would be ruined. The harmonics needed to have delicacy. Precision. Each note, or cluster of notes, needed to have the space to *rest*.

And then the arpeggios, the rolling arpeggios, the cascading, bright high melody. Marguerite was always overwhelmed, every time, *always*, by the pathos in it—she could hear its melancholy, as the D-flat major captured the opening melody and broadened it, made it soar. It gave her goose bumps. She could feel the mind of the creator, all those decades before, gone from this earth now, but still there in his work, in the energy of his work, in the music that she was rendering. She spoke a silent greeting to him then, long-whiskered Debussy, who'd given the world such a lovely gift. A distillation of his suffering, his joy. She thought of the landscape of the lunar surface, the great mystery that she'd stared at, almost inexhaustibly, as a girl. Because she knew the piece so well, her mind was free to travel to these places. It was a part of the piece for her, in the same way that a book inhabited the life of its reader, becoming a part of the story of their life, at a single moment in time. For her, the story of "Clair de Lune" included all of this.

Then the rubato tempo reached up and took her back from wherever she'd gone, focused her attention on the work of her hands. It unified the piece, tied it all together with the highest notes, the ones that always made her straighten her spine, breathe with only the very tops of her lungs. They sounded like a harp. And then—there she was in the last minute, rephrasing the opening melody, concluding it with that single low note, almost like a deep sigh. An exhalation. And directly into the rolling, walking notes, the brief story—Marguerite always imagined—of a walk, a stroll, on a warm summer night beneath a clear sky and a full moon. Then just the last chord. And the gentle final notes—first eleven of them, and then eight more, played with varying pressure, with only her left hand. She'd always wondered about that missing note. Where was it? Surely it shouldn't have been nineteen notes—nineteen notes to conclude the piece? The twentieth was there, but it was invisible, a ghost note, and she was always tempted to add it on to the end, resolving something that Debussy had left—purposefully, of course—unresolved.

She finished. The room was silent. It took Marguerite a moment to realize that it was silent. She turned on the bench and saw why. All of them—*all of them*—were staring at her. Naguib Ghali's mouth was agape, hanging open like the narrow mouth of a fish. Adolfo was smiling. He suddenly began to applaud, and then everyone else was applauding. She scanned the faces in the room. It seemed like everyone had reacted differently. Her father, furious. Her mother, anxious. Ghali, stunned. The prime minister, difficult to read, neutrally pleased, perhaps? Adolfo, joyous—almost triumphant. And her brother Michèl? He was hard to read, too. He seemed to be glaring at her with a version, she thought, of her father's anger. His face, in fact, looked strikingly like their father's face in this moment, with the same features, the same rounded nose, the same space between the eyes, the same line of the jaw.

"Brava!" Adolfo cried. *"Incredible!"*

"Yes," said the prime minister. "Well done, young lady. You have a bright future. What a talented family you have, Monsieur Toutoungi. You should be quite pleased."

"Yes, sir," Édouard said.

Then the party did go out to the balcony to smoke cigarettes and drink Armagnac, the finest bottle that Édouard had in the house. But as they left the room, Michèl grabbed his sister's sleeve. He pulled her to one side.

"How could you?" he hissed.

"What? What did I do?"

"You made a fool of me."

"How?"

"You heard how I played. You made me look like a child by comparison."

"Michèl," Marguerite said. "Nobody is comparing you to me."

"I know that," he said. "It's clear to them who's the more talented musician."

"*Talent?* What good is talent to me? Tell me that. What good?"

"Then why embarrass me? Why embarrass father? And Monsieur Ghali?"

"You're awful," Marguerite said. "Who cares about that man?"

"I do. And your father does. And so should you. After all, he's going to be your *husband*." Her brother said these last words, *ton mari*—your husband—with a kind of vindictiveness. It was as if he were sneering at her from a great distance, a great height. *Mocking me*, she thought. Marguerite wanted to slap him. But she didn't. She simply turned and began to walk away. But then, at the last moment, before she got to the staircase, she turned back.

"You're right," she said. "I do have talent. And no matter what *you* do in life, *that's* something that you'll never—*never*—have."

Marguerite excused herself and left the men to talk and smoke on their own. She went to her bedroom and washed her face. The letter was there, in her dresser drawer, folded twice. She opened it and placed it on the dresser's surface. She looked at it again. It was an impossible problem. How could she uproot her life? Why had she gone to all that trouble to apply—without knowing, for sure, what she would do if accepted? It had all seemed so impossible. Just putting together the application had been a kind of dream. It had been a fulfillment, in and of itself. Her boldness in doing it, in circumventing the rules, in doing so many things that no one—or almost no one—would approve of. It had been a thrill. A *private* thrill. But now it was something else. It was much more real.

How, Marguerite thought, could Michèl have said those things? He'd broken her trust. *Of course* she hadn't meant to hurt him. He'd seen everything that had happened. She'd been goaded into playing by Ghali's remarks. She'd even refused at first. How could he have witnessed all of that and still taken that odious man's side? She loved her brother—but her trust in him wavered slightly. She still thought of him as the boy she'd grown up with—still the same ally and friend—but the impending pressures of adult life were transforming him in worrisome ways.

Tonight, Marguerite had been transported to another place by playing the song. She tried to hold on to some of that travel, that distance, and ignore the things her brother had said to her. But it was nearly impossible. She had the same novel on her bedside table, and again she tried to read it. Again, she failed. She was sitting there, her back propped on a pillow, when the doorknob of her bedroom began to turn. She looked up at the sound. Her door opened, slowly, and there—there was Adolfo.

"You have no idea how many doors I've opened like this, looking for you."

"What are you doing?" Marguerite said, scrambling to straighten her nightgown.

"Your house has too many doors in it."

"You're mad."

"Too many rooms. There should be less rooms." He walked closer to her. He sat down on the middle of the bed. He was close enough to her that she could smell the scent of what must have been his cologne. Applied recently, she thought.

"You shouldn't be in here," she said.

139

"Of course not."

"If you're caught—who knows what could happen."

"Many things, probably."

She put her hand on his arm. "Listen to me," she said. "I'm serious."

"So am I," Adolfo said. And then he leaned over and kissed her. He kissed her once, and then again, and a third time. His lips were soft, she thought, much softer than she'd imagined.

"You can't marry that man," he said. "You should marry me."

"I don't know you."

"I think you do," he said.

"You don't live here."

"And maybe that's a good thing," he said.

Marguerite laughed. Then she leaned closer. They kissed again. "Oh dear," she said.

Meet me this Saturday? he asked her. He was staying at the Hotel St. Georges. He would meet her in the café on the terrace. It had a wonderful view of the harbor. Idyllic. It reminded him of the harbor in Havana Bay, and the view from the Hotel Nacional, where he'd seen Frank Sinatra two years before. Adolfo kept talking, perhaps conscious of the resistance that was rising and falling within Marguerite's mind. In general, he said, he disapproved of the capitalist excess of an institution like the Nacional. But for Sinatra, he'd made an exception—taking the train northeast to Havana.

He kept talking. He asked her if she'd heard Sinatra's most recent album. He was a young singer, but he had an old sound, in Adolfo's opinion, an *old* voice, deeper and more confident than it should have been. And that was when she leaned forward and, taking his face in both of her hands, kissed him again.

"This Saturday?" she said. "At the Hotel St. Georges?"

"This Saturday at noon," he said. "I'll see you there."

She nodded. "I'll see you there," she said softly. But she wasn't certain of anything. She might see him, yes. But maybe not. Surely, he was joking. She could never marry someone she'd just met. He was handsome, sure. His mind was vital and passionate and alive. But who was he? He was from Cuba. His family was wealthy, without question. He was an ardent believer in the Communist cause. But there was much more to a person than a collection of facts. The facts added up to something, sure, but they were only part of the story. How would he *act*—and how would that be different from the things he said? Because, Marguerite thought, Adolfo Castillo was a mystery to her. What did she really know about him, after all?

On Friday morning, Marguerite awoke with a start. She got out of bed almost mechanically, her body awake, but her mind preoccupied and in a different realm. She made her way into the kitchen. No one—not her brothers and sisters, not her mother, not her father—would look her in the eye. She quietly ate a bite of toast, had a sip of coffee. Then she lined up for the calcium shot.

Her mother walked over, as usual, carrying the little box of vials. Marguerite was suddenly filled with a sense of dread at the prospect of the needle piercing her skin. She suddenly felt that this was a tremendous invasion, a nearly insufferable wound. She couldn't bear the thought of it any longer.

"No, *maman*," she said. "Not today."

She stepped out of line. Her mother looked at her, her forehead contracted into disapproving wrinkles. "Yes, today," she said. "Today and every day."

"No," Marguerite insisted. "I have my lesson. I have to prepare."

Her mother frowned. "I work so hard," she said, "to keep you healthy." She looked at the line of her children. "To keep *all* of you healthy."

"Yes, *maman*," Michèl said.

"I understand," Marguerite said, ignoring her brother. "*Je comprends*. But I'm done. No more shots." She paused. "Sorry," she said.

She *did* have to prepare for her lesson. But only psychologically. Because—after the Oum Kalthoum concert at Le Grand Théâtre, her father had written to Monsieur Sarruf and canceled her tutoring indefinitely. She'd be getting married, he told both Monsieur Sarruf and her, as if this were a clear explanation for why her lessons had to end. Her brother would continue, he'd told her, but she would not. Today—this Friday—would be her last hour with her teacher.

While her mother was still thinking—while she was trying to imagine a way to compel her daughter to behave— Marguerite turned away and, again conscious of being watched, left the room. As she walked down the stairs, unsure of what she was doing, she waited for her mother's voice; she waited to be called back to the balcony, called with a tone that she wouldn't be able to resist. But no call came. She made it down the stairs and out the door. She had nothing with her, of course, and this felt like a nakedness, a further vulnerability. But also a freedom. Here she was in the world, on her own. She needed no justification for her body, for its presence on the street.

Monsieur Sarruf greeted her at the door. He was unexpectedly emotional, kissing both of her cheeks, but then taking her shoulders in his hands. *Mon cheri*, he said. *My dear. Congratulations!* There were tears in his eyes.

Monsieur Sarruf wore a bow tie, perpetually—mostly bright red but sometimes blue or gray. *Did he sleep in it?* she sometimes wondered half-seriously. His posture was imperiously straight. He had never slouched, Marguerite believed, even once in his life. His accent was purposefully continental; his bookshelf had a framed photograph of him standing on a stage, shaking hands with Poincaré, the French president, in Paris. Marguerite and Monsieur Sarruf had met once a week for the past seven years in his apartment in the Horsh neighborhood—a grand, sprawling apartment that overlooked the municipal park and its pine forest. Now she didn't know what she would do with this space in her life. This emptiness. It filled her with dread.

"It's wonderful to see you," she said. "Let's get to work."

She started immediately on what she was studying at the moment—Chopin's Polonaise-Fantaisie in A-flat Major. It was a challenging piece—complex in its shades of tone and intonation—and still slightly unfamiliar. But when she made a mistake, Monsieur Sarruf barely corrected her. No sharp admonishment, as usual. He only seemed to be following the sound of her playing, his head moving to the left and the right as the music turned, as if he were being pulled away by a current.

She played the piece once, then twice. After the second time, Monsieur Sarruf paused and looked at her. He was silent. One beat passed, then another. Finally, he said: "What on earth is the matter?"

Marguerite was startled. "Nothing," she said.

"You're so convincing," he said. "Well, no. You are not convincing at all. But also—the music tells the story. It can't lie."

"I'm not lying," Marguerite said. But his concern was moving. He really cared. Now he shook his head and stood up. He took a few sheets of music from the lectern beside the piano. He folded them. He walked to the corner of the room and filed them in the tall metal cabinet in which he kept all the scores. Then he busied himself with some other papers. Marguerite simply looked down at the keys of the piano in silence.

"Will you tell me what's wrong?" he finally asked. "Or do I have to lock you in my house to get it out of you?"

"There's no problem," Marguerite said. "I'm only sad to leave you. That's all."

He sighed. "Fine," he said. "Play it again."

She did. Then a fourth and a fifth time. Her fingers grew tired. The webs of her hands began to ache from playing the scales, from ascending and descending the keys—first with her right, and then with her left. She found it almost impossible to make it through the sequence of rapid notes, through the madness of the beginning of the piece. Through the hunger of winter. The fury of a winter storm. After her fifth attempt, she sagged with exhaustion.

"Maybe something else?" she said.

Monsieur Sarruf frowned. "What do I always say?"

She didn't respond.

"What do I always say?"

"Again," Marguerite said. "Play it again."

"That's right. And that's what we'll do. Until I say otherwise."

"Discipline," she said.

"Discipline," he said, nodding. "The cornerstone of everything I've done. Returning again and again to something—even though it feels like you can't go on."

At that moment, Marguerite realized that—despite all these years with her teacher—she didn't know very much about his past. He was a surface with an imagined depth. Was it all a fiction? Something she'd pieced together from various scraps, from the smallest suggestions he'd made, allusions to one event or another?

But there'd never been an easy way to ask Monsieur Sarruf anything. So much of what they'd done had focused on her playing, on the mechanics of improving her technique, on the deep heart behind her music. It had all focused on her. But him? She wanted to know more, more than just the diploma so carefully framed on his wall, the document that had been so influential in his life—*and* in hers. She looked at him more closely. His onyx cuff links, his starched collar, his perfectly ironed shirt. His pin-striped suit jacket. What forces—what experiences—had created this precise of a man? This exacting?

She began to ask him questions. Had he started playing when he was very young? What was the village like—in the Nur Mountains, she knew, but not much else—where he'd been born? How had his path taken him from that remote place to the Parisian academy? And how had it taken him back? Monsieur Sarruf smiled. "The reasons aren't always clear, don't you think?" he said.

But then he told her a version of his story. He was his parents' only child. His mother had died when he was very young. Only three. He had one memory of her. Walking behind her in the house, holding the end of her long white dress, pacing along with her as she said the rosary. After she'd died, his father had remarried. He'd wanted to start a new family, and so he'd shipped his son off to a seminary in France. *Thonon, France*. "Nothing more than a village," Monsieur Sarruf told her. He'd been five years old.

This was not an unusual gesture for Christians from the region. Often, these sons would become priests, and return home to serve their birthplace in the end. It brought a certain amount of honor to their families. But Monsieur Sarruf had been a terrible seminarian. Undisciplined in every way, except the one he'd loved: music.

"You?" Marguerite said. "Undisciplined?"

"A mess," he said.

Anyway, he continued, he'd written hymns, sung in the choir, played the organ. And at sixteen, when he was supposed to take his vows, the Great War had begun. He'd fled the seminary and ended up—one way or another—in Paris.

"I got tremendously lucky in Paris," Monsieur Sarruf said. "But I can tell you that story some other time."

But what if there isn't another time? Marguerite thought. "I have something to tell you," she said.

And so she told him the whole story. The fact that she wasn't ending her lessons because of her impending marriage. Not really. She told him about her acceptance. She thought he would be angry. He would think that she hadn't trusted him enough to ask for his encouragement. Or that he wouldn't believe her. And she was right. At first, he didn't. Or, rather, he had no frame of reference to understand the situation. But then, when she described how she'd done it, described the acceptance letter in detail, down to the letterhead on the stationery—he began to get excited. He was trembling, shaking with such force that she worried he was going to fall ill, that some calamity would overtake his body. She told him she didn't know if she had the skill to take the requisite classes. The composition students—though they didn't have the same parameters as the performance students—still had rigorous tests. Would she be good enough?

"I'm worried I'd fail," she said.

"If you play the way you can, my dear," Monsieur Sarruf said, "there are no limits. I can imagine . . ." And here he sat down on the piano bench beside her. He looked at her with fervor in his eyes. ". . . almost anything for you."

Marguerite reached out to take his hand. "That's kind," she said.

He pulled his hand back. "No limits," he said.

"I don't know what to say."

"It's the truth. You absolutely must accept. Accept and go. Because, in the end," and here he shook his head, "the work is all that matters."

Sitting on the terrace of the Hotel St. Georges the following afternoon, sitting among the waiters in their bright red coats, among the elegant guests with plunging necklines and straw boaters—hats that were threatening, with each gust off the Mediterranean, to blow into Zaitunay Bay—Marguerite felt a familiar sense of dread. It was formless, shapeless, and incongruous against this backdrop: the city stretching away to one side, the cobalt bay on the other, with its breakwater and the sea beyond it. Why should she feel this way? Among these people wearing their formal clothes so casually? It was a fine afternoon. What could be so oppressive about a demitasse of espresso? Or someone at the next table smoking a cigarette? Why should a four-ounce cup of coffee and a cloud of exhaled smoke feel, to her, inexplicably like a straitjacket?

She'd told her family that she was going to the library. If they'd noticed that she was wearing a new blue dress—one that was different than the wedge silhouettes of all the dresses she had from before the war—no one had said anything. It had narrow shoulders, a cinched waist, a long skirt with a wide hem. It struck her as impractical. The surplice neckline worried her as well; she wanted to cross her arms over her chest, a defensive gesture. She breathed in. Exhaled. Focused on a voice at a nearby table, a man talking—loudly—about politics.

Lebanon, the man was saying. *The whole idea is ridiculous.*

Everyone here was speaking perfect French—seamless, unaccented—which sounded somehow strange to her, artificial. Usually, everyone around her spoke a mixed version of French and Arabic, a creole vocabulary, one that was built from both languages, from whichever one seemed to fit the moment. But here—at the center of European cultural life in the city— the accent had changed noticeably. It was softer, somehow, less abrasive. It wasn't much, only a slight shift around the vowels and velar consonants. No one would notice—other than someone who spoke both languages every day.

She was waiting, waiting for Adolfo. He was late. It was intolerable that he was late because it meant that, quite possibly, he had reconsidered. This idea, to her, was both frightening and simplifying. She would have one less complication in her life. If he never appeared, she would just leave. She would walk through the lobby and out into the afternoon, and that would be the end of things.

"*Écoute*," the man beside her was saying. *Listen*. Glancing over at him, at his strident, sweeping gestures, Marguerite got the sense that he was the kind of person who disagreed with everything. "I am a citizen of France. That is the bedrock truth." His voice was a constant, intense warble, like a siren. "And we will never be able to share power here. Christians and Muslims living together peacefully? A confessionalist government? Never. That time is over."

She'd ordered a single espresso—accented with a lemon peel—like many of the other guests on the terrace. It was the way they used to do it in Italy before the war, she'd heard from a friend. Lemon peel, surprisingly enough, cut the acidity of the coffee. One acid softening another. She squeezed the peel onto the tips of her fingers. A puff of citrus floated out through the air.

To pass the time, she'd brought the proofs of a few family portraits Michèl had done, and which he'd given to her—*before* the dinner with the prime minister—asking for her opinion on which one to frame. He'd been practicing portraiture for the past few months, becoming enamored of it in a way that he'd never been eager to do anything before. He'd talked of opening a portrait studio in the Badaro neighborhood. He'd taken to collecting camera equipment—especially German camera equipment, Leicas and Hasselblads—which he bought from an ever-growing network of local photographers.

Ten minutes passed. *This was a mistake,* she thought. To keep herself calm she kept leafing through the photos, putting the ones she didn't like in her handbag. It had been crazy to do this, to meet him here. She imagined what it would be like for him to come around the corner—to walk toward her table, crossing the room, step by step. She thought of him as luminescent. In her imagination he was luminescent; he seemed to outshine everyone else. Everyone else, in fact, disappeared, slid away, became unimportant.

She glanced upward. The hotel couldn't have been more lovely on this warm day in December. It was the kind of building that—to Marguerite—was the best legacy of the French Mandate. She appreciated this, at least; when they'd left, the French had also left their buildings behind, the buildings designed by architects from Paris and Marseille and Lyon— sculpted to rise from the street in elegance and poise. Adolfo probably hated them, these buildings. Though she didn't know for sure, she imagined that he despised the architecture of the past, that he disapproved of the Gilded Age, with its ostentation and finery.

He's not coming, she thought. Her heart fluttered. He's left the country early, she thought; he's attending to business elsewhere, doing some errand for his father, touring some factory in Ankara, or meeting with some industrialist. He'd felt no real connection to her. Why would he want to see *her* again anyhow? What would make him readjust his plans, change his itinerary—just for her?

And what was the point? This was all doomed. Doubt seized her now, and she decided, with a twinge of relief, that she would forget all about it. She would simply resume her normal life. She would stand up. She would stand up and leave. She would pay the bill and go home, and in two weeks—three weeks, perhaps—this moment would feel distant. And then— just as she was thinking this—she saw him walking across the terrace toward her. He was wearing a crisp white button-up shirt, and no tie.

"Tobacco flower," he said. *La fleur de tabac.* He was smiling, a warm broad smile, one that was both eager and kind, that illuminated his face completely. "How lovely to see you in your natural climate."

She stood up and he took her into his arms, enfolding her completely. "That's a charming thing to say," she said. "Hello."

And, just like that, they'd ordered drinks and were careening through a conversation. It didn't matter *what* they were talking about, exactly, it was more the way that they were saying it. He was irrepressible; he seemed to have an encyclopedic knowledge of his father's tobacco business. She encouraged him to talk. First of all, Marguerite loved to listen to him. His accent was strange, unlike any she'd heard before. But also, it gave her the space in which to conceal herself a bit. It was, really, where she felt most comfortable. Slightly on her own, slightly private.

Adolfo continued talking. The demands on the farms— labor demands, time demands, water demands—were massive. He'd been trying to change the harvest completely, to modernize it in order to help ease the burden on the workers. Diversification, automation, and collective bargaining; he'd done as much as he could, without his father's approval.

"Fifty cents a day," he said. "Since 1934—when they passed the law—*that's* how much a worker makes on the plantation."

Marguerite nodded. "*Your* plantation," she said.

"The plantation *my father* wants me to inherit," Adolfo said. "Fifty cents."

The figure hung in the air between them.

"It's similar here," Marguerite said. She talked about her own father, and how hard the work was that the laborers did in his warehouse. She told him the story of her visit to the wharf, and how the factory was almost deserted, but still palpably an engine of misery, dark and dirty. "Those are the conditions in the whole world," she said.

Adolfo was passionate, earnest, combative. "*Exactamenté*," he said, briefly lapsing into Spanish. "Everywhere I go with my father, all I see in the factories is destitution and slavery."

"Wage slavery," Marguerite said.

"Exactly."

She straightened her back and looked into the distance. The waves of the sea undulated in a steady pattern, one after another. They were deep blue and near black and, in places, cerulean. "Or if the factories are modern," she said, "they're death traps."

"Every machine," Adolfo said, "is a killing machine."

Marguerite was silent for a moment, but then she told him about the tobacco farms in Latakia that she'd visited once, when she was a girl, with her father. She told him about the poverty she'd seen, and the children her age—nine, ten years old—who'd walk the fields in the mornings, topping and suckering the plants, trimming off the flowers and unneeded leaves.

He told her it was the same in Cuba. That it had been built on the labor of slaves—for centuries, the same as in the United States. *Infamia y humillación*, Adolfo said in Spanish. What was worse, he told her, was that there was a myth that the tobacco farms had all been independent, that they hadn't used slavery. But it was a myth. A mythology. It stole away the historical dignity of generations of laborers. And when you stole history, he said, you earned interest in the present moment.

He talked about the money in agriculture. How there was never enough for anyone other than the wealthiest landowners. How the commodity was manipulated from overseas, from the largest cities in the world. Marguerite nodded. She'd seen the auction houses in the city—where men in tailored suits bid huge sums of money for piles of the tobacco leaves, tobacco leaves that had been dried and bundled and stacked on the floor, waist-high. The money. It was hard to see. Especially when she knew how poor the farmers were, almost all of them.

She'd tried to tell her father, at some point, all of this, but of course he hadn't listened. "Why would he listen to a girl like me?" she said.

"I would listen," Adolfo said, "to a woman like you." His eyes—brightly lit by the afternoon sun—had that same burning intensity from the night at the prime minister's residence. "The first thing we need, without question," he said, "is medical care on the farms. Doctors. Nurses. Supplies."

He had a plan for how to do it. He told her that he would divert five percent of the federal agricultural tax to a health fund for workers. *Five percent!* he said. "It's almost nothing." It was a plan that Carlos Zayas supported in the 1944 election. But he'd lost. He'd run a bad campaign and lost, Adolfo said. And now Ramón Grau was president—and he was a thief. Of all people—of every politician on the island—*he* was the worst. And Adolfo was so upset that he leapt to his feet.

The people at the tables closest to them looked over with alarm. He seemed to realize where he was, and then he quickly sat back down. He was blushing. "See what I mean? I'm a fool. A pompous fool. I get too excited."

"Not a fool, no," she said. "I don't think *that*. Pompous maybe. But not a fool." And to her relief, he immediately laughed. It was as if she'd made a leap across a wide and dangerous chasm. It was a small comment, almost nothing, but it had great effect on the conversation. It created a closeness between them; she felt the pull of it, too, almost as if it were a string tightening.

Adolfo was talking then about the fields and his hopes for them. And the lush landscape, as he described it, was the opposite of the land outside of Beirut. Here it was dead. Even the Beqaa Valley to the east of the city, with its wheat farms and its vineyards, could be dry for months at a time. She was thinking now of what it must have been like to be in the middle of such greenery—the city a distant thing, the primary sounds around you the sounds of the natural world.

At one point, he looked down at the photograph proofs on the table. "What are those?"

"My brother Michèl," she said, rolling her eyes. "His new passion. Photography. He took a hundred portraits of us. But that's how he is. Always going from one thing to the next. Almost uncontrollable."

"He seemed nice," Adolfo said, his voice neutral.

Marguerite paused. "I love him very much," she said, and shrugged. She put the rest of her brother's portraits back in her handbag. And then she had an impulse—something that surprised even her. "Listen," she said. "Do you have some time?"

"Today, I do."

"Good," she said. "Because there's something I want to show you."

Adolfo paid the bill and she led him to the taxi stand with its line of modern black vehicles. They got in one of them. "Where are we going?" he asked her.

"Not far," Marguerite said. "Just toward Bab Idriss and then right into the city."

"And what are we doing?"

"I said: it's a surprise."

"Should I be worried for my safety?" he said. "In a taxi with a strange woman?"

Marguerite paused. As the car moved hesitantly through the mixed traffic—through the mass of bicycles and pedestrians and horses and donkeys pulling carts—she saw the reflection of her face in the driver's rectangular rearview mirror. "A strange woman," she said. "Am I that strange?"

"Not at all," he said. Then he pretended to reconsider. "Or *perhaps* . . . ?"

The taxi stopped. "The cathedral," the driver said, gesturing out the window.

"Thank you," Marguerite said. There was a pause—just a momentary pause, but noticeable—before Adolfo realized he had to pay the driver. But then they were out of the taxi and standing in front of St. Georges Cathedral. It towered above them, its elaborate and finely sculpted entryway shimmering with stained glass and sunlight. "St. Georges," she said. "Same as the hotel."

"He's a very versatile saint," Adolfo said.

She nodded and asked him for another bill—*anything small*—and he handed it to her. "Stay here," she said.

He watched as she walked over to the doorman, who was sitting on a little cushioned stool just to the right of the entrance. She talked to him for a few minutes. It was a friendly, jovial conversation, and Adolfo almost missed her handing the doorman the banknote. After a moment, she turned to Adolfo and waved him over.

"*Shukran*," she said to the doorman, and he turned and opened the large, iron-framed cathedral doors.

"*Por la izquierda*," Adolfo said. To the left side. "That's what we call this kind of bribery."

"Bakshish," Marguerite said, thinking of her conservatory application. *A gift*. "It's the only way to get anything done."

They entered the church. Once they were inside, Marguerite saw the pew where she sat each Sunday, immediately beside her father. She was closest to him—on the opposite side of her mother—her brothers and sisters to her left. It was a position of pride for her. When the congregation prayed, when they said the Our Father together, everyone reached out and held hands. As a child, especially, there was no greater joy for Marguerite than that moment—that moment when her small hand fit into the strong, thick-fingered hand of her father. It had been so powerful, and full of life, and warm. It had cradled her—cradled her hand—and held her with a protective, fierce closeness. *Where had that feeling gone?* They'd rolled it up like a scroll and put it away somewhere. But where? She sensed she might never again touch it. She could almost smell the scent of it in the air of the cathedral, the scent of so many Sundays from her childhood: Pinaud-Clubman aftershave and clouds of smoke from the censer. And *hear* it. Hear the Arabic words of the *qurbono*, spoken by the priest in his snowy vestments, hear the congregation singing the *fesheeto*: *From the Father I was sent, as word without flesh.* She shook her head.

"Come on," she said, and walked a little faster.

Marguerite led Adolfo to the side stairs that went up to the loft, where the musicians sat during the service.

"I'm worried," he said, "that you've decided to convert me."

"In a way, yes," she said. "Yes, I have."

"God is dead," Adolfo said.

"Fascinating," Marguerite said. "I'll let him know and see what he thinks about it."

As they climbed the stairs, they passed the paintings of the Stations of the Cross—Jesus submitting to the fourteen stages of his crucifixion. Christ was caught here, frozen in a state of suffering—betrayed, tried before an unjust court, executed. She'd always thought how sad it was that *this* was the most important story—a story of extreme suffering and grisly death. Where were the stories of joy? Yes, there was the Resurrection. But that was only told *after* the story of the crucifixion, of the betrayal.

This had been her parish since she'd been an infant. She loved the sound of the piano, the piano in the loft, and its notes had always felt like they were descending to her, falling from the sky like rain. She'd first imagined writing songs for this space. From time to time—rarely, but as often as she could—she'd come here and play the piano. But the challenge had been getting free of her obligations, finding a way to sneak out of the house. In many ways, it was ridiculous. So many teenagers snuck out of their homes to drink, to gamble, to do almost anything destructive. But she wanted to play the piano in a church. And she was risking the same familial scorn, the same parental anger, the same penalties.

Marguerite explained all of this to Adolfo as they walked to the instrument, as she folded back its front lid, lifted the main lid, fit the prop into its outermost notch to keep the cover open. He walked over and stood beside her.

"I see," he said. "This is what you brought me for."

"Not to convert you," she said.

"Not to convert me."

She began to warm up. She held her right hand still in the shape of a chord—a C diminished seventh—and stretched each finger, first individually, then two at a time. Then she stretched her thumb, tracing circles in the air. Then the left hand, in its own chord. It was boring to watch, she was sure, but necessary. "Are you ready?" she finally asked. Adolfo nodded.

Marguerite began to play her work in progress—the beginning of it, anyway—both loving it and hating it as she moved through it in her mind. Here was the quiet moment, the moment that she loved best, the bars she'd written, in her imagination, while walking down a street in the first rain of the year, the first rain after the dry season, when the streets seemed to come alive.

Adolfo sat beside her as she played. Marguerite couldn't tell who'd begun to lean first, but it was clear after some time that they were both leaning toward each other. She felt the pull of his body flow through her, tightening through her abdomen, spreading warmth upward through her chest. The energy of it flowed into her playing, and now she was reaching a quicker, more energetic passage, and then—it stopped. Mid-phrase. Her body went still.

"That's it?" Adolfo said. "That's how it ends?"

"It's unfinished."

"What is it?"

"I wrote it," Marguerite said with a certain amount of pride. "Or I *am* writing it."

He shook his head. "It's incredible," he said.

She looked at him. She tried to form the thought in her mind—put it into words—how the song was bothering her, how the third part of it, especially, was a challenge. That first part, she had, and of course the second part as well. But the third—it was more elusive. Thesis, antithesis, synthesis. And the synthesis needed a third idea, a third melodic strand, something that would be introduced late, but move the piece to its conclusion. And that was a fragile movement.

She was thinking that, and then—she wasn't sure how—they were kissing again. Marguerite lost herself in the sensation of him. She couldn't have told anyone how long they kissed—it could have been one minute or ten or fifteen or thirty.

"It's a little profane, don't you think?" Marguerite finally asked, leaning back. "Doing this in a church?"

"Not at all," Adolfo said. "I think I've suddenly become a believer."

There was, however, one problem. One significant problem. Adolfo was leaving the next day—believer, or not—for home. His father had decided that the region was too unsettled for investment at the moment; he'd received the telegram just yesterday; his itinerary had now changed. He was taking the SS *Vulcania*, departing from Beirut harbor. He'd stop in Istanbul, Barcelona, and then Havana. He had a stateroom cabin; the ship departed at ten in the morning.

"I see " Marguerite said. "That's not good."

He was quiet. He looked down at the floor. He was clearly thinking something over. He interlaced his fingers, cracked his knuckles. He turned toward her. "There is one solution I can think of," he said. And then he asked her to marry him. It was the second time he'd done it, of course, and it did make her wonder if—*what if*—he was serious. But that thought, that single *what if*, made the moment feel, to her, utterly impossible. *Oh*, Marguerite said, although it was more an exhalation and not a word.

"Be serious." She held him at arm's length. "How?" A gulf of emptiness opened inside of her. It started in her jaw and radiated down her neck into the upper part of her chest and her shoulders. It was in her body, but it was also infinite. "Where would we live?"

Adolfo sighed. His face was pained; she imagined that he, too, was feeling some complex mix of emotions, the deep ambivalence, the fear of such a significant risk. "Pinar del Rio?" he said. But his voice was hesitant, unsure.

"I can't," she said.

"Does that mean yes?" he asked.

"Not quite," she said.

Her mind filled—immediately—with a thousand reasons to say no. First of all, she didn't really know Adolfo. How foolish would it be to even think seriously about marrying him? She and Adolfo fit together *here* at *this* moment, in *this* city—but, even then, just barely. *Secretly*. And nothing so fragile could survive a change of that magnitude.

But also, there was her acceptance letter, sitting on her desk at home. It had its own world within it. It contained a future of an unknown kind. A deep opportunity. She told him that then, describing her desire to take advantage of her talent. To travel far away from this place because of her music, travel far away and never come back. But she wanted to do it on her own terms. Her music—a composition *she'd* written—had already begun that process for her. Other people had read her work and they'd said to her: it has value.

"I understand," Adolfo said. "It's a beautiful thing."

And yet—Marguerite *wanted* to believe in him, in them, in this connection. She wanted to know how this story would unfold. She thought of what to say that might reflect the complexity of what she was feeling. He was looking at her with great intensity. His eyes were bright and trained on hers. His gaze was somehow hypnotic. It made her want to hypnotize him, in turn, to participate in their mutual hypnosis. The moment seemed dangerous. If she reflected her doubts to Adolfo, he would take them as the sum of what she was feeling. But if she was too optimistic, if she expressed anything other than these doubts—she would be lying to him.

In the end, her desire was greater than her caution.

"I think I may love you," she said. As she said it, she suddenly felt lighter, easier. *It must be true, then.* Cuba. What a place that would be to see. She would see the tobacco harvest, a world that was somewhat familiar to her, a world in which she'd always been denied participation, here in the context of her family. She imagined thousands of acres of farmland, producing mountains and mountains of tobacco leaves. What would it be like to be a part of that—part of something she'd always been denied? And music was so unpredictable, a world without maps, a world with no clear outcomes. Who was to say what her fortune might be, in a cold and foreign city, in a country that might not welcome her? But no. This was madness. *Impossible.* "I *may* love you," she said. *"But* . . . it doesn't matter."

"Of course it matters," Adolfo said. "It makes things simple. It means you pack a bag and come with me tomorrow."

"No it doesn't," she said, suddenly frustrated. "That's the last thing it means." She looked at him, took both of his hands in hers. "No. My answer is no."

Adolfo looked broken. He seemed to fold inward, to shrink in size, to contract. He nodded. He understood, he told her. He'd expected that this would be the case. He'd prepared himself for that outcome. He'd just never imagined anything like this—the taxi, the cathedral, the composition. Her music. The beauty of her body, of the physical fact of her, when combined with her music.

"I thought I'd give you this," he said. He reached into his pocket and took out a wrinkled strip of paper. It was his address in Cuba, he told her, the name of the plantation in Pinar del Rio. He handed it to her. He'd be back there in less than two weeks. He hoped she'd write to him soon. He couldn't have seemed more crestfallen. "We have airmail now," he said. "It'll only take a few weeks for your letters to reach me."

It was all unbearable. Leaving him there, in front of the cathedral, walking blindly through the streets with the money he'd given her—crying, clutching the notes in her hand. She finally found a taxi, one that had two other passengers in it, already headed to their own destinations. It would be a circuitous route home, but she was grateful for it.

She knew she'd made the right decision. *The work matters,* Monsieur Sarruf had said as she'd left him. He was right. As the other passengers got out at their destinations—and were replaced by new passengers with their own, new destinations—she knew her decision had been the correct one. Now she needed only the privacy of her room, the quietude of it, and she'd be able to try to put herself back together. This would pass, she thought, this anguish. It was temporary. It would recede and her equilibrium would—eventually—be restored.

She made it home to the Avenue des Plumes. Through the doorway. Up the stairs. Marguerite hung her coat on its hook. She came around the corner of the main living room— the room that was on the way to her own—to find her family, everyone, assembled and sitting on the three couches that surrounded the fireplace. When she appeared, there was a collective, joyous cheer.

"Marguerite!" her father exclaimed. "Back from the library, at last!"

She crept into the room. She tried to understand what, exactly, was happening. There was a bottle of champagne on the little coffee table, she immediately noticed, and everyone seemed to be celebrating. A tic of worry fluttered through her body.

"What's going on?" she said.

"Your brother," her father said, standing, "has had terrific news."

Marguerite turned to Michèl, but he wasn't looking at her. He was talking, instead, with their youngest brother, who had juice in his champagne flute. His face, though, even from the side, looked triumphant.

"What is this news, Michèl?" Marguerite said. But he still didn't answer.

"Your brother," their father said, holding up a piece of paper, "has been admitted to the most prestigious music school in France." And Marguerite saw the familiar letterhead, the shape of the typewritten language, the watermark on the page, translucent in the afternoon sunlight. *Mine,* she thought. *My letter.*

The world seemed to tilt on its axis. She took one step back, then another. She couldn't begin to comprehend—*Our initials,* she thought, *the same initials*—and she felt like she might be sick, she might fall to her knees, right there, in the living room. She could see that her mother could sense that something was wrong, but that only shot a bolt of anger through Marguerite— momentary, searing anger—an anger so strong that it took her breath away.

She thought then of the cathedral she'd just been in, and what she'd just left behind, and how—on all of those now distant Sundays—her brother had been the one sitting imme- diately on the other side of her, closest to her, physically, of all her family. He'd held her hand, too. There were small red pencils in the pews, and Michèl would sometimes pass her silly notes, just one word, a surprising word, designed to make her lose her composure and laugh. *Banana,* he'd write, and when that nearly got her, the next week he'd write, *Pear.*

As she looked at Michèl, standing there in the living room, she saw both the man in front of her—suddenly a stranger—and the boy who'd been squished next to her in that overfull pew, his hair neatly parted, his shirt carefully buttoned and tucked in—and the first image, the image of him as an adult, began to efface and scald the second image away, burn it away with a kind of heat, until there was almost nothing left. The sunlight came through the watermark on the acceptance letter in her father's hand, and—in that remembered past—she glanced over her brother's head and saw the statue of the Virgin Mary that was tucked into a reliquary on one side of the nave, frontlit by a bank of small candles. The two fires—the sunlight and the votives—merged. They became one flame—a devouring flame—that burned her memories away.

She turned and ran, leaving shock—shock and silence—in her wake.

In her room she threw herself on the bed. How could she have been so stupid? She was furious with herself, with her brother, with her family. She bit into her own arm, bit until the pain was almost unbearable. She wanted to feel something, *anything*, other than this.

A knock on the door. She didn't answer, but the door opened anyway. She knew, without looking, that it was Michèl.

"Marguerite—" he began. But she cut him off.

"You thief," she said, spinning around. "You bastard. You snake."

"*Doucement*," Michèl said. Gentle.

"I'll kill you." She stood and hurled herself at him, put her hands around his neck. It startled her, the passion—the fury—that she felt in her body. But also the lack of strength. She couldn't close his throat the way she wanted to. Shut his windpipe. Stop his breathing. She clutched at it, but he brushed her hands away. He took a step to one side, and she crashed to the floor. "How could you?" she cried. "How?"

"I didn't think—"

"Shut your mouth," she said. "Shut it. Leave right now. Get out of my sight."

"I'm only saying—"

"I said leave!" she yelled.

"It's not your future," he said. "This would all go to waste unless I took it."

She couldn't believe his betrayal. Why had she confided in him? Trusted him? Shown him the letter? It was her fault. "I was so naive," she said aloud, more to herself than to him.

"It's done," he said. "It's over. You're going to be married." This way, he continued to explain, he could take a break from the business, a business that he wasn't really suited for. He had a direction now. And Naguib Ghali might be better off running it on his own for a while—just to stabilize everything.

At the mention of Ghali's name, Marguerite stood back up. Again, she threw herself at her brother, but this time more carefully, keeping her weight even, her balance centered. She was able to shove him back a few steps and, with one hand, pull the door partly closed. *Go!* she screamed, and he took a final step back and she slammed it shut. In the hallway, her brother said her name—once, twice—and then left.

Marguerite began to pace back and forth. After a moment she could hear them celebrating again, laughing out in the other part of the house. How could he have done it? *How?* And how had she not seen it, expected it, understood this central weakness in him? She'd been torn. Torn open. She knew, of course, that what was torn could be repaired, remade, repurposed. But now, in her bedroom, she was simply in pieces. The pieces of her were everywhere.

How could a person's fate be so fragile? Marguerite thought of *all* the precautions that her mother took—the calcium shots, the cod-liver oil, the constant washing and rewashing of hands, of her own hands, of her children's hands. The vigilance against disease. All that work, daily and exhausting. Yet Marguerite's enemy hadn't been something foreign, something microscopic. It was the person she'd trusted most in the world, her own brother. Her brother and her father, who saw her as a commodity, something to be bought and sold.

The evening passed in agony. She tried to imagine ways out of her situation, ways to punish her brother—and her father as well. She idly thought of suicide. The thought had never crossed her mind before, but now everything was collapsing. What if she flung herself off a balcony? Ate arsenic like Madame Bovary—but in the living room of their house? Begged God for forgiveness, like Anna Karenina, and threw herself under a train? She couldn't sleep. By the time the roosters started calling out she was even more miserable. Perhaps she could write a new composition—more brilliant than the last—

and apply again, this time under a pseudonym? But how could she get the papers to travel if she was using an assumed name? It was going to be incredibly difficult under her own name—a challenge that she hadn't yet fully planned out. She couldn't imagine adding another degree of difficulty for herself.

Later, she'd consider that it was the shock of it all, the suddenness, that had prevented her from immediately understanding what to do. It was why she'd lost those fourteen precious hours. Because by the time she realized that she had to find Adolfo, that she had to go to the harbor and find his ship—*What had he said? The SS* Vulcania?—by the time she understood her course of action, it was too late. Or almost too late? *Pack a bag*, he'd said. *Pack a bag.* And so she stood up from the floor—the floor where she'd spent the night, lying on her back—and pulled a small satchel from her bureau. It was barely big enough for anything, just a few clothes and toiletries and one thin book, a book of poems, a volume she'd just bought, in Spanish, by the Chilean poet Pablo Neruda, *Viente poemas de amor y una canción desperada.*

Frantic, she looked around her room. There were the artifacts of her childhood—the banner she'd made in her grade-school classroom for a group project, the long black banner that she loved so deeply, the one that said: CREATURES MYTHIQUES. *Mythical Creatures.* There was the art deco print of a girl walking through the woods, holding a walking stick in her hand, a walking stick with a skull on its crown—the eye sockets shining out light, like a lantern, on her path. There was the photograph that Michèl had taken, just last week, of the house on Avenue des Plumes. The tall, cream-colored house that would forever only live in her imagination, animated by memories that she'd never really be able to touch. *Michèl.* His

Leica portraiture. Barely understanding why, she opened her handbag and pulled out the small stack of portraits of her family. Unable to look at them, unable to really think about it, she stuffed them all in her bag. They were light, after all. Mere grams, all of them, they fit easily into the satchel. They weighed almost nothing.

And now: Michèl's room. If *he* could violate her space— well, then she could violate his. She didn't knock. Some part of her hoped that he'd be there. But he wasn't, of course, not at this time of day, on a Sunday. She knew where he kept money, gambling money for the casinos downtown, money for his burgeoning collection of German cameras. He rolled the notes together, tied them with a piece of fabric, and slipped them into one of his shoes.

Into his closet. She searched one pair, and then the next. *Nothing*. There was a third pair—located farther back, just under the slope of the closet's interior wall. She slipped her hand in one of those shoes and—there it was. A bundle of notes. It must have been close to a hundred Lebanese pounds. There was foreign currency, too, she saw, francs and liras and even a few dollars.

Marguerite stashed the money in her bag. She turned, straightened her spine, brushed the bangs from her forehead, and walked out the door. She tried to move quietly through the house. It was a Sunday morning. The main rooms would be deserted, she thought. She'd make it out and down the stairs and be absorbed into the body of the city.

Except it wasn't like that. Her mother was sitting in the kitchen, unexpectedly, sitting there and drinking a cup of coffee. For a moment, Marguerite thought she'd make it by without being seen, but then, on the landing, she heard her mother's voice, ringing out like a clarion through the house. "What are you doing?"

"Nothing, *maman*," she called. Could she leave? Would she be able to walk down the stairs without saying anything more? She paused. *No.* It wasn't possible. For a variety of reasons—it wasn't possible. She froze there, ensnared like an insect in a gauzy web. She heard her mother's footsteps, heavy and fast, coming toward her.

"Édouard!" her mother called. And then she was standing a few feet away and saying: "Your father and I have been waiting for you." And then her father appeared, summoned from another part of the house, and his face was strange, an admixture that she couldn't quite read. But then he spoke, and things became clearer.

"Our neighbor's cousin, Ashraf," he said. "He's a taxi driver downtown."

"Yes," Marguerite said. "And?"

"He told us that you went to the cathedral yesterday," he said. "With a man." *Avec un homme.* "A strange man." Marguerite didn't move. She was poised on the top step. Her hand rested on the banister, gripping its curved, lacquered wood in her palm. Her grip on it tightened. She felt herself squeeze it, almost involuntarily, and then—once she'd noticed—she increased the pressure, clutching it, trying to imagine that she was big enough to crush it to wood pulp in her hand. "I'm assuming he wasn't Naguib Ghali?" her father added. There was, she thought, a slight hopeful note in his voice.

"No," Marguerite said flatly. "No, it wasn't Ghali. It was another man. A beautiful man. And I'm in love with him."

Her mother seemed to collapse downward. She seemed to be diminished, notably diminished, in some significant way.

Her father had the opposite reaction. His body seemed to expand, to grow larger and longer, almost as if he were being inflated.

"Love?" her father said. "What do you know about love? You're a child."

"Édouard," her mother said.

"What?" he said. "It's true. She's a child. She understands love as much as any one of her brothers and sisters."

"That's not true," Marguerite said. "I understand it more than you do. And what about Ms. Ayrout?" She looked at her father. "What have you taught her about love?"

"*Khalas!*" her father screamed in Arabic. Enough!

"You don't want to talk about it because you know what you've done."

"I said enough!" her father yelled. *Khalas! Khalas! Khalas!*

He was panting, taking in great gulps of air. Her mother looked like she was about to break down. It all added to Marguerite's feeling of being ripped apart, torn into pieces. *Honore ton père et ta mère. Honor your father and mother,* she thought, *so that you may live long in the land that God has given you.* It was an involuntary thought, an impulse summoned from the hundreds of times she'd said those words, week after week after week. It had been instilled in her since she'd been a little girl. But what was it? She thought. What was it—other than propaganda? "I understand it and I'm leaving. And I'm never—ever—coming back."

"She's been possessed," her father said, turning to her mother. "She's been possessed by a demon. And it's your fault."

"Mine?"

"You're the one who pushed to send her to school."

"You think this is because of school?" her mother said.

"This is her. This is our daughter. *Your* daughter. School had nothing to do with it."

"Stop," Marguerite said. "Stop fighting. It's done. It's over. I'll never marry Naguib Ghali and I'm leaving."

"If you walk out that door," her father said, "you're dead to us."

Marguerite stared at him. She seemed to hear his thoughts then, behind the words that he was speaking: *The father is the God of the family.* And she knew what he believed: an ideal family structure mimicked the structure of God, the Father— presiding over the world, protecting his people, making their lives better and more orderly. His authority was not to be questioned. His power was absolute. When he was pleased, the order of the world was in place, things could proceed as they should. When he was angry, it was someone else's fault, and someone had to apologize. He'd gone bright red in the face. A vein was standing up along the side of his neck, bulging underneath the skin. He waved his hand in a swiping motion like the windshield wipers of a taxi. It was as if he were threatening to wipe her away.

"I will never," he added, "speak to you again."

"Édouard," her mother said.

"No," he said. "It's true. If she leaves right now, I have one less daughter."

After she did leave, after she took the first step down the stairs—immediately following that proclamation—Marguerite told herself that she would not cry. There was no reason to cry. It wasn't necessary, or appropriate. She was tough, capable, strong-willed. The emotion she was feeling now was self-indulgent. It was misplaced. *Inappropriate.* As she walked away, she heard her mother's voice—wailing, terrified—calling her name. She ignored it. Marguerite would always remember that—a sound that was otherworldly in its pitch, that couldn't have been more saturated with grief. But her mother had made a choice, too, Marguerite thought. She'd decided a hundred—a thousand—times to defer to her husband. She'd refused to intervene in his moods. And this was the result.

She found a taxi relatively quickly, peeling the bills from the folded money with a sense of raw power. It was incredible what money could do. With money, she was suddenly capable of anything; she could chart her course through the world. It was a relatively small amount, but still: it represented freedom. And, conversely, bill by disappearing bill, her freedom would slowly erode.

Beirut harbor. Quay 5. Turning Basin 2. The scent of stagnant water, the piers that had been restored, periodically, for centuries. A palimpsest of shipping history—cargo and people and the cultures of the world, arriving and departing in a steady procession. Marguerite scrambled to find the harbormaster's office, running, breathing heavily, pushing herself to go as quickly as possible.

She was too late. *That ship left four hours ago.* But when she showed them the tightly rolled notes, held them in her hand like a talisman, they reacted almost immediately. Out came logbooks, clipboards, timetables. A roster of departures. There was one—the SS *Marine Carp*—that evening. It was bound for New York. But she could transfer to Havana, and the ship harbor in Guanabacoa, immediately afterward.

She thought about her painful departure from the cathedral. She thought of Adolfo, sealed away in his expensive cabin, having little to do but reflect on what she'd done, how she'd refused him, turned him down twice. Would he even want her anymore? She hesitated. Who knew, she thought, what the future held? No one. It was a mystery, something impossible to predict. She bought the ticket. It took almost two-thirds of the Lebanese pounds.

"Are you single or married?" the harbormaster asked her. He wasn't even looking.

"I'm sorry?" Marguerite said.

"Single or married? It's for the paperwork."

She paused. "Married," she said.

"Husband's name?"

She paused again. She somehow couldn't bring herself to say it. The harbormaster looked up at her.

"I'm assuming," he said, "that you know your husband's name."

"That's a safe assumption," she said. "Adolfo Castillo," she added.

The hours passed with interminable slowness. She'd boarded, but the ship was stationary. She put Adolfo's address—on the worn strip of paper—on the little table next to her bed. She looked at his handwriting. *Carlos Jorge Castillo Tobacco Plantation. San Juan y Martinez. Pinar del Rio*. It was a promise, just like the letter of admission had been a promise. But, this time, she wouldn't let anyone steal it from her.

Marguerite couldn't stay in her cabin, though; it was too tiny and claustrophobic. She waited, instead, on the deck of the ship. Hours passed. Finally, finally, the ship lurched away from the pier. The deep baritone of its horn echoed through the night air. One tone. Then a second. Then a third. *Underway*.

Sailing across the Atlantic on the SS *Marine Carp*, Marguerite was awed by the massive scale of the ocean, the sheer immensity of its watery expanse. In some sense, she used this immensity to fill the vacant space inside of her; she filled it with the vista of the sea. It washed into her, ponderous and vast. But what most surprised her—astonished her, for some reason— was how much the smell of the open ocean was like the smell of fish skin. Like the scent a fish left on your hands if you touched it. Of course, it made sense. But for some reason Marguerite had never thought of fish as smelling like water—like the liquid in which they were immersed for their entire lives.

Her parents. Though she'd promised herself that she would return—*someday*—that she would retrace this journey across the ocean, she never did. And eventually, her parents would both be dead—lying beside each other in the same sarcopha- gus at Ras el Nabeh—their bones forever united in a way that their flesh never could be again.

On that first night of the trip, Marguerite awoke covered in cold sweat. She'd just dreamed her mother was standing in the doorway—standing there but not looking at her, look- ing down at the floor instead. *You haven't eaten*, her mother had said. *I'll make you an omelet.* Marguerite awoke in a panic. She looked around the cabin with a frenzied, frenetic energy, glancing again and again at the door, afraid that the dream would come true, that the net of her family would somehow ensnare her again.

She lay, wide-eyed, on her mattress. She turned her head and tried to see anything through the tiny circular porthole window. *Nothing.* Just a swatch of black that might as well have been a piece of fabric. Questions began to crowd her mind, but they were too disquieting. She pushed them away. They were all unanswerable. They led not to answers but only to other questions.

Her mouth was hot and dry and sticky. She went to her

tiny bathroom, where she turned on the light and rummaged for the water glass that was stored in its rimmed alcove, safely tucked away, in case of rough seas. Despite the humidity of the saline air, the environment inside her cabin was somehow moistureless. Still groggy, she poured herself a glass of water. She drank it greedily. And there—in the bottom of the porcelain sink—was a spider.

It was a large, fragile-looking creature. A cellar spider—its body was impossibly tiny, compared to its legs—its long awkward legs that were light brown and jointed twice. Each joint, she saw, had a small dot of white, the exact color of the sink, a partial camouflage. The faucet seemed to have surprised it, though. Its feet seemed to be stuck, somehow, in the water's surface tension. It was struggling to free itself.

Had she brought this creature with her in her bag? Had it been curled at the bottom of the satchel? Her father was terrified of spiders; he couldn't abide even the sight of them, and he'd always summon her mother, yelling in fear, when he saw one. Her mother, however, was superstitious about killing any animal—except, of course, roaches—and so she would often catch the spiders in her hands. Marguerite thought of her mother releasing the spiders outside—placing them on the branches of the lemon tree in the courtyard.

The spider struggled. *It's scared of the light*, Marguerite thought. It was trapped by the water and scared of the light. Marguerite reached out and turned off the overhead bulb, plunging them both into darkness. After a few moments in the black, Marguerite's eyes began to adjust. She perceived a faint line of illumination beneath the bathroom door; it was the ambient light of the stars, which she hadn't been able to see when she'd been in the other room.

After a few moments, Marguerite realized that she was crying. Tears were streaming from her eyes, covering the planes
of her cheeks. She was thinking of home, of her home that
she'd just chosen to reject. She was thinking of Adolfo, crossing the ocean just ahead of her, unknowing, unaware of where
she was. *This is ridiculous,* she thought. *Pull yourself together.*
But her body felt vulnerable and raw. She felt adrift in the cur-
rents of time. They pulsed all around her, surging and abating
with the movement of the steady, inexorable waves.

Naïm

Naïm had been silent all day. Silent as he landed at Washington Dulles—silent as he walked through the vast daylit interior of the airport—beneath the tall windows that were something from the architecture of his dreams. *Two, three stories of glass. Almost like no walls at all.* He was silent as he handed his passport to the customs agent and glanced at his own name written in Western characters—so strange and foreign and unfamiliar. The boy in that passport photograph looked guarded, wary. He stared at the camera like it was a hungry animal.

Naïm stayed close to his mother. He followed her toward the frosted doors of the International Arrivals Hall, which opened to admit them like the curtains opening on a stage. As soon as they'd stepped across the threshold, Naïm and Fatima had officially entered the state of Virginia. The doors closed behind them with a deep hydraulic sigh.

A group of American strangers stood there. His mother greeted the first woman in line. Naïm saw a half-dozen bilingual signs, signs in Arabic and English, and at least ten onlookers, many of them holding flowers or helium-filled red, white, and blue balloons. Naïm glanced over and saw the side of his mother's face. And even as he did this—even as he mimicked her friendly gestures—he began to lose track of his body. He was physically there, but his mind was leaving; it was going somewhere else, wandering into the living room of the family apartment in Aleppo in another time. There, his father was smiling, lit from within with joy. Naïm saw a clutch of balloons held in his father's right hand. Bright green, for luck. *Mabruk, habibi*, his father was saying, *mabruk. My dear beautiful son. I love you so. Getting so tall now—God is good.*

The moment fractured. And his father's shirt started to smolder. A small orange flame rippled over the woven white fabric. It touched his father's cheek so that his skin reddened and bubbled. Naïm touched his own cheek, as if to brush the flame away. He blinked and looked down. He made himself breathe. *Ghosts.* Naïm's mother had always believed in them, but his father hadn't. *Tawhīd*, he'd said whenever someone— someone in the family usually—had mentioned anything supernatural. *Tawhīd*, the oneness of God. One holy being, one divinity, one arbiter of justice. Nothing supernatural, other than God.

But then, what was this? *Who* was this? Green balloons still bobbed at the edge of his vision.

"*Come back!*" his father said. "*Come home, my beautiful boy.*"

"No," Naïm whispered in Arabic. But he didn't say it loud enough for even his mother to hear. His lips barely moved. *La*, he said again. "I can't."

Naïm was afraid to look. There was smoke now, curling up near the ceiling of the terminal, above the tall windows. His hand throbbed; his missing fingers itched like they were growing back. He stumbled after his mother, joining another line. Did anyone else see the smoke, smell the accelerant—the burning air? They had bombs here, too. Even in America.

I need you, his father said. And though he was far away— his father's voice was clear and immediate. *Come back, Naïm. Come back.*

"I can't." But Naïm felt the resolve inside of him breaking, and before he knew it he was dropping his light blue UNICEF backpack—pushing it at someone who was momentarily in his way—and then he was sprinting, long-limbed and awkward, running toward the vision of his father. He worried that if he looked away, even for a moment, Salah would disappear. Because, what if, in this new country, on this new side of the world, he'd never see him again? And so he kept running—sprinting back through the door to customs, ignoring the huge red placards declaring that entry, beyond this point, was forbidden.

Naïm's mother shrieked his name; an alarm cut through the air. "Code Blue!" someone was yelling. "Code Blue!"

Nearly two hours later, Naïm sat in the cold basement of the airport.

"You were lucky!" the TSA agent said. He had a name tag that read: OFFICER AIME. He was trying to smile. "Thank God you weren't carrying anything we might have thought was a weapon."

Naïm nodded. Fatima had finally been allowed to see him—to visit him after ninety minutes in the claustrophobic interrogation room deep within the interior of Dulles. She'd given him half of a Valium. His body was calmer now; the agitation in his mind wasn't manifesting anymore in his muscles, in his joints, in his skin.

They were waiting for some final clearance. A bureaucratic necessity. A piece of paper that had to be signed and scanned and sent to a supervisor. And Naïm sat there, almost motionless. He closed his eyes. He wished that he had his cell phone.

He wanted to play Candy Crush.

That's what he really wanted. After all—he was right on the verge of passing Sugar Shrubs. After that, it was on to LEVEL 1701. And after LEVEL 1701, who knew what might be next? It could be anything. He didn't even know how many levels there were. Perhaps they were endless? Perhaps they'd grow and adapt their difficulty to his skill? Perhaps they'd have no limit? *That's* the kind of game he would have designed, if he'd been a game designer; an infinite climbing game—a game of windows—one window leading to the next and the next and the next. A sonata that didn't conclude, but just started again. A revolving keyboard. A landscape that, because it was infinite, would be free from time.

Highway 267—heading away from Dulles. The resettlement agency's host—Annabel Crandall—hadn't been there to greet them; she'd apparently fallen earlier in the week and was being evaluated in the hospital. The woman who met them was Annabel's next-door neighbor, Janice. *It's nothing too serious,* Janice assured them in English that was bewilderingly fast and hard to follow. *But at eighty-five, you can't be too careful.*

Naïm's mother looked at him with concern. "What's wrong?" she said in Arabic. "Did she say *hospital*?"

Naïm nodded. "Do we help?" he asked.

"Bless your heart," Janice said. "But she won't need anything from you."

The neighbor had a large Chevrolet SUV, and they drove along the implausible ribbons of highway—concrete ramps that looped over each other with geometric precision. Naïm stared out the window, amazed by the sheer size of everything.

Its scale. "Well," he said, summoning his English resources, "I hope that she is recovering soon."

They arrived in West Falls Church. 815 RIDGE PLACE. A white brick rambler with a sunken driveway and a sprawling lawn. Naïm and Fatima were going to live in the basement apartment, which had a separate entrance. But because of the events of the past week, Janice told them, the apartment still had to be cleaned—and they'd have to spend the first night in Annabel's actual house.

Naïm watched the neighbor pull a spare key off a little ledge and open the door. They stepped inside. It was a lovely, well-maintained home, and Naïm walked through its interior in shock. The kitchen was a spectacle of gleaming appliances; a refrigerator that was impossibly large, a sink that glittered with the sheen of new porcelain. He noticed a pantry in a little alcove beside the stove; it was filled with dried noodles and rice and various cans of food.

This was also the home of someone elderly; there were dozens of vials of medication on the kitchen counter, a cane in the umbrella stand, a walker folded at the foot of the stairs. When he used the bathroom, Naïm noticed the grab bars—one in the tub, one on each side of the toilet. Janice told them that Annabel didn't like a lot of noise—so, no music, and no guests at night. No parties. *The woman has ears like a bat*, Janice said.

The image stayed in Naïm's mind. After Janice had closed the door, after he and his mother were alone in this large, formal space, he kept imagining an elderly American woman with animalian hearing, hearing that required—that *demanded*—silence. His mother unpacked their toiletries: the toothbrushes, the small bar of lavender hand soap. She rolled their suitcases into the hallway; since they'd be moving in the next few days, there was no reason to unpack completely.

Eight p.m. *A knock on the door.* Fatima was immediately worried, nervous. *You answer,* she told him. She took a step back into their bedroom—the little guest room with twin beds, where they were supposed to sleep that night. Naïm crept to the door. He hesitated as he pulled it open, discovering a short, heavy-set woman in a bright yellow vest standing in the buggy circle of the nightlight's illumination. She held a clipboard in one hand, batted away a moth with the other.

"Hello?" he said.

"Great, yes," she said, gesturing to her badge—a little laminated card that was clipped to her vest. "I'm from Inova Fairfax. I'm here to prepare the house for Ms. Crandall's arrival."

Naïm looked at her. He didn't say anything. "You weren't notified?" the woman said after a moment. She sighed. "We called twice."

He stepped back and let her come into the foyer. Fatima stood behind her son as he explained their situation as best he could. They'd only arrived a few hours ago; they were strangers in a stranger's house.

"I see," the woman said, frowning.

Oh no, Naïm thought. "I have all of our documents available," he said.

The woman shook her head. She looked perplexed. *Well,* she finally said, *I suppose I can still go through the checklist.*

It took ten minutes. But in those ten minutes, Naïm toured most of the home. He trespassed throughout Annabel Crandall's life, looking through her bedroom, her closet, opening drawer after drawer, accidentally touching her clothes, her jewelry, her small crystalline bottles of perfume. Carpeting.

Thick carpeting. A padding underneath his feet that seemed almost unreal. He took step after step across it, sinking into it, marveling at its depth and cushion. He went upstairs and downstairs, helping the official check boxes on her form. And then—at the far side of the house—the room farthest from the front door: *a solarium*. And, in it, a Steinway grand piano.

A grand piano. An almost unimaginable object. What he would have done, in a previous life, just to sit down at its keys. Naïm walked over, forgetting everything else. He sat down. Some part of him wanted badly to play; he was surprised how badly, actually. But of course he couldn't. He hadn't since the day his family had been killed. Because now, instead of a pinky finger on his left hand, there was a smooth-cut callus, and instead of a ring finger, there was a half-rounded digit. And who had ever heard of an eight-and-a-half-fingered concert pianist? This wound on his body, this brokenness, it felt like it had inhabited him. It had become his sense of himself, had expanded to become almost the only way he could imagine himself. It crowded everything else out. He *was* this damaged hand. Nothing more. Completely diminished.

He stared down. Sitting there on the bench, Naïm was suddenly angry—furious—suffused with a formless, burning anger at the cruelty and stupidity of the world. He didn't move, but his heart concussed itself against the margins of his chest. He was conscious of something newly broken—some feeling inside of him that was messy and ragged and seemingly limitless. He wanted to cry.

"Are you going to sit at my piano all day," a crackly voice said, "or are you going to get me a damn gin and tonic?"

Naïm swiveled around. He saw the woman from the hospital—standing behind an elderly woman in a wheelchair.

"Now, now, Ms. Crandall," the official said, her voice cloyingly sonorous. "You know your medication doesn't permit it."

"Until you leave it doesn't," Ms. Crandall said. "Then this nice young man is going to be my angel."

Naïm looked at his mother. Fatima stepped forward and shook the woman's hand; Naïm hung back, unsure what was appropriate. Ms. Crandall said that they were welcome in her house; she was excited to meet them; she'd actually been looking forward to it for many weeks. "But then my goddamn body started giving out on me."

Naïm nodded. "I see," he said, even though he didn't understand.

"Let's get you settled, Ms. Crandall," the official said, her tone shifting somewhat, becoming more aggressive. "I'm sure these fine folks want to get some rest—after all the traveling they've done to get here."

Where were they now? Naïm wondered that night as he lay on his mattress in the guest room. *Salah. Omar. Aysha.* Names so painful that he struggled to even imagine them. He couldn't put them into language, somehow—he could only *see* them, imagine their essence, some part of what they'd meant to him, in a closed and inaccessible past. *Salah, Omar, Aysha.* Father, brother, baby sister. And hundreds more, and thousands more. Their names an invisible list, floating over the city always—not quite ghosts, but something else. Not quite shadows, but something else. Or were they something different? Some combination of elements, a combination that he couldn't even begin to understand. That nobody could. Or were they simply missing because—because they'd been delayed? *Delayed.* The word sparked something in

186

his imagination. It was so much better to think of them that way. Not dead. Not pulverized. Not vapor and smoke and dust. They'd only been delayed; their smuggler had taken them to the wrong border crossing. They'd been captured. *That's* what had happened. It was only a matter of time before they arrived.

Naïm sat up in bed, startled by the clarity and focus he suddenly felt, imagining his family in this circumstance, imagining his father there—*safe*, but on the other side of the world. Omar in a little cell. Naïm began to tell himself a story about these feelings—about the things his brother was thinking, that his father was doing. Omar, Salah, and Aysha sat in a cinder-block detention cell together. Salah put his arm around his youngest son; it was an easy gesture for Naïm to remember. His body remembered it. He knew what that had once felt like. Salah's other arm caressed Aysha's head. They'd waited there like that for hours, and then—a miracle, the work of the Prophet (peace and blessings upon his name)— they'd been released. A woman had shown up, wearing the cerulean beret and neck scarf of the UN peacekeeping force, carrying a black plastic clipboard, just like the official from Inova Fairfax. *Come with me,* she'd told them. *We will get you back on track.* For a moment Naïm was elated, but it was hard to keep all the details straight. It was a war, after all. And war splintered families, just like this. And so Naïm imagined that they had called him from their new camp. *What did it feel like to be separated from us?* But his father didn't answer him. His brother didn't answer him.

But wait, he thought, *I haven't really arrived, either.* His body was there—in that bed, in America, surrounded by a new language, a language that had only existed, for him, in You-Tube videos. His *body* was safely in the suburban home of this elderly American woman, Annabel Crandall. A woman whose possession of her house was so complete, so total, that she didn't have to even be here to occupy it. Naïm understood, at some level, this manifold existence. He was in Za'atari. He was with his dead family, who were both dead and gone but also with him, who haunted him, visceral and embodied, people he could see and hear but never touch. He wished he could control it—keep his imagination yoked to a single time, a single place. But he couldn't. *Hit the water*, his father used to say, *and it stays water.* But if you were submerged, Naïm thought, it was impossible to breathe.

Looking over at his mother—his mother who was sleeping soundly on her own little cot—Naïm stood up. He stood up and decided to go back downstairs. To the solarium. He would just sit at the Steinway, he'd decided. He wouldn't play it. It would hurt too much to play, wouldn't it? Not physically. It wasn't the pain that he was most afraid of. He'd faced worse. His body stuffed into cramped spaces, thirsty, freezing, lying on the ground, shot at, concussed. He was afraid of something else entirely.

Still, within minutes, Naïm was seated again on the black leather cushion, sliding his body into place. And, doing this, he felt an immediate panic. *Push through it.* He spread the web of his hand open, but there it was—he gasped—the burn, the fire along his skin, the nerves scalded as if they were exposed to air. He touched the fingertips of his right hand, his uninjured hand, to the keys. He pressed downward and played a string of notes. Quietly, so quietly. He heard the beginning of a melody, and then the complication of this beginning, and he thought, for the first time, of all the songs he'd played, lying on the floor,

during the first months of the siege. And then he heard something strange.

He stopped. He started playing again and then—at that
same note—something was wrong. It was the tiniest thing. But
still he noticed. It wasn't an out-of-tune flatness. It was something different. Something unusual.

Naïm played that single key, just a bit louder, just to see if
he was imagining it. But no—there it was—a rustle almost. A
sizzle at the margins of the sound. *What was that?*

He looked over his shoulder at the darkened house. If his
mother had heard him tapping gently at the keys, she hadn't
come out of their room. And so he stood and walked over
to the light switch. He turned it on and then went back and
lifted the top of the piano. He folded the first lid at its metal
seam, then propped the second lid fully open. He stared at the
insides of the instrument—at the dampers and the rosettes and
the cast-iron frame. He hit that note one more time. He saw its
three strings vibrate—traced them from one side of the case to
the other—scanning them with his eyes. And that was when he
noticed it: jutting from beneath the frame of the piano, a scrap
of sepia-toned whiteness, just barely visible.

It was the tip of a piece of paper—thick and yellowed—and
it was attached to the stanchion of the piano's frame, tucked
inside an alcove in one of the frame's posts. *Strange.* He pressed
the key again. And the string vibrated just enough to snag one
of the paper's edges.

Naïm leaned over and reached into the piano; he pulled
the object out and held it up in the air. It was, he saw, a small,
rectangular, black-and-white photograph—the image of a family. One of the younger boys looked, Naïm thought, a bit like

Omar. The boy's expression was mischievous; his thoughts, clearly, were somewhere else, engaged in their own distant daydream.

Though he didn't know why, Naïm shivered. Something seemed to pass through the photograph—to rise from its surface and travel through the length of Naïm's arm, into the center of his body. *It's old.* Someone had put it in the piano years ago, Naïm decided, but it had only recently come loose—slipping from some place of concealment. He flipped the photo over. *Nothing.* No identifying marks.

He turned the photo over again and looked—sequentially—at the faces of the family. Naïm studied them now from the safety of his own perspective. He kept returning, though, to the young woman standing to one side of the group. She was smiling in a sweet way, with a slightly unusual smile. Was it happy? Or was it a forced look of frustration, a facade put forward for the camera? Or both? In this one moment—captured from a life and passed forward, through time, into the hands of an anonymous stranger—what was she thinking? After a moment's pause, Naïm reached down and tucked the photograph into his pocket. It wasn't wrong to take it, was it? After all, it had been here for so many years. It had been hidden away, gathering dust. He was giving it a second life. He was its collector, its curator. In a way—he had set it free.

MARGUERITE

The RCA Radiogram arrived in Havana in the middle of the night. *A Sea-Letter. Ship to Shore. Speeded on by Mail.*

Marguerite had worried that she wouldn't—couldn't—say enough. There was the fact that the right words were elusive, that every draft was further from what she hoped to say. That she only had feelings, not words, and that every time the feelings entered *into* words, they failed. So she'd said as little as possible: ON MY WAY. LOVE, M.

From Havana the mail took it south and west—the little slip of paper with its navy masthead and RCA logo, with its three embossed letters, its tiny, line-drawn graphics of a ship, and a train, and a plane. It arrived in Pinar del Rio, carried by hand, shuffled into the midst of a hundred other small single envelopes, arriving at the plantation only a few days after its addressee. *There's a letter for you, Adolfo.* And he was distracted, thinking about something else, until he unsealed the message, and looked down at the text, and breathed in with shock, and let the paper fall to the ground, stunned.

When the ship docked in the harbor at Guanabacoa, Marguerite collected her luggage, cleared customs, and walked down the gangway, arriving in the center of an unfamiliar city. One step after another. Flat-soled shoes on a rubber mat and then on a broad sweep of concrete. The smell of the harbor, but also the smell of the docks, of the wood itself. The call of seagulls, spinning overhead. She had just the single, hastily packed bag, but as soon as she'd disembarked, she was surrounded by a swirl of men on bicycles. The bicycles had baskets on their front handlebars.

"Taxi," the first rider called out.

But he was cut off—almost immediately—by a second rider.

"Don't trust him," he said. "He's a liar and a cheat."

"He is, too," a third man said. He threaded between the other two and pulled up beside her. "I'm the only honest bicycle taxi in this whole city."

Marguerite stopped. She paused. She drew herself up until she felt substantial enough to face them. She summoned the right words, in the right language. "No thank you!" she said. "Leave me alone."

And with that the men turned their bicycles around and disappeared. She shook her head, turned back toward the city, and took a single deep breath. The train to the southwest—that was the next step. She knew it—but she couldn't think about it, not too closely. If she stopped to consider what faced her, the uncertainty of it, she'd be overwhelmed.

The afternoon was loud. *Dissonance and consonance.* Any chord, Marguerite knew, was only as dissonant as your perception of it. Because nothing was objectively unpleasant. Every note, every combination of notes, had a context—in relation to her, to the music of her time, to the other notes and chords in the piece. It was safer to think, now, of Schoenberg—rather than meals and taxis and train tickets. Schoenberg, whom Monsieur Sarruf couldn't stand—because he couldn't hear the sound of it, couldn't hear the way the compositions fit together. *There's no melodic thread,* he'd complain, *nothing pulling you through from one end to the other.* But—for Marguerite—that was exactly the exhilaration. *The subtlety of it.* The way you had to listen for it, had to make up the through line, yourself. The city was like that, right here, in front of her. Its capacity for dissonance matched her ability to understand it.

Marguerite found a bank and changed her little remaining money. She asked for directions to the train station and started walking. She followed the line of the harbor to the Malecón—heading along the seaside esplanade and the perimeter of Havana Harbor. She was hungry. She passed a couple of tiny restaurants with signboards on the sidewalk in front of their doorways—daily specials written up in colorful chalk. But anything was too expensive; she wanted to save everything—or as much as she could, for the trip to Pinar del Rio—even if it meant going hungry now.

But walking toward the center of the city, she heard a street vendor—the plaintive tone of voice that was so familiar from her own childhood—everything nearly the same, except the language. Marguerite stopped. She felt a stab of nostalgia, almost crippling in its intensity, a longing for mango juice and *malabi* and *ful medames.* She turned the corner and saw it: a little wheeled cart, surrounded by barefoot children. Later, she'd learn the vendor had been selling *buñuelos*, little donuts made from cassava flour. But now she simply watched the transactions for a moment and then, when it was her turn, quietly held up one finger, and said, *Una, por favor,* and handed over exact change.

The donuts were hot and dripped with sweet oil. They came in a little newspaper cone and Marguerite ate them quickly, voraciously, her hunger barely allowing her to taste them. Walking down the Malecón immediately afterward, she noticed something moving along the cracked sidewalk. She looked more closely. A shell. She stopped, bent down, picked it up. It was a hermit crab, and still alive; it had evidently washed over the seawall on the crest of a wave. Marguerite frowned. Here on the Malecón, it was certain to be crushed, or to dehydrate, or—more likely—be eaten by a bird. In one quick motion, she pitched it back into the sea. First a spider, now a tiny crab. She would be their protector; she would give them what no one had given her.

She found La Habana Central. There was an overnight train— a long, slow passenger train—that cut down along the valley to the south of the city. Marguerite rode it for what felt like an eternity. At first, sitting in her uncomfortable seat, she couldn't sleep. Her body wouldn't settle. She thrashed to the left and the right, her limbs hot and uncomfortable, her ribs itching, her spine stitched with cramps.

Finally, she drifted away. She began to dream. Among the many things Marguerite had left behind was her beloved woolen doll, a gift—in childhood—from an aunt. It was small. Its eyes were buttons; they were painted a bright Prussian blue. And so—in her dream on the train—her doll became a living girl. She was small but strong. She could go almost anywhere, unnoticed. She could negotiate herself into nearly any space. She went back to Beirut and sat in her family's house, felt the sorrow of the room, the room that lacked her presence, that was—without her—lifeless and cold. Marguerite's father sat at the dining room table, alone, his arm slack at his side, blood coursing from a wound—a cut—near his elbow. There was so much blood; it flowed and covered everything in their house; every surface was tinted with it, dark-stained and transformed.

Then Marguerite, herself, became doll-sized. And she wasn't safely in the apartment on Avenue des Plumes, but out on the road in front of it, lying on her back in the path of a dozen—two dozen—marching tobacco factory workers. They were coming unstoppably toward her. She tried to run—but she couldn't manage to stand; she couldn't get traction on the ground. And then she realized: running would be futile. She was too small and the column was too wide to outflank. They were going to crush her. They would grind her fragile bones to dust; they would pulverize her skull beneath their boot soles. She covered her head with her hands, said a quick prayer—and awoke.

She sat up, gasping for air. She was on the edge of tears; she felt the panic of the dream in her neck, felt a deep ache in the glands along the sides of her jaw. She couldn't shake it off. She stood up, hitting her head on the luggage compartment. She walked down to the back of the train. Everyone else—all of the passengers—were asleep. There was just the steady sound of the wheels on the tracks, the gentle sway of the cars as they made their way through the rural night. The last car was an observation car and entirely deserted. It had a curved glass roof on each side of the compartment, and Marguerite could see the nearly full moon through the windows. The constellations seemed to pulse above her—hanging close and dusty and immediate in the sky.

At the station in Pinar del Rio, there was an old man with a flat-bottomed cart and a solitary, overweight horse. He offered to take her to the Castillo tobacco farm for nearly nothing; he seemed relieved not to be sitting in the hot sun, waiting for someone to need his services.

The roads were terrible. The vegetation on either side of the roadway seemed constantly on the brink of engulfing them; insects roiled through the air in great clouds. Marguerite was conscious of the fact that she hadn't bathed in many days; what a terrible impression she would make on the people who were to be her new family.

But then they came around a curve in the road and there it was—the house. She'd been imagining it for weeks now, and it did in fact resemble what she'd imagined. Set back from the road in a thicket of tall mahogany trees, it was a collection of elongated rectangles, with large, screened-in porches on each of its sides. Before she knew it she was gathering her things and stepping down from the cart and walking—incredibly—up the stairs. A man greeted her; he wore an open-collared shirt and dark gray trousers, and when she told him her name, his eyes went wide. *She's here!* he called over his shoulder.

And then people were appearing from everywhere, one after another, and there—suddenly turning the corner and looking at her, stopping ten feet away and staring directly at her—was Adolfo.

"It took you long enough," he said, and smiled, and then he crossed the room and took her in his arms and kissed her.

But then there was a shout—and a girl was yelling something, and somebody else had brought out decanters of red wine, and Marguerite had a glass in her hand and everyone was demanding a toast. His father would be back soon, Adolfo said, *and he was eager to meet her*, and then Adolfo had a glass in his hand, too, and someone clutched him from behind and lifted him up into the air with a shout of jubilation.

They were surrounded. Marguerite watched Adolfo talk. Standing here, in the middle of the room, talking to one person after the next, he had a deep, overarching confidence. He had confidence in his intellect, in the physical form of his own body. His voice reflected what he was feeling—what she was feeling—pure relief and joy. As they were surrounded by a crowd of well-wishers, Marguerite felt something she'd never felt before. She wanted to stand beside him and talk with him—about anything—forever.

How had it all happened? It made her a little afraid; it made her feel apprehensive. Adolfo shifted his weight and, for one moment, their hip bones touched. The impact sent a spiral of electricity through her body, a rattling, crackling sensation.

And then there was a pause—and he put his hand on her arm and asked, in French, *Can we flee?* And she said, *Probably not.* And that's when she realized most clearly what this moment was; it was a chance to start over. Someone was laughing nearby, and someone else refilled her glass of wine, and the chemicals of love surged from some hidden part of her body, spiraling through her nerves and veins and bones; they made quick work of her intellect, they demolished it and began to set up their own space, inside of her, a vocabulary that was both hers and Adolfo's, partly her voice, but partly his, too—a cadence of bright vowels and rolling foreign consonants.

Naïm

The Food Lion on Columbia Pike in Annandale, Virginia. Naïm couldn't get used to its name. *Lion.* Bashar al-Assad had misused this image for so many years. *Al'Assad—of the lion*—fierce, fearless, violent. A creature that had given him a mythic power. Given him the ability to do almost anything he wanted. To hunt whoever he chose to hunt. *Food* and *Lion*: these were two words Naïm would never have imagined fit together.

Naïm walked through those doors into the order and peace and prosperity of the American grocery store. Meters and meters of food, obsessively cultivated, organized, and aligned in displays and on shelves. A miracle. But who believed in the miracle of the grocery store anyhow? No one in this nation, this country where everything was taken for granted, where everything was expected, where people didn't die from thermobaric bombs dropped on them while they were asleep—after they'd spent all night dodging snipers to get water for their children. No one got on their knees, Naïm thought, like they should have, when they entered this space, when they walked through the produce aisle. No one said prayers of thanks over the tomatoes and avocados and papery bulbs of garlic.

He did, though. Floating through the Food Lion on a Saturday evening in December, praying the *tasbih*, counting the prayers on the knuckles of his fingers: *Subḥān-Allāh*, thirty-three times. Then *Al-hamdu lillāh*, thirty-three times. Then *Allāhu Akbar*, thirty-four times. It had never seemed as important to believe as now, in this foreign nation, where everything seemed to disintegrate and fall away as he walked through it, where memories were constantly threatening him, pushing against him, catapulting him out of the present. *Hyperreal.* That was his description of it, borrowed from the books he read at night when he couldn't sleep, the Arabic science fiction novels that peppered their text with terms directly translated from English—the novels by Youssef Rakha and Mostafa Mahmoud and Ahmed Tawfik—novels that gave him this word, this description of the way each step sizzled as he walked through the supermarket, a condition that was destroying him, and only getting worse.

He got a gallon of milk, ground beef (eighty percent lean), a bag of dried lentils, a bag of jasmine rice, a few cans of kidney beans, a loaf of French bread in a long white paper sack that had a print of the French flag on it. And then he was standing in the produce aisle, looking down at the varieties of tomatoes. There were small tomatoes—red like tiny jewels—and absurdly large pale tomatoes that were the size of his fists. And bright tomatoes on vines, connected to one another with their verdant green stems. Stems like green bones, he thought.

"You done?" It was an aggressive masculine voice. "Or you gonna stay here all night?"

The man was large. That's what Naïm noticed immediately, turning toward the voice. He was large and wore sunglasses—narrow polarized sunglasses that looked like an insect perched on his face.

"You even speak English?" he said. "Where you from, jackass? Habla Anglaisy? Move it—I want some goddamn tomatoes."

Naïm still couldn't bring himself to respond. In part, this was because if he did—if he allowed his body to react in the way that it wanted to—he'd probably start laughing. Not a joyful laughter. Not laughter at something that was funny. But laughter of a different kind. The kind that would lead, in moments, to uncontrollable sobbing. Naïm didn't move and, with one quick motion, this man reached out and swept Naïm to one side, shoving him as hard as he could, clearing him away from the tomato display. And Naïm was light; he sprawled sideways and stumbled and fell to the linoleum floor.

"Son of a bitch," the man was saying, and he was glancing around, looking for witnesses, even as he stuffed a few tomatoes into a slick plastic sack. He walked away, glancing from side to side, muttering something under his breath.

Naïm picked himself up. He looked for someone to help him—to see if anyone had noticed—but no one had. He stood there for a moment. Classic rock kept playing softly over the speakers recessed in the ceiling. Grocery store smell surrounded him—a numbing cloud of it. Naïm walked toward the checkout aisle, his head throbbing. Once he'd reached the cashier, he managed a small smile.

"Did you see that guy?" he said, happy to have summoned the right English words, in the right order. "Crazy guy."

"$42.51," the clerk said. "Will that be cash or credit?"

Naïm's smile faded. Maybe they hadn't been the right words after all. He reached into the pocket of his sweatpants to find the debit card that his mother had given him to buy the groceries—and it wasn't there. The pocket was empty.

Alarmed, Naïm held up one hand and walked back to the produce aisle—looking down at the linoleum floor as he moved along. Nothing. He walked back to the cashier, searching around his feet the whole time. He was aware that the other customers in the Food Lion were staring at him now, and he glanced up and saw that the illuminated number at the end of the aisle he'd used was flashing off and on, off and on. He froze.

The cashier stared at him. Naïm imagined what he might do if he were on the other side of the register—instead of standing there, without any money, with three paper bags of his groceries pulled to one side of the long black rubber conveyor belt. He'd hand the groceries to the humiliated version of himself. And if his manager complained, he'd silence him with a quote from the Sūrat al-Insān: *They give food, out of love of God, to the poor and the orphan and the captive.*

But he wasn't on the other side of the register. And so nothing like that happened. "I can't pay," Naïm said, remembering the contraction, remembering to make his voice sound informal.

The clerk shrugged. He picked up an intercom. "Restock in aisle 5," he said. "Restock in aisle 5." After a short delay, the clerk's voice echoed through the cavernous interior of the store.

Naïm walked home in a panic. His mother would be *so* angry with him, he thought, when she found out about the lost card. How could he lose such a precious thing? he imagined her saying. *How could you be so careless?*

It had been two months since they'd reached the end of their allotted stay at Ms. Crandall's house. Ms. Crandall had been hospitalized, *again*, after a fall in late July; she hadn't been released from the rehabilitation center by the time the resettlement agency had required that Naïm and Fatima move into independent housing. Their federal resettlement stipend of $1,925 a month had expired, and there was nothing extra— *nothing at all, j'hani*—in the budget. Fatima worked fifty-five hours a week to try to earn enough to pay for food and rent and transportation and, more recently, her blood pressure medication.

She'd found employment—through the job placement program for refugees—at Sheetz, the convenience store and gas station. She worked in the store and, sometimes, she pumped gas. Naïm had laboriously translated the *Sheetz Employee Handbook* into Arabic for her, using both his English textbooks and Google Translate. "Above all else," he'd read, "Sheetz is about providing kicked-up convenience while being more than just a convenience store. Sheetz is a mecca for people on the go." The reference to Mecca—while disconcerting—was also comforting, somehow. The rest of the document had been more difficult to translate. "Road warriors. Construction workers. Soccer moms. They all have a special place at Sheetz." The word for road, *altariq*, seemed completely wrong. *Sharī*, street, was more appropriate, when paired with warrior, *maharib'*, but then—it brought up the question: Street warriors? Why would Sheetz want to serve street warriors? He didn't want to upset his mother. And as for *soccer moms*—once Naïm had read that, he'd decided to skip the paragraph entirely.

Naïm walked past his high school. FALLS CHURCH HIGH. HOME OF THE JAGUARS. It was just a few more blocks to his apartment complex on the other side of Arlington Boulevard—but he decided to go down the little embankment and take the grassy path over to the baseball diamond. He was still having the problems—the visions—and he worried that going home with this much anxiety would only make them worse. The thing that Naïm wondered—as he walked along the little access road—was: How did he heal his own mind *with* his own mind? He was trying to use the defective instrument itself as a healing tool. And what was the point of that? In November, Donald Trump had won the American presidential election and, since then, things had been getting worse and worse. His symptoms had intensified. Trump reminded Naïm so much of Assad; he didn't understand how the voters hadn't seen it, seen *all* of it—the classic dictator's megalomania, the cult of personality, the appeal to anger and patriotism.

It began to rain. It was hard for Naïm to get used to the rain. After so many months in the deep desert, where water was such a precious commodity, it was still shocking to see precipitation so frequently. In Aleppo, most of the rain fell in one month—Naïm was still surprised by the feeling of being consistently soaked by rainfall, the smell of the petrichor, the clatter of thunder.

There was no baseball game, but the lights were on and, in the twilight, the air around the field had a misty, refulgent glow. He'd spent a significant amount of time this fall watching the Falls Church baseball team while he'd walked back and forth along this road. Even though the enclosure was empty now, Naïm could envision the players taking batting practice, or running through fielding drills in small groups. The sound of it—his memory of the sound of it—rose up and carried out over the diamond. The figures were ghosts; they glitched in the silver light, coming in and out of existence, images in a stop bath, half-fixed, half-vanishing. And then, in his memory, he was back in his tent at Za'atari, on a winter night with no heat, and the temperature near freezing, and the cold leaked in through the seams in the canvas tent, through the ground itself, which chilled his feet if he walked on it. And Naïm was sitting on a chair that had been left next to the dugout. He rested. This was an old wooden schoolroom chair—one with a solid metal frame—and Naïm was looking through the chain-link fence that surrounded the baseball field, he was looking through the loops of barbed wire on top of the chain-link fence that surrounded the refugee camp, and he was remembering the first time he'd seen a game of baseball, he was remembering the first time he'd seen a man pay for *harissa* with an iris scanner—the large cylindrical EyeCloud camera that linked to the Bitcoin wallet for refugees. Naïm had marveled at the way the players threw the ball from third base to second to first, their bodies fluent in the game, almost effortlessly so; he'd marveled at the way the man had done this so casually—presented his eyes to a machine for photography; he'd wondered if he'd ever learn a game like this; he'd wondered if he, too, would someday grow accustomed to paying for things with his body, itself. There had been a time, in the first days after arriving in America, that Naïm had questioned why he'd been chosen, of all the eighty thousand people in the camp, why he and his mother had been selected, along with so few others, to come to this new country, to have a new life. There'd been a time, in the first days after the bombing, that Naïm had wondered why *his* building had been chosen for destruction, why *his* father—and *his* brother, and *his* baby sister—had all been incinerated, pulverized, massacred, and not his neighbors' families, or any of the families just down the road. And there, in the cooling night air, in the deepening Virginia dark with its ceaseless sound of crickets, there in the memory of watching other teenagers play a game he didn't quite understand, but sensed the easy joy of, there in the memory of the stench of the rubble, the dirt and broken sewer lines and torn bodies and charred plastic and ash and charcoal of the attack, Naïm looked—he looked through the present and into the past, and back to the present again, back to this *always* of his current moment, his constant raw loss, and he thought: *Why?* He didn't know who he was asking but, despite that, he couldn't stop. *Why?* he thought again. Why choose me? Didn't you see how young I was? Didn't you care? Anyone, anyone could have told you. I'm nothing. I'm nobody important. I'm just a boy.

Naïm went home. Coralain Gardens, Building 7, Apartment 2C. His mother was waiting for him in the front room. *You're late, you're wet, where are the groceries?* All three right away, in quick sequence, without the chance for him to reply. *You're late.* Yes, I am. *You're wet.* Yes, I am. *Where are the groceries?* That was harder to explain.

Naïm detailed his experience in the store and Fatima listened quietly. He couldn't tell if she believed him or not. And, honestly, he almost wondered himself. He left out the part where the man had taunted him in Hamza's voice, with the insult that Hamza had—from the very beginning—chosen as Naïm's special nickname. Naïm braced himself for his mother's anger. But she just shook her head sadly. *Let's call the bank,* she said. They'd chosen SunTrust for its seemingly auspicious name.

Sitting there in the living room, Naïm dialed the number he'd found online. A recorded message answered, and he navigated the phone tree, selecting the option for lost or stolen cards. Finally, after he'd waited on hold for nearly ten minutes, a cheerful woman answered. How could she help? she wondered. What could she do for him?

"I call—" he said, and then he stopped to correct himself. "I have called because I have lost my mother's debit card."

Once he'd passed the phone to Fatima to verify that she was—in fact—herself, and that he had permission to speak with this call center representative, Naïm explained the situation. They were alone in a new country, and they had no other way to pay for food.

"I'm so sorry, sir," the representative said. "We can send the replacement card immediately."

How immediately? Naïm asked. *Could it come today?* he wondered.

"I'm sorry, sir," she said. "The soonest it can arrive is in five to seven business days."

Naïm was silent. His mother looked at him. She shook her head. *What is it?* she said, mouthing the words. What is she saying?

"Do you have anything else I can help you with?" the representative wondered.

He didn't.

"You have a great day, then," she said, in a way that seemed slightly aggressive. Why order him to do this? Naïm thought. What if he wasn't having a great day? What if his day had been terrible? Or simply mediocre? What if she made him feel shame, by requesting, in her enthusiastic voice, that he try to feel one way—and not another? Shouldn't she have taken all of that into account? Shouldn't she have been more careful?

There was no food. They had a bag of rice and an onion, half a carton of milk. They'd been buying groceries week to week—trying to understand the unfamiliar structure of prices in America. Naïm immediately suggested that they call Sairah Khairouz, the interpreter who was their liaison with all state and county services. But his mother shot down that idea. Absolutely not, she said. They were guests in this country. What did it say about them that they lacked the fundamental skills to survive?

"But," Naïm said, "we've had a crisis."

"What will they think," Fatima said, "if you have a crisis every time you buy groceries?" The consequences, she told him, could be significant. What if they revoked their visa status, or no longer allowed them to apply for a green card? What if they sent them back to Za'atari?

To Naïm, this was ridiculous. They wouldn't kick him out of the country for being the victim of a crime. Though he'd learned some hard lessons about America over the past year, the country was more generous than that. The local government wasn't capricious and vengeful in the way it had been at home. And yet: the fear did nag at him from time to time, whispering to him—floating on the margins of his senses. "That would never happen," Naïm said, shaking it away.

"I'm telling you no," Fatima said. "Absolutely not. No charity! Believe me, *habibi*, nothing is free. Every good deed has an inner darkness."

His mother diced the onion and cooked the rice. She wouldn't be paid for another week; he already knew she was occasionally skipping meals; what was she—what was he—supposed to do now? Eat two tablespoons of rice per day?

The next day was Sunday, and when his mother went to work, Naïm went out looking for the free food pantry. Their interpreter had mentioned it as they'd driven past it, but that had been months and months ago. He knew it was *somewhere* in the neighborhood—he just wasn't sure where.

Northern Virginia had not been designed for pedestrians.

Sidewalks were few and far between, which made walking on almost any street a psychologically uncomfortable experience. Traffic passed by at dangerous speeds. Each car brought a rush of air, a burst that buffeted him and sometimes threatened to throw him off-balance. This lack of space for people, for human bodies: Had it just been an oversight?

He wandered through a few strip mall parking lots. No rain today, just a cold sun, a clear cloudless sky. He walked past the Food Lion as well and, when he did, he was surprised to see the indifferent clerk from the day before rushing out toward him. The man was waving his arm, flagging Naïm down. "Hey!" he was yelling. "I can't believe I saw you! We found your card! We saved your groceries! Well," he added, "some of them are in the walk-in."

Naïm looked stricken.

"What?" the clerk said. "It's good news, right?"

Naïm felt like he was going to cry. "I canceled it," he finally said. "It won't work."

"Oh," the clerk said. "Well . . . Yeah. I'm sorry about that."

The temperature seemed to drop. Naïm wished he'd worn a sweater. A wave of hunger rolled through his stomach as he walked away from the Food Lion, thinking of the groceries waiting for him, right there, in the store. Even in Za'atari, they'd had the daily bread ration: four loaves per person, often hot and pillowy and slightly dusted with flour. It wasn't the best bread in the world, but it was consistent; Naïm certainly had never imagined that he'd miss it once he came to America. He swallowed to try to make the hunger go away.

He walked blindly for a bit, thinking he'd reached the point where he should turn around and go home. He turned onto Dahlgren Road and suddenly—the area started to look familiar. Then he saw it, the little sign he remembered: EBT FOOD DISTRIBUTION CENTER, AMERICAN LEGION, POST 622. A thrill replaced the hunger. He began to salivate.

The American Legion Hall was mostly deserted on Sunday afternoon. There was just a single car in the parking lot. As he came closer to the building, Naïm saw a monument in front of the entryway—a small quartz pyramid. It was, he realized, a monument to American veterans. A statue of an artillery mortar sat nearby—a mobile howitzer that had been built to scale. And between these two statues—a black flag.

Naïm shivered. The last black-and-white flag he'd seen was the flag for Da'esh, the Islamic State—with the words from the Shahadah, and the circular seal of the Prophet beneath them. He stood there, looking at the flagpole. POW—MIA, he read. YOU ARE NOT FORGOTTEN. Naïm looked up at the image of a man in profile—with a guard tower behind him in the distance.

The power of flags had always surprised Naïm. It made no sense, how much emotion could be conjured by a strip of colored—or, in this case, colorless—fabric. They were concentrated, condensed embodiments of so many feelings: the longing for home, the anger—or the heartache—of having a country, a nation that you believed in. He'd felt it many times: seeing flags burned in the street in Aleppo, seeing the Jordanian flag at Za'atari, seeing the American flags in customs at Dulles. Seeing this flag now. He felt it in his body. It was visceral, strong.

He moved past the monuments and walked toward the building. There was no obvious indication of where he should go. But as he got closer, he could hear a scratchy radio playing a song with a regular backbeat. He walked up to the front door. Locked. But the *music* must have been coming from inside the hall; there were no other buildings nearby.

Hesitant, he went around the corner. In the back there was a narrow stairway leading down. He descended the concrete stairs and found a door—a two-part basement door, split down the middle by a seam. He turned the knob; both the top and the bottom halves swung open. A man in a baseball cap sat at a long folding table, a table that was covered in cardboard boxes of food. He had a portable radio, and his feet were up. When he saw Naïm, he immediately turned the volume down. "Can I help you?" he asked.

Naïm tried to come closer.

"Whoa," the man said. "First time here? Nobody's allowed inside."

Naïm could see the shelves of food behind the man, stacked from floor to ceiling.

"Is this for the food?" he said.

"Right," the man said. "You need to fill out this form."

The man handed him a pen and a piece of paper on a clipboard. Naïm looked down at it. There were several English words he didn't know; he'd become verbally fluent much faster than he'd acquired words on the page. This had been the case for him when he'd been a kid, too. But Naïm didn't want to say anything. The man wasn't overly friendly; as soon as he'd given the paperwork to Naïm, he'd turned his radio back on.

It was a laborious process. As Naïm shaped the letters with agonizing slowness, a few other people arrived at the door. The manager seemed to know them; after a quick exchange he handed each of them a box of food. Everyone glanced at Naïm as they went past; their collective gaze shamed him. He couldn't concentrate on what he was doing. His palms began to sweat. Finally, he just checked a few boxes and signed his name and hoped for the best.

The food bank worker glanced down at the form. "That's it, then?" he asked.

"Yes."

"Okay—you qualify for a single bag. And you can return in two weeks." He sorted through the groceries and pulled out a series of packages. He filled a bag and handed it to Naïm. It felt like the material was too thin to support its weight, like it might split at any time.

"Thank you," Naïm said. He wanted to look through the bag immediately, but made himself wait until he was out of sight of the pantry. He walked a short distance, then sat on a bench and went through it all. There was a single package of limp celery, four cans of creamed corn, a box of Cocoa Puffs cereal, and a bar of Dial soap. And two cans of cocktail franks, in broth—something neither he nor his mother could eat. He was stunned. It wasn't much of anything.

Naïm went back to the pantry and knocked on the door. The worker answered—except this time he'd clearly locked the door's bottom half. Only the top part opened. Naïm set the bag down on the ledge.

"I am wondering," Naïm said. "Can I pick out a few things?"

"That's not how it works."

"I just . . . We can't eat some of these things."

"Look," the man said. "This isn't a restaurant."

Naïm was startled by this. He was so hungry. The hunger made him tired as well.

"I thought you were supposed to be nice," he said. "I thought you were supposed to *help* people."

"I am nice," the man said. "If you don't like our food—you can go somewhere else."

"What?"

"I said, *you can go somewhere else*." And before Naïm could say anything, the man took back the bag and shut the top of the door. Naïm heard the lock click into place.

He knocked again. "Hey!" he called. "You took my bag."

But no one answered. He felt increasingly desperate.

"We're closed," the worker called through the door.

It was, to Naïm, a warning. Two words—delivered in a tone that forecast more trouble, more suffering, if he persisted. So he waited quietly at the door. One moment, then another. Then he ascended the stairs and walked back toward home.

The next day at school, Naïm couldn't concentrate. All he could see was food, food everywhere. He craved it, wanted to beg his classmates for it—but his mother's admonition echoed through his mind. When the last bell rang and the day was over, people flooded the hallways. Making his way through the crowd, Naïm spotted a candy bar—a Skor—sticking partly out of another student's backpack. Skor candy bars were, Naïm had decided, one of the great joys of life in America, and he'd been eating one a week, an indulgence he couldn't resist. *Delicious milk chocolate. Crisp butter toffee*. Naïm imagined this would be true happiness: buying as many Skor candy bars as you wanted and not worrying about how much they cost.

Now it seemed like an imperative; he *had* to follow this student—a boy he didn't recognize. They made their way through the crowded hallways. He felt the magnetic pull of the candy bar; he could taste its sugar, hear the snap of the toffee as he bit joyfully down. Naïm got closer and closer. On impulse, he reached out and plucked it from the side pocket of the backpack, staying in step with the other boy.

It was just an empty wrapper.

Things would soon get better, he knew; his mother had a job; she was going to bring home some expired bananas that very evening from the Sheetz. She'd be paid in six days. But it was still a torment. He had to go to the Fairfax County Public Library that night to research a project for his American history class; at least because of his bus card he didn't have to walk. But on the bus back home he saw someone eating a Subway sandwich. And, getting off at Arlington Boulevard, he immediately passed a Thai restaurant; the scent of the frying noodles nearly drove him out of his mind. At the entrance to his housing complex, he saw a half-eaten bag of french fries sitting on the lip of a trash can. He hesitated. They'd be cold, but—at some level—salty and delicious. He shook the temptation off. He kept walking. But as he climbed the stairs to their apartment, he continued thinking about the fries and how he'd be less hungry if he just made himself eat them.

Fatima worked late that night, and—after he watched ABC's *World News Tonight with David Muir*, which Naïm had taken to watching every evening, mainly for the calming, serious presence of the anchor—Naïm sat out on the balcony, quiet and subdued. He'd eaten some of the last rice, saving some for his mother, and this had at least calmed the hunger momentarily. Though he wondered if it was possible, he did feel like he was losing weight in just this short amount of time, like he could feel his stomach contracting, dwindling inward.

He sat on the balcony and, as he'd taken to doing more and more recently, he took out the photograph that he'd found in the piano at Ms. Crandall's all those months before. Naïm had begun imagining a life for the people in this image, a life in some city in the distant past—some place unlike this place, the one he'd been sent to by the war. It was a counterpoint to his imagining of his dead family—*Dead,* he thought, *dead, gone, but no—no—still coming, still on their way.* Narrating the story of *this* family, to him, had become easier than narrating the lives of Salah and Omar and Aysha, in part because he felt he was running out of things to imagine for them. Or, no, the things were infinite—they could take any shape at all—but increasingly he came up against the stubborn fact of the laws of physics. A body in motion, a body at rest. How could he, with his skinny arms and legs, his muscles that were less and less strong, bring the resting body into the world of momentum? How could he provide an overwhelming force? *Every good deed has an inner darkness.*

More and more, Naïm's eyes were drawn to the image of the young woman on the margin of the photograph. She looked to be a few years older than him—in her early twenties. He wondered what *her* life had been like, what she'd hoped for, what she'd dreamed about. But he was afraid, too, of imagining too much, thinking too closely about anything at all. What if her life began to take up space in his? What if he began to remember her memories instead of his own? What if her family—the one in the photograph—began to blur the faces of his own father, his own brother, his own baby sister? What would they say then, when they finally arrived in his life again?

An idea shot through Naïm: *Ms. Crandall.* The spare key. He remembered those first moments so clearly, when he and his mother had entered Ms. Crandall's house for the first time.

The entryway. The kitchen. The pantry. The shelves and shelves of food in her pantry. But the moment Naïm thought about the indignity of asking for it, of returning to her house and admitting to his situation, he began to sweat; his body started to shake, almost uncontrollably so.

What was the good of asking someone—anyone—for help? Help was temporary. Whatever condition it alleviated would invariably return. But the shame of not being able to solve your own problems? That would linger. You'd understand yourself as incapable, a failure—less than the people around you. And what did that invite? *Almost anything*, Naïm thought. There was no real limit to the catastrophes that he could imagine; his speculation knew no boundaries in its darkness. Why did the sniper target one person—instead of the next? Was there something magnetic about trouble? Was life and death, in war, linked to your sense of who you were—your confidence, or your lack of confidence? Your shame? Or was that a vile thought? All Naïm knew was that as soon as he began to imagine asking Ms. Crandall for help, he began to imagine being strafed by sniper fire on Al Mutanabi.

Besides, he could easily manage to sneak in—to *break* in—to the house on his own. Surely there would be no consequences. He could get in and get out within minutes; even if he were caught, there was nothing an old woman, living alone, could do to stop him. She was frail. He'd be safe, fine—a hero, even—a young man with luck and confidence. As he thought more about it, he became increasingly certain; this was the easiest way to solve a time-dependent problem.

Was stealing even wrong if it was something that you—that your family—needed? The answer was no. Quite simply: no. There was nothing that separated one human being from another. Made one human being inherently superior to another. And so when, in a situation like this one, Naïm was surrounded by people who, through no fault of his own, had *so* much while he had so little—he shouldn't feel guilt over taking what he needed. It was in some ways the *most* fair thing he could do. Because, really, all of these people, with their decadent, obscene wealth—their abundance of food, of money, of property—while, just a few miles away, in *their* city, people were hungry, people were starving: this had to be a heavy burden for them to bear. Even if they didn't understand it explicitly, even if they ignored it with their conscious mind, at some level they *had* to understand. *I thrive while he suffers. That is unfair. How can that be?*

Naïm would break into Ms. Crandall's house and get what he needed. What *his mother* needed. He'd be caring for himself and, he thought, caring for Ms. Crandall, too. Her immortal soul—when it stood in judgment before God—wouldn't have anywhere to hide. God would sear her with the fire of truth, and any excuses she made would be just language. *I had so much while others had nothing*, she'd be forced to tell him. *I was rich while all around me was suffering.* And what feeling would that be? What torment would that bring her? It was extreme rhetoric, Naïm knew, but beneath its exterior surface he perceived a bedrock of truth. He'd been looking for a clear lesson, but the truth was simply that there wasn't a clear lesson. The world wasn't a fixed-format image, a print derived from a negative and put in a chemical stop bath. Its levels could constantly be changed. They could all be adjusted. Updated. Maybe everything that happened in the past could become something else in the future. It could be transformed completely.

Within twenty minutes, he was standing in front of the little painted brick house, his backpack slung over one shoulder. He reached up onto the ledge outside of the doorway. And there it was, metallic and cool against the brick surface: *the key*. Naïm let himself in.

Everything was the same as he remembered it. A dark hallway. Thick carpets. A little musty. Silence. He walked past the piano and paused. He lifted the dustcover on the keys, but no more. He told himself that he just wanted to look at them for a moment—to see the string of notes, the potential sound of the scales, the escalating and plummeting tones. *Nothing more*. He walked into the kitchen. Nobody had been in here recently, he thought. He grabbed a bag of pasta and a jar of marinara sauce. There were a few packets of microwavable lentils. A bag of tortilla chips. Unable to contain himself, he opened it. He ate one chip and then another and another, feeling the glorious way that the salt and oil filled his mouth. He found a stack of paper grocery bags underneath the sink and put what he'd gathered inside of one. On a nearby shelf, there were two jars of tomato sauce that said PRODUCT OF ITALY. Probably they'd been expensive, he thought. He tucked them in his bag, nestling them carefully into place, being cautious not to accidentally break them. Despite his earlier certitude he was still trembling as the thrill of what he was doing took possession of his body.

It was no different than what his father had done, after all, going out into the dangerous city to find provisions for his family. Naïm imagined the pride his father would feel when Naïm told him what he'd done, how he'd responded to the adversity of losing the debit card. The thought made him pause. He could feel the pressure of something—the pressure of reality—against the edges of this idea. He knew, of course, the truth. But belief in the lie was important, too.

Naïm didn't see Ms. Crandall watching him, sitting in her wheelchair beside the couch. It had taken Annabel an hour to get from her bedroom to this place, and now she sat completely still, blending in with the room around her. She'd been reading a novel by Elena Ferrante, and she held it in her lap, open to her page.

She didn't know what to do. She'd recognized the young man immediately—the young man with the damaged hand, the son from the last family she'd hosted in the downstairs apartment—a mother and her child. *What were their names?* Fatima. Naïm and Fatima. Through the doorway, she could see everything the teenager was doing. He moved furtively, looking through cabinet after cabinet, taking things down and reading their labels.

It was so strange: taking food from her kitchen. What on earth was he doing? Annabel didn't care about the food—she was just confused. And mainly, she was jealous, watching Naïm move around so easily. He looked in every cabinet, moving with the grace and ease of youth; Annabel couldn't move without her joints aching—her knees, her hips, her back, all of it.

Naïm turned to go. Annabel watched him walk past the piano and then—he slowed down, almost as if he couldn't resist. He waited there, perched above the open keyboard. He seemed to be debating something, thinking of something, turning something over in his mind. Then he came to a decision. He put the brown paper grocery bag down on the bench and sat down. After a moment, he let his right hand glide over the keys, tapping softly against them—not quite hard enough to create sound. He held his left hand behind his back as he did this. Annabel watched him construct a rolling series of pantomime scales, his single hand ranging up and down the surface of the keyboard. She could see his other hand twitching, too, as if it were dying to play. Finally, she cleared her throat.

Naïm was completely startled. He jumped to his feet—turning his body and nearly stumbling over himself. He saw Annabel and began to stammer an apology. But she just shook her head.

"My dear," she said. "I just want you to actually play the damn thing."

"Ms. Crandall," Naïm said after a moment. "I'm so sorry."

"There's nothing to apologize for," Annabel said. "Clearly, you're a hardened criminal. I feel like I'm in danger."

He waited, looking at her. "Are you calling the police?" he asked.

"What do you want to play?" she said.

Finally, he said that—because of his injury—he couldn't. He wanted to, but he couldn't.

Naïm paused. He waited.

Nonsense, Annabel said. "Just sit back down and do it."

And so Naïm followed her instructions. He sat down and played for her then with his single hand—running through some of the simplest scales he remembered. He kept glancing over as he played. The fluidity of it—the ease with which his hand was able to negotiate the keys—surprised him. He didn't really organize it into a melody, though; doing that, he felt, would bring something closer to him, something that he didn't want to look at. Even as it was he nearly slipped through that darkened gap;

he was running a scale with his right hand; he was playing the keyboard without batteries in the darkened rooftop alcove of Tuhama Street. After some time, Annabel stopped him.

"That's enough," she said. She pointed to one side of the solarium. "On the top shelf of that closet is a box. It says 'Cleaning Supplies' on the outside. Go get it for me."

"You need cleaning supplies?" he said after a moment, wondering if he'd heard her correctly.

"I need the box."

Naïm went over and opened the closet. He saw her shoes and coats, neatly organized, aligned in careful rows. The box she'd requested was there on the shelf, and he pulled it down. It was rather heavy. He carried it over to Annabel and saw a plastic container of uneaten, cold food on the table beside her. On the top of the container was a sticker that read: *Restricted diet.*

Annabel saw Naïm looking at it. And—with a shockingly adept gesture—she swept it off the table with the tip of her cane.

"Don't mind that," she said.

Naïm set the box down. She asked him to open it, and he did, seeing that it was—in fact—full of chocolate. Not cleaning supplies. There were dozens of candy bars, but also sampler boxes. Some of them looked expensive.

"Oh," he said, suddenly inhaling the scent of the sugar. Annabel smiled.

"What are you waiting for?" she said. And she extended her open palm.

They sat in silence and ate. Naïm seemed to be trying not to shove the candy in his mouth all at once. He took tiny bites, but quickly—one after another after another.

"I'm so sorry," he said again. "I can explain what I'm doing here."

"Please be quiet," Annabel said. And so they sat in silence for a while. Finally, she said: "Where did you learn to play?"

It was a simple question. A straightforward one. There was nothing malicious in it. But the complexity of the memory—the way it was folded and refolded within pain, the way that pain moved through it, a seam in its center, a bright vein of anguish—made it almost impossible for Naïm to know how to answer. *Think of a time when you were happy*, a well-meaning teacher had told him in an ESL class at Falls Church High. The resulting thoughts had devastated him for days.

Where did you learn to play? He'd learned in a place that didn't exist any longer. The International School had been destroyed, wiped away with a violent flourish. It was difficult to think about the way it was now: a blank space between buildings—a vacancy.

Where did you learn to play? It was easier to think of when he'd begun to fear it—fear the keys, fear their terrifying order and almost limitless melodic possibility. Terror of the white keys. Terror of the black keys. Terror of scales. Terror of the staves. Terror of legato and staccato, of diminuendo and crescendo. Terror of—*especially*—dynamic markings. Because whatever controlled the dynamics controlled the emotion of a piece of music. And what dark power was that?

ANNABEL

Annabel waited in the quiet house, sitting still, breathing slowly in and out. It felt like she could never get enough air, like she was trying to suck the oxygen in through a straw. Her heart would begin to flutter with the smallest exertion, leaving her fighting just to stay awake. *Thirty minutes.* Thirty minutes after the boy left—she tried to stand up. If she could walk a little bit each day—even once or twice around the room—it would make a difference. On the days that she did manage to walk before the home health aide arrived at seven p.m., she felt much stronger. How she hated this body, frail and unreliable, with its skin like crepe paper, skin that blossomed into bruises at the slightest touch.

She pulled herself to her feet. Using the arm of the wheelchair as a stabilizer, she managed to maneuver her hips to arrange herself in her walker. She paused to rest. If Naïm hadn't broken in, she reflected, she'd have been sitting in the same place, thinking about her unreachable chocolate. She looked up at the print she kept in her hallway, the painting by Wyeth, *Christina's World*, the portrait of the woman—Anna Christina Olson—who'd had a degenerative muscular disorder, but who'd refused to use a wheelchair, instead choosing to pull herself wherever she could, indomitable. Annabel stood there in front of the painting, gradually catching her breath. In the Wyeth, of course, you couldn't see the woman's face. It was hidden, held in secret, turned away.

They'd take her out of her home soon, Annabel knew, place her in an assisted-living facility. Inova had a caseworker visiting her regularly, and Annabel could feel the woman's anxiety in the subtext of the questions she asked. Someone was probably already preparing the paperwork. But where could she go that was anything like her home? A ninety-year-old woman who couldn't take care of herself anymore. They'd stick her in some hideous loud room, warehoused with other unfortunates. It was so unfair. No matter what you did, you gave up control in the end.

Annabel had made it her life's work to help people from war-torn countries start over. She'd taken the money from that single American Tobacco ad campaign and stashed it in the bank; she'd used it to fund an organization—a volunteer-based organization—that helped resettle refugees. She'd spent decades wrestling with social services, navigating layer after layer of bureaucracy, simply because that was the price of admission. She'd never believed it would be her turn.

She took another step and another. Each one hurt, but soon she'd walked a little circle. She could still smell the sweet powdery scent of the candy. She could hear, too, the reverberation of Naïm's playing, or at least imagined that she could—those ghost notes, those reminders. It was remarkable. Just when she'd thought she'd known what would happen next—and how everything would end—she'd felt something new. She was surprised and grateful. It was worth all the whole wheat pasta she had.

The barrier between the living and the dead had winnowed for her recently, become less substantial. Annabel had seen Marguerite the other night—the vivid image of Marguerite standing at a window and running her hand over the gauze of a sheer curtain, looking out into the distance. Annabel wondered what it meant. She'd had a friend who'd started seeing ghosts and she was dead in a week. Annabel wasn't sure what to think about that. If it was going to happen soon, she hoped it happened the day that they tried to stick her into a van and drive her to the warehouse—to its hand-sanitized version of purgatory. *No thank you*, that's what she said. Who wanted that fate? Not dead but not fully alive. Barely embodied. Living in memory alone.

Anybody got a match? Lauren Bacall, lighting a cigarette, standing in the doorway of Humphrey Bogart's hotel room in *To Have and Have Not*. And then her next line, after she lit it—a single word—somehow smoldering with disdain and coolness and desire: *Thanks*.

Annabel had seen that movie on the day it opened in 1944, and then she'd gone back again and again, at least ten times, until she'd memorized most of its dialogue. It had started Annabel smoking at age twelve—stealing single cigarettes out of her mother's engraved silver cigarette case—the one she kept tucked in one corner of the dining room sideboard. MARLBORO CIGARETTES, the case read, MILD AS MAY.

Annabel would sneak out into the open field behind the dairy barn. She'd light her cigarette and imagine kissing Humphrey Bogart. *You know how to whistle, don't you, Steve?* she'd say, inhaling. *You just put your lips together and blow.* Then she'd exhale and try not to cough.

These lines had always, for some reason, lingered in her mind. They were almost the first thing she'd thought of when—nearly fourteen years later—on a hot summer morning in June of 1958, while she'd been waiting for the municipal streetcar at Rosslyn Station, she went to light a cigarette but realized that she'd forgotten her lighter. There was a man standing next to her, a tall young man in a gray pin-striped suit, and she'd turned slightly in his direction. *Anybody got a match?* she'd said, and he'd smiled, and rummaged in his pocket, pulling out a matchbook. And so of course Annabel had done her best *To Have and Have Not*. She'd lit her Chesterfield and thrown the match over one shoulder—before turning sideways and thanking him, channeling, with every gesture, Lauren Bacall. The man had kept smiling. *Do you model?* he'd asked. She'd laughed. *I'm a secretary*, she'd said. He'd only nodded and handed her his card.

The John Powers Agency was recruiting. They needed candidates for a new Lucky Strike campaign. A spokesmodel: sophisticated, beautiful, alluring. Someone who would play internationally. But the catch was simple: The whole process, from audition to publication, was to be a competition. Held in Cuba. Covered by *Life* magazine. It would be a full-color, four-page advertisement—one that would read just like a feature article. The industry was going global, Annabel was told, like never before. Airfreight was expanding the reach of durable light goods, and the American Tobacco Company wanted to be the global market leader. A photographer took a series of pictures of Annabel in the John Powers offices. It was all done in a few hours.

It had been a stressful year for Annabel. She'd just left her longtime boyfriend in Culpeper and come to the city; she'd seen no future for herself in that tiny town. Her boyfriend had wanted to marry her, to marry her and start a family, but she'd clearly seen the outcome of that process—all of her friends were married, had at least one child. There was nothing surprising about it, nothing at all. Annabel had worked as a cashier at Baby Jim's Snack Bar since she'd graduated from Culpeper County High; she couldn't imagine that job being the sum total of her experience of the broader world.

And so she'd moved to the District of Columbia, and worked hard to get a position in the typing pool at the *Washington Star*'s offices on Pennsylvania Avenue. She'd taken the Tuch-Rite Typing Course at home, teaching her fingers to fly over the keys, listening along to the monotone voice of Dr. Philip Sidney Gross, hour after hour, on the accompanying LP record. She'd memorized the *Gregg Shorthand Manual*, staring at the pages of the little green book until she'd thought the images would be burned permanently into her mind.

But after a while even that job had become monotonous. And so when the call came in, Annabel had hardly believed it. She'd had three days to quit her job and pack her bags. She'd flown first class; Pan American World Airways Flight 32. Washington to Miami to José Martí International in Havana. When the first flight rose into the air above suburban Washington, Annabel had felt like she was falling, not rising, falling into an abyss that had no limit. She could barely breathe.

What a thing it had been to land—so easily, so seamlessly—in *another country*. She remembered it so clearly, remembered standing in the little bathroom at the back of the DC-6 and applying another layer of lipstick. She'd looked disapprovingly in the mirror. *Too orange.* She'd wanted Cherries in the Snow, but the Revlon counter at Woodies had inexplicably been out of it. She'd chosen Hot Coral, instead—but looking at it now, she felt it made her lips look like the skin of a pumpkin.

They'd just landed and there had been some problem with the gate equipment; beyond the bathroom door, Annabel could hear both English and Spanish as the cabin crew prepared the passengers to disembark. It was early—only nine a.m.—but the sun was bright and Annabel knew it would be at least ninety degrees. Maybe her lipstick would melt off, too. It would run

down her chin and then she wouldn't look like a vegetable—
she'd look like a vampire instead.

"You ready?" Someone knocked on the bathroom door. It
was one of the other girls. *Her competition.* There were four
others—all of them younger than her, without question. The
girl knocked again. And tried the knob.

"Yes," Annabel called. "I'm ready."

She checked the shoulders of her dress and looked in the
mirror. The money—for the competition winner, for the next
spokesmodel—would easily be enough to buy a house. It would
be more than her salary for the next ten years. Even the fee for
participation was more than she was scheduled to earn for the
rest of this year, and the next.

But now—she'd reapplied her lipstick in the restroom at
the back of the plane—and everyone was waiting. Annabel
took a deep breath. She stepped into the cabin and saw them
standing in an expectant line: the four other women—Cleo,
Nancy, Blanche, and Sheila—the photographers, the agency
reps, the American Tobacco executives.

They disembarked. "We have to go through as a group,"
someone was saying. "Have your passports out," someone else
said. It was late September, but the air was immediately heavy
and hot. Even as they came down the stairs onto the tarmac,
another plane landed on the runway behind them, its propel-
lers roaring and uncomfortably close, loud.

Soldiers everywhere—armed soldiers, soldiers with auto-
matic rifles slung across their chests, with ties tucked inside
the front panels of their uniforms. Annabel noticed them. It
was impossible not to. She stayed close to the middle of the
knot of Americans, jostled on every side by the uneven motion
of the crowd. Now, here, she was anonymous. But what if she

was on the precipice of something else—on the edge of fame? If she won this competition, her image would travel out across the world. They might put her on the cover of a magazine and then no one could ever again tell her that she was disappointing or dull or stupid. People wanted to be close to fame. They approved of it. And if American Tobacco gave her the contract, the honor would be like an umbrella that she could stand under. *No*, she thought, *it would be like a shield.*

The immigration officer asked for everyone's documents. Annabel got hers out and then noticed Cleo—the young woman standing to her left—staring down at Annabel's picture. "I just hate my passport photo," Annabel said, putting her hand over the image, laughing like she'd said something funny. She was trying to obscure her birth date, since—as she'd immediately noticed—she was at least a few years older than the other women. Cleo, herself, looked very young—she couldn't have been more than seventeen. She was skinny like a racing dog and pretty in a wide-eyed, anxious way.

Annabel had told her mother—had told herself, even—that she was doing this for the money. But now, standing in line, she wondered if that was true. What she actually wanted, ultimately, was something more abstract; she wanted to be known, to have pride in something she'd accomplished. She wanted to feel like, in the end, something that she'd done had actually mattered.

The Hotel Nacional rose from a hill overlooking the Caribbean—built on a broad, flat purchase of land at the top of that hill, a small plateau that rose directly above the rocky shoreline. But somehow, even so, Annabel didn't see the building until their open-topped, cream-colored 1953 Chrysler Windsor pulled into its driveway. They'd hidden the approach. This was purposeful, she thought. Once you were there, you understood the grandeur of the place. But it wasn't supposed to be seen from the city. Not clearly. Its wealth was meant to be held in private.

American Tobacco had paid for a suite on the fifth floor; all the women's bedrooms were connected to a shared living space. Annabel hesitated when she opened the door to her bedroom. There was something astonishing about the plain-stated luxury, the bed with its mountain of pillows, crisp sheets, the vase of fresh-cut white orchids on the bedside table. High ceilings. Big windows. A row of crystal decanters that held amber-colored liquors. Rum? She opened one and sniffed its mouth. The scent of molasses and oak. Looking back at the still-open door, she lifted the bottle to her mouth and took a drink.

Annabel walked to the window. There was a sliver of Havana visible to the east—a single street that teemed with pedestrians, people who were tiny from this distance. The entire experience, she realized, was meant to separate her from the city; the group arrival, the ride in the beautiful new car, the check-in at the castle-like hotel. *Tiny distant humans.* Door still open, she stowed her clothes in the dresser, carefully removing her two dresses from their garment bag and hanging them in the closet. She noted the wrinkles with dismay; she'd been so careful when she'd stowed the bag in the overhead compartment. She knew that they'd have wardrobes for the shoots; she imagined that every detail would be carefully managed. But still—she wanted to always look perfect. If she didn't look perfect, then she was risking failure.

In the main room there were two couches and a small

kitchenette. The interpreter assigned to the five contestants—her name was Bianca—sat on the sofa closest to the door. She was an interpreter, yes, but she was also supposed to be a chaperone. She wore a pillbox hat and elbow gloves. She somehow managed to look both more poised and more rugged than Annabel had imagined was possible. Annabel made a mental note to look for flats, to buy them if she ever got the chance. She walked over to the other woman.

"When can we see the city?"

"The city?" Bianca said. "I'm not sure. The schedule is quite full."

"It can't be *that* full," Annabel said. "Can it?"

"You'd be surprised," Bianca told her. "They don't want any of the girls getting into trouble."

"What kind of trouble?" Cleo asked, appearing from her room. "I like trouble."

Bianca looked her up and down. "I'm sure you do," she said after a moment.

Annabel used the opportunity to walk over to the sink. She was startled that her conversation had been overheard. But *of course* it had; no one had their doors closed; everyone had been listening to every word she said. She took one of the little glasses from the silver tray that sat next to the sink. She reached for the faucet, turned on the cold water.

"Oh," Cleo said, still standing in her doorway. "You're not supposed to drink from the tap. You'll get sick."

"That's a myth," Annabel said.

But Cleo didn't respond. Instead, she clutched her forehead as if remembering something.

"I shouldn't have said anything. Why did I say anything?"

Annabel moved her hand—steadily, slowly—until she'd positioned the glass beneath the stream of running water. She took a long, deep drink. "You can pretend," she said, "that you didn't."

Annabel went down to the lobby. She'd argued her way past Bianca, saying she'd be right back—that she just needed a breath of fresh air. She'd ordered a pineapple juice at the bar and now she was waiting for the bartender to return. Annabel looked out across the grass of the little, oval-shaped lawn. A brace of palms. Beyond the palms, a slope heading down toward a boulevard. And the sea. What a bright blue. And a strip of turquoise just a little farther out. From this distance, the sea was silent. There was no wind today and it looked almost like a sheet of glass. It was difficult to believe that it could ever be in any other state.

After a time, Annabel became aware of a presence nearby. She turned and saw a handsome, tall man in a black suit standing just out of arm's reach. He was looking at her. How long had he been standing there? There was no way to tell.

He smiled. "You must be . . ." He took his time scrutinizing her.

"You don't know which one I am, do you?"

"Ah," he said, blinking. "No."

"Which one are you?" she said.

The man looked confused. "Which one . . . what?"

"Which suit?" Annabel said.

"I'm Henry Dobbins." When she didn't react, he added, "I'm the one you have to impress."

She nodded. "Annabel Crandall," she said. The waiter arrived with the glass of pineapple juice. It was improbably long and accented with a yellow flower. It looked like a column of concentrated sunlight. She took a sip.

"Ah," Dobbins said. "The secretary."

"No," she corrected him. "The next spokesmodel for the American Tobacco Company."

Dobbins asked her if she'd like to take a walk. As soon as he did, she knew she didn't really have a choice. It was part of the interview. Part of the selection process. He'd seen her separated from the rest of them—on her own—and he'd seized his opportunity. She was tired. But now this was a necessity.

"I'd love to," Annabel said.

She finished her drink. Earlier, walking alone through the lobby, Annabel had felt watched. The employees she'd passed had followed her with their eyes; though they'd said nothing, she'd felt the pressure of their attention. Now they looked anywhere *but* at her; walking together with Henry Dobbins, she'd become invisible.

They came out into the sunlight in front of the building. She was suddenly afraid that she didn't know this city. It was a replica of what she'd felt, rising into the air above Washington. Now, though, there wasn't even the container of the plane around her. Her dress felt suddenly flimsy, like the barest piece of fabric separating her nakedness from the world. Dobbins walked with purpose, striding southwest along Calle 21. Annabel didn't know where they were heading; she didn't know how far she would go.

They walked up through a small commercial district. They passed the skeleton of a large building—a structure that was mostly concrete and towered above everything else in the area. There was a fence around the perimeter of its lot; dozens of workers moved from place to place within the construction project.

"The Havana Hilton," Dobbins said, looking over at Annabel.

"You don't say."

"It will be the first *truly* world-class resort in Cuba."

"And are we going to be staying there next year, you and I?" Annabel asked. "When we come back?"

They were standing at a stoplight. Dobbins—who'd been imperturbable up until that moment—smiled. But only slightly.

"They've been having trouble finding an honest contractor to run the casino," he said. "Hauser called a press conference in DC to say he couldn't be bought."

"Usually that means," Annabel said, "that he can be bought."

"Usually," Dobbins said, nodding. "But in this case—I don't think so."

And then they were in a residential area. *Vedado*, Dobbins told her. Family residences, set back from the road, ornamented with art deco designs. They were talking about his work, and the idea for the spokesmodel competition, which he'd rejected at first, but then warmed to, as they'd lined up more and more publicity. Annabel strained to understand what Dobbins's position was at the company. She didn't want to ask him directly, because that would display too much interest on her part. It would cede even more power. And she had so little power to cede. There was only her mind—her thoughts—and, of course, her body.

He talked about the history of the American Tobacco Company. Dobbins was passionate about what he did, passionate about the history of his corporation. It had been one of the first companies listed on the Stock Exchange, he told her. It had survived the Panic of 1893, the Great Depression, and two world wars—increasing in profitability the whole time. Its contracts extended to every part of the globe. Annabel got the sense that he loved his work. What would it be like to feel that? she wondered.

As they walked, the sound of hoofbeats grew louder and louder behind them, and then a horse and cart overtook them. It was a tall, wrought-iron cage that rested on a handmade wooden frame—an open wagon in which half a dozen kids were riding. An older boy stood on the wagon's back step; he was ringing a large handbell, calling children out of their homes to pay a coin and take a seat. The kids were loud, and churning over one another to reach out and touch the horse's tail. The whole scene was bedlam. Annabel and Dobbins stepped aside. They let the wagon pass.

"Is this the part," Annabel asked, "where you put your arm around my waist?"

Dobbins laughed. "This is the part where I offer you a Lucky."

"No, thanks," she said. "I don't smoke." She waited a beat, to see how he'd react. But he was good. Unreadable. "Only joking," she said gently, putting her hand on his arm.

The unfiltered cigarette tasted like hickory. The flavor of it was big and immediate; it burned her throat as she inhaled. Bits of tobacco flaked out onto her tongue. What did you do with the tobacco an unfiltered cigarette left in your mouth? How did you get rid of it demurely? She decided not to worry. She exhaled a cloud of smoke and spit into the street.

They kept walking. Annabel wondered aloud if they'd been gone too long. Dobbins told her that he was, in fact, in control—and that the schedule would accommodate whatever he wanted it to accommodate. They passed a large, grassy park on their right, a park with, in the distance, a carousel.

A new house was going up here. Because it was late afternoon, the workers were cleaning their tools before heading home. Dobbins asked her where she was from originally. He said he'd read it somewhere, but now he couldn't remember.

"Culpeper, Virginia," she said. *Out in the country.* She told him a little bit about growing up next door to a dairy farm. How the workers would wake her up every morning at three, leading the cows to the milking barn. Though Dobbins made the appropriate sounds as she spoke, she wondered if he was really listening. Or—more importantly—what was he looking for? What was he hoping to hear? And how could she say it to him?

He talked about how she wouldn't be used to life on a photo shoot like this one. That it would be a whirlwind. That everything would be scheduled. That—after a day or two—tempers would flare. It happened every time. And with a concept like this one, an advertising concept *designed* to pit people against each other, who knew what might happen. They'd be in Havana for a few days, and then they had some other locations to visit. It would be a fast-paced itinerary. Dobbins wouldn't be on set the whole time; he had to conduct some business outside of Viñales, near Pinar del Rio, on one of the company's satellite farms.

They stopped at a *heladería*. Waiting in line, Annabel became aware of skinny, hungry animals in the shadows of the nearby alley. Cats and dogs, lumpy under their fur. The dogs hanging back in a cluster; the cats sprawled wherever they chose to go. It was a matter, she realized, of where she looked. She could look into the alley and see one thing. But out on the

242

street, in the full sunlight, the world seemed quite different. What she saw depended on where she focused her attention.

Dobbins got them two tall cones of sweet vanilla ice cream. Walking with the cone became slightly more complex; the ice cream melted quickly in the heat. They took a left and another left; they were headed back to the hotel, she realized. Her cone was dripping; she could feel the sticky sugar of it coating the skin of her hand.

"I want to know," Dobbins said, "what you would tell people about American Tobacco—if you were chosen as its representative."

"That's easy," Annabel said, suddenly sure of herself. "I'd tell them all about this. The competition. The flight. The arrival. All of it. I'd tell them a story."

"What kind of a story?"

The sun had started to set. The light had an indigo hue; it made every surface—natural and man-made—glow with an internal brightness. It was as if the envelope of the horizon, with its quicksilver illumination, had expanded to contain everything. Annabel thought about what she really believed—that she'd tell whatever story they wanted her to tell. Of course, that would be the worst response. Dobbins would probably think that, for it to feel authentic, the story had to come from her. But, in fact, that wasn't true. She was a talented mimic; she could be whatever he wanted.

"A story about a young woman from humble beginnings." She leaned into her drawl. "Who grew up shooting rabbits in the country. Went to school in a one-room schoolhouse. Came to Cuba. To this glamorous tropical island. All on the dime of the generous folks at American Tobacco." She paused. "That's why I love to smoke my Luckies."

Dobbins smiled. "They're toasted."

Annabel knew, though, that she was a hypocrite. It was easy to see the money here—the lush lawns and gardens of the homes in the residential district that they were now leaving, the construction projects going up in the commercial core— the hotel itself. And most of it, she guessed, was on its way out of the country, taken by people like Dobbins. Annabel tried not to care about this too much. In order to survive, right now, she felt like she had to see only what was on the surface.

As they neared the Havana Hilton again, they were some-how discussing a speed-reading course Dobbins had taken— many years ago—at Johns Hopkins in Baltimore. He was telling her how difficult he'd found it, how hard it had been to change a fundamental behavior: the way he read. And then she told him about the Berlitz School of Languages records she'd just checked out from the municipal library—trying to learn some amount of Spanish, in preparation for the trip. She'd been unsuccessful. But she'd enjoyed the sound of it; the mystery of having the most basic things, the simplest phrases, transformed.

"And what was your favorite word?" Dobbins asked.

"In the entire language?"

"Sure," he said. "Why not?"

"I don't think I have one," Annabel said. "Do you have a favorite word in English?"

"I have many," Dobbins said. "But mostly I couldn't say them in polite company."

"Is that what I am?" Annabel asked. "Polite company?"

"I assumed you were," he said. "But I could be wrong."

There was a café nearby, an open-air café, and a four-piece band was playing; the music of it drifted through the open front windows and out onto the street. Annabel sensed something changing; she felt a spark of something, a flare, move between Dobbins and her body. They stopped walking. They were standing on a street corner, in the shade of a sprawling mangrove tree. Its roots hung down from its sprawling branches. She had the image of the mangrove as a witch—some variety of ancient sorceress, holding her arms out wide, her blood circulating outside of her body, ropy veins reaching for the nourishment of the dirt. Dobbins was now looking at her quite intensely. *This is wrong*, she thought. *This is a bad idea.*

But then he was talking about the schedule again, moving forward, and then—out of a sky that barely seemed overcast— it started to rain. Where had it come from? It wasn't unpleasant, just unexpected, and then Dobbins broke through the space between them and took her hand in his.

"I'm going to kiss you now," he said.

What a wild power, she thought. She wanted to turn her face away—she *would* turn her face away, she decided—but then, at the last moment, she didn't. She couldn't. His mouth had, she noticed, the slightest scent of alcohol. They kissed once, then a second time. She pulled back and glanced down— purposefully—at his left hand, which, she'd noticed hours ago, had a golden wedding band on its ring finger.

"And what about your wife?" Annabel asked. "What would she say about this?"

"She'll forgive me," Dobbins said. "She always does."

Annabel came back to the hotel in a trance, her mind unable to focus on any single thing. She left Dobbins downstairs and took the two flights up to her suite. Bianca was nowhere to be found and, at first—even though it was just nine o'clock—neither were any of the other women. There was a bowl of fruit on the counter in the kitchenette; Annabel didn't recognize any of it. No apples. No citrus, even. She took a pendulous, pear-shaped green globe from the bowl and looked at it. A knife. She needed a knife.

The drawers were empty. She was looking through them, pulling them out one at a time, finding nothing, when she sensed, once again, someone close behind her. She turned. Cleo stood there, wearing a nightdress, her hair in curlers.

"What are you looking for?" Cleo asked.

Annabel turned toward her. "That's a complicated question," she said. "Isn't it?"

The other woman paused. "No," she said. "Not really."

"A knife," Annabel said. "To cut this . . ." She held up the fruit.

"Guava."

Annabel nodded. "Maybe they don't give us knives," she said, "because they're worried about what we might do with them."

"I'd kill you if I could."

"You might not be joking," Annabel said.

Cleo turned and walked back into her room. She was gone for a moment and then returned—holding what looked like a butter knife. She handed it to Annabel, blade-first.

"Where'd you go?" Cleo asked. *And why wasn't anyone looking for you?* she seemed to be implying.

Annabel thought about her options. If she told the truth—or any version of it—she would immediately arouse suspicion. And news like this would be exactly the kind of thing that would spark alliances among the women; Cleo could gain one of the other competitors' trust by telling them where Annabel had gone. Or, perhaps, Annabel could create a bridge, a bridge to Cleo; she could bring her closer by confiding in her. But that, too, had its risks. Annabel had no idea how the other woman would react. What if she was angry rather than empathetic? Where was the power in this situation? Annabel guessed it was with her, but it wasn't anything she could be sure of.

The heart—the emotional world activated by an intimate conversation. This might be a kind of insurance. But thinking of this, she felt something more complex build inside of her. A cold fury. *He'd known what he was doing*. He'd chosen her because he knew she was likely to keep her silence. He'd left her with a confusing array of emotions—a sudden blank wall inside of her, undecorated, unornamented. This thought chafed. It eroded her sense of this moment, when she was standing there, in the kitchen. *I'm unreliable*, she thought. *I'm weak*.

She looked down at the fruit and the blade she was using to slice through the guava's skin. She pressed the tip of the knife into the yielding fruit. It broke its surface, drove through the flesh and revealed its pink, seeded interior. Juice dripped down the handle and onto her fingers. A residue. The white porcelain of the sink—just to her left—looked like a glowing ice platform. She turned and offered half of the guava to Cleo. The fruit had an intense floral scent.

"I went for a walk," she said.

Cleo looked at her and frowned. "Must be nice," she said. She didn't take the offering; she walked back into her room.

Annabel did, too. It would be a long time until the sun came up, and she had no idea how she would sleep. Once she'd closed the door, she took off her clothes immediately. *The relief*. She lay on her king-size bed, naked, and stared up at the ceiling. The fan spun in a relentless circle, rotation after rotation. What had she done? She'd made a decision—a critical decision in her life—with no real sense of the consequences. Or, rather, she'd tried to imagine the consequences and failed. Anxiety moved through her body and seemed to ring out—to fill the empty room—this darkened space beyond the farthest margins of her continent. She hadn't done anything wrong, nothing that couldn't be undone. Maybe Dobbins would take *each* girl out on a walk. Maybe she wouldn't be remarkable.

Annabel covered her eyes with the back of her hand. Would she come out of this the victor? Or maybe she'd be vindictive—determined to find a way into Dobbins's core, swim like a worm in the blood, diastole sucking her into his heart, where she could explore from the inside. She closed her eyes. She opened them. None of these personas, though, felt natural—so she would use them as emotional skeletons. They could bolster her as needed, while, inside herself, she would be quiet and wait.

If she followed her thoughts to their extreme, though, she could get as dark as she wanted to and nothing would matter— not her mother, not anyone waiting for her, waiting to hear what happened during her time in Havana. Someone had told her once, long ago, *We all die alone*, and it was a phrase that stuck in her mind, that wouldn't let her go. She thought about it often, this solitary end that she, that everyone, would come to. There was nothing to do about it, though, except choose life—choose life, always and every day, until your last.

The next morning brought a photo shoot at a market—an open-air market on Calle Obispo. There was a great deal of commotion, getting everyone ready for their part in the shoot; all five women—someone had decided—would take the same photos in the same location. Level the playing field. All equal.

"Coffee!" a production assistant was yelling as Annabel came down to the lobby. "Coffee and cigarettes, right now, for Mr. Jenkins!"

Who Mr. Jenkins was, Annabel didn't know. But it was jarring to hear the strident American voice, calling for something, demanding it, echoing out through the enclosed interior space of the hotel. Annabel stood to one side and watched. The area in front of reception had filled with—as if they'd blossomed overnight—several dozen workers.

American Tobacco had been, apparently, building its own elaborate set on Calle Obispo so that the photographers could control the look of everything. The set was a short walk from the Hotel Nacional. Down to the water—and then east along the waterfront esplanade. But Annabel couldn't go alone, even if she'd woken up before everyone else. *No.* Nothing—nothing— could be done alone. She had to have a retinue of handlers around her, a structure that could control her movements, and the movements of the other potential spokesmodels. Nothing could be left to chance. A team of young, attractive professionals from an advertising agency—J. Walter Thompson in New York City—were in charge. They shepherded the contestants from the hotel, through the streets, to the make-believe market stall.

Once Annabel reported to the set, a young assistant escorted her to wardrobe. A designer put all the women in peasant shirts and wide-brimmed hats and skirts pinned up beyond their knees. The idea was that they were selling tobacco at a farmer's market; dried tobacco leaves hung down decoratively from the ceiling, alternating with braided ropes of onions and garlic. It was hot. Everyone was sweating. Nancy, Blanche, and Sheila looked uncomfortable; they seemed almost boiled by the tropical sun. Cleo looked good, however. She looked too good—and as Annabel considered her more closely, she noticed something. Flexing jawline. An almost otherworldly brightness and enthusiasm in her eyes. *Speed*, she thought. Speed of some kind. Benzedrine, maybe? Or diet pills?

People at the neighboring market stalls were confused as to what was happening. Someone had started a rumor that they were filming a movie and so a group of kids had gathered, drawn out of the urban neighborhoods that surrounded Obispo. Everything moved quickly. A designer would dart in from time to time and adjust things; at one point, he tied Annabel's hair in a colorful rag. She held a lit cigarette and let it dangle casually from her hand. She was doing well; she could feel her own magnetism, drawing admiration out of anyone who was watching.

Dobbins was one of those onlookers. Annabel hadn't seen him arrive, but at some point she became aware of him watching her, observing her as she smiled out at the camera lens, trying to look wide-eyed, despite a drift of silvery smoke. Whir of the shutters. The instructions of the photographers. And the hush of the onlookers, whose silence was an almost palpable thing.

Annabel's turn to be photographed ended. She knew that those images would be scrutinized by men in office buildings far away; they'd discuss her in God knew what kinds of ways. Who knew what they might say? What terms they would use? She tried not to think about it.

There was a small storefront that had been repurposed

into a dressing room. Just inside the door was a table of food for the workers, for the personnel on the shoot. Kids scurried in and out, snagging slices of ham or small, sweet pastries. Annabel walked over and poured herself a cup of coffee. Dobbins was there, talking to a little group of executives from the advertising agency; they were looking at something—a poster that they'd put down on a table—and discussing a font.

Annabel saw, on the edge of her vision, an older woman. She'd stepped inside that same unguarded doorway and was taking fish, smoked fish, from a plate at the far end of the food table. She had a basket on her arm, a basket that she'd lined with a towel, and she was carefully placing the fish in it. Annabel watched her. Then Annabel saw that Henry Dobbins had noticed the older woman, too. He was staring at her. He didn't look pleased. *Stop!* he said. But she didn't.

Before Annabel knew what was happening, she saw this man—the man who'd dominated her thoughts throughout the night—cross the room and grab the woman by the arm.

"What are you doing?" Dobbins asked her. "Is that yours? Is it?"

But the woman said nothing. Dobbins shook his head and used his grip to lead her away—but not out the door. Instead, he took her deeper into the building. The woman looked alarmed. Her hair was white and it was gathered in a loose bun on top of her head. She tried to yank her arm free. But Dobbins shoved her into what appeared to be a back room and then—from the outside—locked the door.

Annabel was shocked. At first, she looked to the other people in the room, one after another. Nobody would meet her gaze. *What's he doing?* she said. Silence. *Where is he taking her?*

As soon as Dobbins returned, she confronted him.

251

"Do you know her?" she said. It was a ridiculous question, she thought—but who would grab a woman they didn't know?

"Why do you care?" Dobbins said.

"Because she might be frightened."

"Frightened?" he said. "I'm calling the police." He had the woman's woven basket in his hand. He tossed it through the doorway, out into the street. Dobbins's nostrils flared with each breath; a wrinkle cut through the center of his forehead, folding his features into a furious mask. When no one said anything more, he finally turned back to the people he'd been talking with a moment ago. *Let's tackle this one later on,* he said, and stepped out into the street.

Annabel approached the cluster of men.

"Can he just do that?" Annabel asked the one closest to her, a young man—not more than twenty-five, who was wearing a light blue linen suit, a pressed white shirt with no tie. He shrugged. "Should we let her out?" Annabel asked.

The man shook his head. "Henry has a temper," he said. "Careful or you'll get in the line of fire."

"But she's just an old lady," Annabel told him. "Someone's grandmother."

"You want a piece of advice?" the man said. "Forget about it."

But after about ten minutes—ten minutes when she'd left the storefront and then returned—Annabel could hear the woman crying behind the closed door. Everyone else had cleared out; probably they were afraid of getting involved and angering Dobbins. Annabel felt a sudden urgency; what if something went terribly wrong in there?

"I've got a wardrobe change," one of Dobbins's assistants said, hurrying in. He was carrying a bathing suit on a hanger. It was small—a yellow bikini with pointy breasts and low-waisted pants. There was barely anything to it. It was, she thought, utterly scandalous.

Through the door, Annabel could see Dobbins. He stood in the street, talking with two policemen. He pulled his wallet out of his back pocket and gestured with it, pointing from door to door; Annabel was far enough away that she couldn't hear what he was saying. The three men turned and walked a little distance away. *Where's he going?* Annabel thought. She reached out and took the bathing suit.

"Fine, fine," she said. "But I want to change in here."

The man gave Annabel a lewd smile. "Okay with me," he said.

"*Not*," she said, "with you watching."

"Oh," he said. "Sure. Of course, doll, of course."

He left and closed the front door behind him. As soon as he was gone, though, Annabel rushed over to the back room and unlocked the door. She knocked. *Hola?* she called. There was no answer. She waited. She repeated the word, this time a little louder.

When she opened the door, Annabel found that the space was empty. She frowned; she'd heard the woman only moments before. But then, at the back of the room, Annabel spotted the window. It was open. She walked closer. There was, on the windowsill, a single footprint. The muslin curtain—gauzy and white—seemed to shimmer in the bright afternoon sun.

Annabel always wondered what would have happened in her life if she'd made different choices. If she'd somehow negotiated the next few days differently.

Dobbins was nowhere to be seen for the rest of the morning. But something—some current of some kind—was moving through the air. She wasn't sure what it was, but Annabel noticed a subtle shift in the feeling of the shoot. She sensed people moving out of her way as she walked through the hotel lobby. And when she returned to her room afterward, there it was.

A short note. Hotel stationery. Wild handwriting, blue ink from a fountain pen. Written without pause, without doubt, without hesitation:

Lunch tomorrow
Room 432
—HD

And that was all. Four words—three words, really—that transformed her life. Nineteen letters, three numbers. *On a note card*. It did have, Annabel thought, a certain charm.

She took a shower. When she stood under the faucet, holding it above her head to rinse out the shampoo, she didn't feel the sting of the water—hot or cold. She experimented on herself in a detached way, turning it to one extreme or another. *Nothing*. She felt untouched. Her skin was just a shedding device, like a gutter. Her body would absorb no temperature. It would not be modulated.

Annabel dried herself off. She lit a Lucky Strike and stood at the window. The same dark sea waited for her out there, with its implacable, inky waves. She wasn't the first person, she realized, to look out over the sea and think about the way that the waves came in sequentially, constantly, trailing one another, a steady inevitability. There was infinity in them, of course, a measure of immortality—or rather something beyond that, something that wasn't really immortality because it wasn't living, because it was a constant and ever-churning organism. World without end, amen.

She did feel solitary, though. A vanguard, an advance patrol. The cigarette was a speck of orange in the general black. The smoke moved quickly out the window. Annabel had read a newspaper story about a big British study—Doll and Hill—that found that smoking twenty-five cigarettes a day increased your chance of developing lung cancer. But these were just rumors. The president still smoked. Her mother still smoked. *And yet.* It was difficult not to notice the yellowing of her nails if she smoked too many cigarettes. The faint discoloration of her front teeth. The way she craved a Lucky Strike first thing in the morning.

Last night, Dobbins had asked her what she'd say when someone told her that smoking wasn't healthy.

"I'd say: 'If it's so bad for you, then why's my doctor got an ashtray in his waiting room?'"

It was the kind of thing he was looking for, and his laughter had been a balm on her anxiety. Why hadn't she remembered that feeling? Why hadn't she possessed it, held on to it, guarded it within herself, nurtured it, like a fragile flame? Now she just had the open expanse of water—and the water was no refuge. To get to this island, Annabel had flown above that water in a luxuriously appointed cabin, drinking cocktails and pretending to be entertained by boorish conversation. She was no Amelia Earhart. Or maybe she would share Earhart's fate? Maybe Annabel would see the water, and its shimmering bulk would open upward to consume her. *KHAQQ calling Itasca. We must be on you, but cannot see you. Gas is running low.*

• • •

Annabel found herself in the appointed hotel room at the appointed time, wearing her coral lipstick and a bright red dress that she'd bought from the Sears Christmas Book for $19.90. Almost one-fifth of her weekly salary at the *Washington Star*. Dobbins looked relaxed and comfortable; he had a glass of liquor in one hand when he answered the door. He was wearing the same style of shirt as he had the day before; he must have half a dozen of them, Annabel decided, hanging in a row in his closet. The sight of him did initially affect her in a way she hadn't expected. She felt a small flutter of nervousness in her pulse as he crossed the room and bowed his head slightly to kiss the back of her hand. "I'm glad you could make it," he said.

"You set the schedule," Annabel said, recalling his words from their night together.

"True," he said. "I do enjoy that power."

His room had a balcony overlooking the Gulf of Florida. It was a large, tiled space, and there was a table set up on it, and a little umbrella canted to one side to shade that table from the sun. White tablecloth. Decanter of chilled wine. He gestured toward it all. "Have a seat," he said. "The view is fabulous."

Their first dish was already plated: a tomato aspic with mint. There was a parsleyed cottage cheese sauce on the side, and Annabel could taste the onion in it, and the chive. It was a dish she'd grown up eating; that she could close her eyes and see her mother making, opening the packet of lemon Jell-O— with its bright red lettering, and its slogan: *Delicate. Delightful. Dainty.* She wondered if they'd used the real thing, or a bulk gelatin product, sourced locally in Havana.

After a few bites, Dobbins put down his spoon.

"I know I can be intimidating," he said. He waited for her

to agree with him, but—when she said nothing—he continued. "I need someone who can stand up to me. Someone with courage. With grit."

Those were not, however, words that Annabel would have used to describe herself. She smiled at him, as if she were too shy to admit to her better qualities.

"That's why I can trust you with this," he said. He took a briefcase from beside the table and opened it. Inside were a series of photographs—of her.

She, Dobbins explained, had already been chosen as the winner. It had all been done *before* the competition, he told her, to eliminate uncertainty. "This is the picture for *Life*," he said. Annabel looked down. Sure enough, there it was, that yellow bathing suit. She was smiling, and holding a Lucky in her right hand, a look of pleasure and joy on her face. Dobbins waved the photograph in the air with a great flourish, like an artist signing a masterpiece.

"You brought me here to tell me," she said, "that it's all a sham."

Dobbins sighed. "In a way," he said. "But it's a sham that favors you. You've already won."

Annabel's breath caught in her throat. She stared at him. "If you're lying to me . . . ," she began.

"I can assure you I'm not lying to you."

"But if you are . . ."

"I'm not," Dobbins said. "You see—there's something else." He made a show of removing the wine from the decanter, examining the label. It had been uncorked earlier and now he poured them each a large glass. "I said I had to travel, starting tomorrow," he told her. "And I could really use someone where I'm going."

"Hell?" Annabel said. She said it so deadpan that it took him a moment to realize she was joking.

"I hope not," he said. He told her the name of the farm. "We're having a real problem with morale there."

"What do you mean?" Annabel asked.

"It's been," Dobbins said, "a tough period. It's just important that we seem *solid*. Like nothing can move American Tobacco."

Annabel took a big drink of her wine. "*Grit. Solid.* You sure know how to charm a girl, Mr. Dobbins."

"And a pretty face will boost everyone's spirits," he said.

"That's a little better."

"I have other ways," Dobbins said, setting down his wine, "to charm a girl."

It was all so clear in Annabel's memory—all of it—even six decades later. The color of the tile floor, the brightness of the summer sky, the feeling of Dobbins's body, his strength—which had surprised her at the time. His aggression. Of course he'd planned everything, imagined her role from the very beginning; it was as if he'd been following a script all along.

That moment. The yellow light mantling over everything, giving it a bright gloss in her mind. She'd felt so timid at the time—frightened and debased and afraid in a way. Aware that she'd made some kind of decision, on her own, and that she was now dealing with the consequences. It was as if she'd split, split as a person, and some part of her was trapped, trapped by the circumstances of the moment. She'd taken her body to this place, and now—now she'd fallen into bed with a married man. It was what she'd expected, but it also wasn't what she'd wanted.

But then: what happened next—it always hurt to think of that. It hurt and so she'd kept it hidden, secreted it away in a compartment of herself, a place that she could barely look at, barely touch. Memory would surface and cause her anguish, physical anguish, if she wasn't careful. It would cut through time like a voracious blade; it would reduce decades to pieces, cut half a century into ribbons.

PINAR DEL RIO

Cuba
August 1958

As she sat at her vanity, combing and recombing her humidity-damaged hair, Marguerite's pulse raced, raced simply from remembering the sound of it—the four-propellor Martin M-130 that had banked that afternoon through the fusillade of bright silver clouds five thousand feet above their tobacco fields. At first, she'd thought it was thunder. But no— not thunder—commercial air travel. Probably a flight headed toward Havana.

She couldn't get used to it. A new technology, a bridge across previously unbridgeable distances. Pan American and Trans World Airlines, flying everywhere. Each time she heard one of the planes it created a discomfort inside of her, a feeling that was hard to identify—or shake off.

"Do you think we'll ever take a trip like that?" she asked, trying to keep her voice light and casual. *Steady*.

Adolfo stood in the bathroom of their little home—a small, renovated house on the Castillo plantation, a former workers' cottage. Adolfo was trying to fix his tie in the cracked mirror in their low-ceilinged bathroom; Marguerite could see him bending down, adjusting the knot of black fabric, loosening and straightening it, then cinching it tighter around his neck, then repeating the process. "Would you like that?" he asked after a moment.

Marguerite put her hairbrush down. "How do those people not go deaf?" she said, half-joking. She stood up and walked over to the table next to their bed. "It would be like living in the guts of a piano."

Marguerite opened a drawer and took out her folder of music—the compositions she'd written in the last few months. She began to page through them, thinking eagerly of the expensive Steinway in her father-in-law's living room. She was excited, humming a few bars of her most recent piece. Even just looking at these scores had the power to preoccupy her; she took a pencil from the same drawer and made a mark on the page, noting a place that she wanted to revisit tomorrow.

A cramp fluttered through her stomach. She wasn't feeling well and, as soon as Adolfo reappeared—his tie approximately the same as it had been—she put the composition on the bed and went into the bathroom. She shut the door behind her. Once it was closed, she leaned against it and checked her underwear. *Spotting.* Just as she'd suspected. She was starting her period, and so she thought the same thing now that she'd thought last month: by thirty-two, her mother had seven children. Marguerite felt a momentary surge of despair.

"Everything okay?" Adolfo called through the door.

"Fine," she said, just managing to keep her voice from breaking. She didn't want to tell him the news just yet. She'd been a week late, and so they'd been hopeful. And tonight, the dinner with his father was going to be stressful enough.

She arranged her clothes and stood at the tiny window with its slatted glass. A guava tree had grown through the aperture while the previous tenants had lived here; though Marguerite had converted this space to a bathroom when they'd moved in, she'd refused to cut the little branch that was growing into their house. Her secret dream, which she hadn't told anyone, was that it would flower and fruit inside. Then she wouldn't have to leave the house to harvest her breakfast.

"You don't need to bring your music," Adolfo called from the other room. "It's not that kind of party."

"It's always that kind of party." She stepped out of the bathroom. "And I finished something. I want to see how it sounds. I'm tired of just humming it."

Adolfo stared at her dress. It was green silk; it accentuated the curves of her body, bright and lively to the touch, almost like a second skin. "You shouldn't wear that," he said.

Marguerite looked at him. He'd never cared about what she'd worn in the past. "Why?" she asked. "Too scandalous?"

"It's too expensive."

"It's just a dress."

"You should wear the blue one I got you." He gestured to a dress that was lying across the bed. It was a blue cotton button-down and very plain—almost like a man's work shirt.

"It's boring," she said.

"It's honest," he countered.

"And boring." She laughed. "I'm not a matron yet." She pulled on her wedding ring that sat in a little dish on the dresser. Adolfo was acting a bit strange, and it made her apprehensive. "You're not fighting with your father again, are you?"

"No," Adolfo said, glancing away. "I just liked the color." She sensed there was some meaning in all of this—but she just didn't know what it was. She stepped closer to her husband. She took the bottom of his tie in one hand and slid her palm up along it until her fingers brushed the side of his jaw.

At her touch, he seemed to relax. Something came away from his eyes, some obscuring layer, and he kissed her gently on the lips. "I love you," he said.

"Next time," Marguerite said. "I'll wear the other one next time."

They hurried out the door.

The Castillo plantation was—easily—the largest in the province. As hacendados, they supplied the critical, sun-grown, central leaves for the Partagás and Montecristo brands, for the cigars that eventually traveled, from their loamy soil, around the world. Their tobacco fields were the legacy of the Indigenous tribes—the Igneri, the Arawaks, the Taíno—who'd used the plant in religious rituals, and had been systematically massacred by the Spanish, in the first days of colonization.

Marguerite had been astonished when she'd arrived, to learn this history, to see the evidence of it, written in the grain of the land. To understand so much about this product, tobacco, that she'd always assumed to be her own. It was her name, after all. A fundamental part of her heritage. To see the farms here, with their vast differences from Latakia—with their history of labor that had come from the slave ships, with their Bantu-speaking prisoners from the Gold Coast of Africa. When the slavers had crossed the ocean they'd led a chain of sharks, sharks that had followed the ships to feast on their discarded human cargo. A blood banquet. And she, herself, had followed that same route. There was a highway on the ocean floor, she sometimes thought, built from the sacred bones of the dead—the ones who'd sunk to the bottom in chains, the ones who'd had no ceremony, whose souls patrolled through salt and brine forever.

They walked along the dirt path to the main house, stepping carefully, trying to keep their shoes clean. Several workers stood aside to let them pass. One made eye contact with Adolfo and nodded. He nodded back.

"My love," Marguerite said. "Tell me who'll be there."

"A pack of American jackals," Adolfo said. "The American Tobacco Company. A few board members of Cuban Land and Leaf. The usual."

"Give me a name," she said, "other than American Jackal."

He laughed. "Do they need a name?" he said. "Do they care what our names are? It's better to greet them on their own terms, don't you think?"

Marguerite sighed. She was clutching Adolfo's arm to steady herself as she walked.

"If you didn't want to go," she said, "you should have told your father."

"He said he needs me there."

They were on the edge of one of their most common dis-agreements. She couldn't help herself. "You know change has to happen slowly."

He stopped walking.

"You just had to say it," he said.

"Because you don't seem to understand," she said. "That's why I have to say it again and again."

"They aren't draining our country slowly," Adolfo said. "That's happening quickly."

"Anything that happens quickly can't be sustained."

"Which is why we need to stand up to them," he said.

Marguerite shook her head. She believed in it all—believed in the ideals that Adolfo held so dear, his deep engagement with the cause. Because—after all—a person was not a com-modity. A person was not the same thing as a tobacco plant or a stalk of sugarcane. Not a natural resource waiting to be

267

harvested and consumed. A person was something different. A person was the whole of the species at once: seed and stalk and blossom and soil. And rain. And worms. And the wind that carried the bees. And the heat that evaporated the sea and sent it, in fog, over the island.

But Marguerite was uncomfortable with the more radical approach that Adolfo was increasingly interested in. Last year, he'd moved them out of the main house into a worker's cottage. Marguerite had objected at first—but he'd just been so *relentless*—and so she'd finally agreed. She'd demanded, though, that they put in a private bathroom of some kind, and then wire the cottage with electricity. The project had turned out better than either of them could have expected. The electricity had extended to all the workers' cabins; they'd become the first farm between Viñales and the coast that was fully electrified.

But Marguerite missed living in the big house with its running water and fans and, of course, the piano. She loved her husband, loved his restless mind and his good heart—but she felt like his love of politics had edged ahead of his love for her. Or for anything else. And they'd done so much good here. They'd increased wages, hired a doctor for the staff. They'd sponsored regular school for the children in the area, hiring a young, idealistic teacher from Matanzas. And so Marguerite thought that it was, possibly, good enough. It was better, without doubt. But better—Adolfo had often told her—wasn't freedom.

"I know what you're thinking," he said. They could see the house in the distance, every window ablaze.

"If you argue with your father at dinner—"

"Argue?" he said. "I'm not going to argue with him. Why would I argue with him?"

But over the last few months, as talk of an actual revolution had increased, Adolfo's relationship with his father had deteriorated. They'd fought over everything, everything and nothing, or—rather—not the right things, the irreconcilable things, the differences that truly separated them. Fidel Castro's party—the Partido Socialista Popular—had been, in particular, a source of strife. For all of his generosity of spirit, Adolfo couldn't see that his father had his son's best interests at heart.

"He just wants to protect you," Marguerite said. "He believes in incremental improvement."

"That's a coward's perspective," Adolfo said. "It's the residue of the colonial superstructure."

"You know what I mean," she said. "If you aren't supportive, he'll see it as a betrayal. And he'll be less likely to listen to you in the future."

He sighed. After a moment, they continued walking. They reached the grounds of the estate—the garden around the neoclassical home, the home that had been built in 1830 by Adolfo's great-great-grandfather, built before the railroad had connected this part of the country to Havana, when the roads had to be cut out of the wilderness yearly with machetes. "I'm not going to do anything drastic," Adolfo said. "I won't take any wild chances."

"Whenever your father expands the business," she said, "we can take some of that profit and roll it into the plantation. We can pass some of it along. He'll always allow that. He's trying to meet you halfway."

"You're thinking too small," Adolfo said. "But it's not your fault."

This made Marguerite angry. But it wasn't the time. She

took a deep breath, feeling the heavy cramping that had started to move through her belly. "You can't build something," she said, "and simultaneously tear it down."

"I just want a better world for us," Adolfo said. And he let his hand slide around her waist to touch the side of her belly. "For our family,"

He was looking at her hopefully and Marguerite couldn't bear to say anything. *Later*, she thought. *I'll tell him later.* "Yes," she said. "Now, tell me again who'll be there? Your father, and Hector Diaz from next door."

Adolfo nodded. He went down a roster of names. They were there to finalize the details of a new ten-year contract. Henry Dobbins, the representative of the American Tobacco Company. His two associates, Michaels and Stephenson. A few others—men who were coming directly from the Cuban Land and Leaf board meeting in Santa Clara. And Annabel Crandall—a guest added by Dobbins at the last moment.

"A woman," Marguerite said. "Then it's a good thing I wore my best dress."

"We don't need to impress them," Adolfo said.

"Women notice clothes," Marguerite said. "Silk is wasted on the rest of you."

The Castillo home was, that evening, a study in luxury. There were buckets of champagne on ice, crystal vases of flowers spilling from every surface. Fans whirled overhead, making the pendants of the chandelier tinkle softly—a subtle music. Though it embarrassed her, she experienced all of this as a relief. Her father-in-law, Jorge Castillo, greeted them warmly, with a kiss on the cheek.

"So good to see you," he said. He shook Adolfo's hand. "Thank you for doing this."

Adolfo squeezed his father's hand but couldn't bring himself to look him in the eye. Most of the guests had arrived over the course of the day, taking the agonizingly slow train from Havana—then transferring to private cars in the city. But the four representatives of American Tobacco had only just arrived—flown in on a Piper PA-23, landing on the dirt runway just outside of town. Annabel, the last-minute addition, looked tired, in particular; as they sat on the veranda drinking Santiago rum, she seemed out of place, as if she were somehow surprised to be there.

Marguerite introduced herself. "It's nice to meet you," she said in English.

"Likewise," Annabel said. "I feel underdressed in my traveling clothes." She was wearing wide pants and a blue cotton shirt.

Annabel commented on the beauty of the house. And—for Marguerite—it was nice to be reminded of this; the building *was* almost shocking in its beauty, with its sweeping columnar terrace situated in a lush landscape. When she'd first arrived, Marguerite had felt as if she'd moved not just to another country but to another planet. In the distance, the tobacco fields undulated to the horizon—rolling hills that would soon have their geometrically precise installations of the bright green plants, the ones that had been raised from tiny, tiny seeds. And this moment of the day was particularly remarkable. The San Juan y Martinez river trickled by. Cricket song. Bulls and horses in the fields. Soon the air would fill with *libélulas*—the bright green fireflies. The sunset had begun; its first tentative colors washed out over the twilit sky.

As Marguerite and Annabel talked, the steady sound of hoofbeats approached the house. The veranda had a view of the main road, and Marguerite saw the plume of dust that always announced an impending visitor. There was a clutch of rubber trees at the last bend in the road, and as the flat-bottomed wagon came around the corner it scared a flock of meadowlarks from their branches. The birds were bright yellow. They rolled and careened through the air.

This was their last guest. Father Ignacio Soto, the priest from the village, the man who'd baptized Adolfo, who'd married Adolfo and Marguerite, wearing his brightest white vestments, ones Adolfo's father had ordered specially for the ceremony. Every time that Marguerite saw Father Soto, she remembered him this way—unnaturally bright, his stole embroidered with golden crosses and fringed with golden tassels. He'd been like a second sun, standing on the altar, singing the words of the wedding mass. She'd looked at him through her lace veil and felt like his image would scald her eyes.

As Father Soto approached, though, she saw that he wasn't smiling. He looked concerned. He seemed to be hurrying. He took the little gate to the side yard—where he was greeted by the butler and offered a drink—which he peremptorily declined. By the time he reached the party on the veranda, he seemed to have regained his composure. Marguerite was standing closest to the entrance.

"Father," she said, bowing her head slightly. "How nice you could join us."

"My dear," he said. "Such a pleasure to see you, as always."

A thin, gray-haired man, the priest was popular in the village—he'd been known for decades as an arbiter of disputes, a judicious counsel, a freethinker. His door was open to every-

272

one, and he was often seen sitting at a little table on the transept, playing dominoes with one of his many acquaintances, drinking little cups of homemade aguardiente long into the night. His homilies often referenced the Santeria orishas who his congregants had honored for centuries. And, over the last five years, he'd started saying the Mass in Spanish, facing the congregation, rather than the way it had always been done before, in stentorian Latin, back to the crowd, facing only the figure of Christ.

Soto looked very serious, almost downcast. Even so, Marguerite was grateful for his presence. In a wash of faces that were largely unfamiliar, it was a relief to see someone she knew. He was a pocket of safety in an exhausting performance. She confessed her concerns about Adolfo's relationship with his father, about how it simply seemed to be worsening. They could argue, she said, about whether water was wet. He nodded.

"The two of you," he said, gesturing to Adolfo, who was standing nearby. "Do you have a plan to protect yourselves?"

"Protect ourselves?" she asked, taken aback. "From who?"

"From everyone," the priest said.

Marguerite was shaken. She didn't know how to respond. *We'll be fine*, she said, trying to brush the moment off.

They joined the rest of the group and soon everyone was talking about this season's rain, and the new crop that would be planted in a few months, and the ways that they were modernizing the plantation's infrastructure. Thanks to money from the American Tobacco Company, Adolfo's father said, they'd installed a new boiler in the workers' recreation hall. It would be powered completely by *bagasse*—the fibrous sugarcane pulp that remained after the mill pressed the cane. There was a sugarcane farm outside of Hermanos Saiz that would give them the fuel for free—even *paying* to have it hauled away.

The party moved from the veranda to the dining room to the great room, with its vast brick fireplace. The conversation continued; Marguerite listened attentively. She was holding her sheet music rolled in her hand—she'd been using it as a fan—and now she tapped it against her leg. She was gauging how long it would be before she could sneak off and play her composition. She imagined the roll of the opening crescendo, the notes opening and consuming her. She'd be transported.

Then Henry Dobbins was saying that yields were down slightly, and that he'd been looking into various ways of modernizing the curing process. There were new ventilation machines, he said, that mimicked the natural variance of the wind and allowed you to cure tobacco in half the time.

"Then we'll have twice the profits," Adolfo's father said, and everyone laughed, except Adolfo. "It's going to be a great year." Adolfo's father turned to Adolfo for reinforcement. "And tobacco futures in New York are only going up."

Father Soto interjected something here. "It would be smart," he said to Dobbins, "if you'd consider meeting with a few *other* people—while you're here." He told them that there had been a killing, less than twenty kilometers away, by the Cuerpos de Defensas Rurales, the Rural Defense Corps. A well-known coffee farmer had been shot; he'd been an active organizer for the socialist parties in the region. The next week there had been demonstrations in town—and all along the road through the mountains. The crowds had chanted, "¡*Abajo Batista!*"—Down with Batista!—all day long.

"Yes," Adolfo exclaimed, sitting up. "They did. Because they are tired of being the subjects of a dictator." Marguerite looked sternly at him, though, and so he added: "That's what I hear, anyhow—that many of them seem to feel quite frustrated."

"Frustrated?" one of the other Americans asked. "Why?"

"Look," Dobbins said, "if there's anything ATC can do, we're all ears."

"The truth is they're just malcontents," Adolfo's father said.

"Not necessarily," Adolfo said.

"Some of them have ideological motivations," Father Soto said. "They're believers, in a sense."

"They're opportunists," Adolfo's father said. "They want Communism for everyone else—and wealth for themselves."

"That's not true—" Adolfo said, but Annabel interrupted him.

"I think that, motivations aside," she said, "it would be useful to collect some further information. For your shareholders." Dobbins looked at her gratefully. This seemed to lower the temperature in the room.

The conversation turned to the fighting happening in the Sierra Maestra. The consensus was that this rebellion wouldn't last, that it would be temporary. *So much talking.* This social animal wasn't Marguerite's authentic self. Not really. She would gratefully shed it, in exchange for almost any other skin. She watched Annabel Crandall. The American woman seemed to be walking a fine line as well, contributing to the conversation carefully—letting the men occupy all the space they wanted to, but asserting her presence at certain moments. Marguerite noticed that, unlike the other three Americans, she wasn't drinking. The men all had large full glasses of rum, and they drank them incautiously—their bodies reflecting the amount of alcohol they'd consumed. The conversation became less and less serious. Eventually they began to discuss, with great enthusiasm, the World Cup—which Brazil had just won—and Pelé, Brazil's seventeen-year-old phenomenon, who'd scored two goals in the final.

Marguerite turned to Annabel. "Do you have any children?"

"No," she said. "Do you?"

"Not yet," Marguerite said. And then suddenly she wanted to change the subject. She glanced around. "Can I ask a favor?" she said, and then she asked Annabel to come with her into the main room—where her father-in-law kept the piano. She'd been working on something for quite a while, she told Annabel, and everyone in the house was tired of listening to it. It was almost done, but she was trying to decide on an ending. Annabel looked over to Dobbins, who had just stood up and gone to pour himself a generous glass of rum. Annabel nodded. *It's fine*, she said.

They walked out through the house, which—at night—was mostly lit by candles. Though there was electricity, Adolfo's father preferred the look of the candlelight, the way it had all been lit when he was a child. Cream-colored, honey-smelling tapers—they gave the air a slight sweetness, and a redolence of smoke. Stalks of white ginger bloomed on every side of the house, filling the air with their sweet perfume. On the wall above the Steinway, Adolfo's father had hung a landscape by Miguel Arias; the oil of the paint caught the candlelight and seemed to shimmer.

Marguerite collected herself and looked at the sheet music, on which she'd written *Untitled*, and printed her name: *Marguerite de Castillo*. She played the sonata. At first, she was self-conscious, worrying about some aspects of the construction, a few particular moments, as she made her way through them. But then she began to sink into the melody, point and counterpoint. How she missed this! The benefits of living like a member of the proletariat did not eclipse the benefits of a well-tuned piano. Midway, as she played, Marguerite chose one of the two endings that she'd been considering. And when she rendered it, it felt right—though she did have a certain sorrow over her other, now discarded, ending. Why couldn't she have them both simultaneously?

She finished. There was a long pause. And then Annabel sprung to her feet, applauding. "Bravo!" she exclaimed. "Bravo!"

"It's strange," Marguerite said, "but I wrote this piece for a lizard."

Annabel laughed. "It must be quite a lizard."

"He was," Marguerite said. She felt so ebullient then, so joyful. She'd played her work for a stranger, and it was clear that she'd loved it. And so Marguerite explained that every morning when she drank her coffee on the little patio outside of the house where she and Adolfo now lived—a small lizard, a brown anole, would climb up the wall and watch her. He'd been a tiny creature—he could have easily fit in the palm of her hand. But every minute or so, at unpredictable intervals, he would flex his neck and inflate a flap of bright orange-and-yellow skin. It was a dewlap, and it was colored like a variegated sun—a sun with a bright rim and a dark core.

"He probably thought you were a predator," Annabel said.

Marguerite nodded. This had happened for several weeks. And then one morning, on impulse, she'd dissolved some sugar in a tiny dish of cool water and placed it at the foot of the wall. Incredibly, the anole drank from it—that first day, and every day afterward—for at least a month.

"Then what happened?"

"Then," Marguerite said, "he was gone." Later she found out that the brown anole was the most aggressive of all the lizards—and that it ate all the other subspecies in the ecosystem. But that made him valorous in her mind, made him fiercer. "Do you want me to play it again?"

"Of course," Annabel said. And so she did. It was such a haunting melody and such a beautiful night that, when Marguerite was done playing, Annabel said: "I wish I could stay in this moment, always. Do you ever feel like that?"

Marguerite ran through a few fragments of something else she was working on. "Do you play an instrument?" she asked.

"I always wanted to," Annabel said. But she'd somehow never had the chance. Her parents had been poor; she'd been a child in rural Virginia during the Depression.

"Do you think American Tobacco will offer us good terms?" Marguerite asked.

Annabel suddenly looked hesitant and nervous; Marguerite didn't understand why. "They were saying—on the trip up here—that they like what you've done with the local village." She paused. "And . . . that this is some of the best soil in the country."

"Do you think they'd be interested in investing in more than just the crop?" Marguerite was uneasy, trying to think of a way to make Adolfo happy. To make him see what was possible. "I think that might spark a lot of goodwill, make America seem like less of a . . ." She tried to think of the right word. ". . . a problem."

"Do you think we're a problem?" Annabel said. "Americans, that is."

"Some people think so."

"But do *you* think it?"

"I don't know," Marguerite said. "I don't know what a problem is anymore."

"Sure you do," Annabel said. "For example, out here. What's the root of the problem out here?"

"Poverty."

"But what else? It can't be that simple."

It was true. It *was* complex. So many factors—including, of course, the legacy of slavery. Of a system that, until a few decades before, had treated so many people as property. Marguerite remembered with great clarity the moment that she'd first understood this. Writing music in the library of the plantation, she'd taken a moment away from her piece and walked to the bookshelves that had surrounded her. She'd looked through the leather-bound volumes, and she'd come across a census for the plantation—for the little village of Mayarí that was just down the hill from the house. *Población residente en vegas,* she'd read.

The town was divided—she immediately saw—into *blancos, negros y mulatos libres,* and *esclavos. Whites, free blacks and mulatos,* and *slaves. 34%, 55%, and 11%.*

She'd looked at the categories. Not only was *esclavo* a gruesome word—the categories, themselves, disturbed her. *What am I?* she'd thought. She was certainly not one of those available things. *Maybe I am? Have I* become *this because I'm living here now, and that's the reality?* The next Cuban census would include her. But she was an Arab. An Arab Christian. In the country where she'd been born, the color of your skin wasn't a determining factor in your life. Religion, language, social class—these were much more important. It was hard to adjust to a different way of looking at the world.

"I think that problems can only be solved in music," Marguerite said.

"Ah," Annabel said. "But then they stay in music."

They returned to the great room. Marguerite sat beside Father Soto, and he asked her about the garments for the Good Friday Procession of the Cross. She'd been sewing the black lace robes for the statue of the Virgin Mary. They were moving along slowly, Marguerite said. But the lace was of tremendous quality. Adolfo's father had imported it from Venice, from the House of Morenos. It sounded convincing, Marguerite thought, but the truth was that she'd given almost all her free time to writing her music.

Adolfo seemed nervous and she was trying—but failing—to catch his eye. Stephenson got up to use the bathroom. Marguerite asked her father-in-law to pour her a rum, just one line—*una línea, solamente*—and she sipped it slowly, enjoying the warmth of the alcohol. It was fifteen minutes before she realized that Stephenson hadn't come back.

"You think he got lost?" Marguerite asked the room in general. "It's a big house."

"I'm sure he'll find us," Adolfo said.

But Adolfo's father got up to go check on him. Marguerite noticed that Adolfo was sweating, despite the relatively cool evening.

A shout—a shout in the hall. There was a commotion of some kind in the hallway and then two men surged through the doorway into the room: her father-in-law, and the man they'd passed on the path to the house, the one who'd nodded at Adolfo. And this man had a gun—a pistol—pointed at her father-in-law's temple. He'd grabbed a handful of his shirt as well, and he was using this to pull him into the room. Adolfo got to his feet. "What are you doing?" he said.

"We will not be occupied!" the man yelled. *"Patria o muerte!"* Homeland or death! He pointed the gun at Michaels and pulled the trigger. The shot hit the American squarely in the chest; the impact of it made him fly backward, still sitting in his chair.

Everyone was screaming. The gunman disappeared, but two of the representatives of Cuban Land and Leaf ran after him, leaping over a table and following him down the hallway.

Marguerite couldn't look away from the wounded man. There was a ragged hole in his chest, and blood surged from it, and from his mouth, as he struggled to breathe. Dobbins was at his side; he'd taken off his shirt and was using it to stanch the bleeding. She lost track of her father-in-law; he left the room, but then ran back in, moving with astonishing quickness. He was holding a shotgun. *Run!* he said to Annabel and Marguerite. *Hurry!*

But Adolfo grabbed Marguerite's arm and pulled her aside. "This wasn't supposed to happen," he whispered. His face was white. "I swear."

"What?"

"That isn't . . ." he said, shaking his head, but not finding the words. ". . . that wasn't the plan."

Marguerite couldn't believe what she was hearing. "How much of this," she gestured around the room, "is you?"

He grabbed her shoulders. "We have so much to do," he said. "Don't you see? Everything has to be remade. And it has to start here. Nowhere else but here, with us." He looked panicked. "But not like this."

Marguerite tried to process what he was saying. She shook her head, stepped away from him, and then there was a surge of activity; three people had lifted Michaels and were carrying him to a car out front. She took one step forward, losing track of Adolfo, transfixed by what she saw in the other room. The man's blood had left a terrible stain on the rug in front of the fireplace; brown, almost black, it was a map of some unholy territory, the territory of violent death.

Then Annabel was there; she clutched her face; her eyes were stunned and terrified. "This way," Marguerite said. She led the other woman to a closet in the hallway. The door wasn't immediately obvious—it looked like paneling. They stepped inside, flicked on the light. The closet was huge, with a bench and many coats hanging on the wall. At least a dozen pairs of boots were tucked beneath the bench.

They sat side by side.

"You have blood on your face," Marguerite whispered. She reached over and wiped the dots off Annabel's cheeks. Then she turned out the light.

Marguerite heard footsteps in the hall. *Running.* She heard voices shouting, at first nearby, but then farther away, and then—gunshots. Marguerite took Annabel's hand.

"Tell me about your life in America," Marguerite said. The other woman didn't know what to say, but then she talked—as quietly as she could—about a job she'd just left, a job as a secretary at a newspaper. Marguerite was only partially listening to Annabel's answers. She was horrified by what Adolfo had done, what he'd helped plan. And then she realized that she'd felt it coming—felt that little seam of evil growing wider and wider, even tonight, even as they'd walked to the house. *O, Adolfo,* she thought. *O, my dear*. What did it even mean to do good? And how much evil was done in the name of good—before the initial goal was transformed, was changed into something else entirely? She lost herself in these thoughts. It was a moment until she realized that Annabel had said something.

"I'm sorry?" Marguerite asked.

"It's quiet," Annabel repeated. "Do you think it's safe?"

"I don't know," Marguerite said. They sat in silence for ten, fifteen minutes. The silence expanded around them, became a cloak, a fabric, a gauze. It grew and grew. Finally, Marguerite felt she might go mad, hunched there in the darkness. "Let's talk," she said.

"About what?" Annabel asked.

"About anything."

Annabel leaned closer to her and nodded. "Okay," she said. "Are you . . . Are you from the area?" She asked if Marguerite had lived here her entire life.

Marguerite was grateful for the distraction—but—the question threatened to split a vast gulf inside of her. She thought momentarily about her parents, and how they'd returned her letters unopened. She thought of her father, standing in the living room, saying, *If you leave, you are dead to me*. A black flower, she thought. There's a black flower here, rising up out of the darkness—part of the darkness itself. A black orchid. She'd found it once—one evening when she'd been walking down along the extremity of the tobacco fields. She imagined her brother—*Was he even still living in Beirut?*—pictured him lined up on the balcony above their courtyard. Or was that world gone? Were they still in the same place? Was everyone still alive? And then she had a thought, an impulse: Maybe the music could do what a letter couldn't? Maybe it could be the apology they needed—but wouldn't accept—and finally they would hear their daughter's, their sister's, true voice?

"No," she said, "nowhere near here."

"Havana?"

"Farther than that."

"The East?"

"Yes," Marguerite said, "far, far east. Lebanon, in fact." But there was no way for her to see the other woman's reaction to this. It was too dark. And so she reached out and grabbed Annabel's shoulder. "Listen," she said. "I want you to mail this to my family."

She handed Annabel the sheet music for her sonata—the music that she was still clutching—that she'd swept up from the table when they'd fled. That would be her apology, she thought, it would be her way of communicating with them—*This is who I became. This is the beautiful thing I was able to render.*

"What is this?" Annabel asked.

"My work," Marguerite said. "Send it—when you get home."

"You can mail it yourself," Annabel said, and tried to hand it back.

But Marguerite wouldn't accept it. *No,* she said, *no.* She said the family name would be enough, and Beirut, and the Avenue des Plumes. "Don't say who it's from."

"That's ridiculous," Annabel said.

"Please," Marguerite said. "Take it."

"I'll write down the address," Annabel finally said. But she didn't have a pencil. She put the music in her handbag anyway.

• • •

It had been hours and they hadn't heard anything for a while. They crept out of the closet. The house was dark and empty. Room by room, they edged through the house.

"Where is everyone?" Marguerite whispered.

She picked up the telephone—the line her father-in-law had installed himself, fifteen years before. It was silent. No dial tone.

"I think we need to get out of here," Annabel said.

The women held hands as they walked. It was comforting, creeping along one of the paths through the margins of the tobacco fields. They were headed to Marguerite's house, where—she hoped—they'd be safe. The sun was about to rise and, incongruously, it was beautiful in the fields. Rats scurried through the furrows, headed on their mysterious errands, darting in and out of sight. They lived, Marguerite knew, in any provisional stack of vegetation, natural or man-made. Their homes were makeshift and improvised, not generational.

Marguerite and Annabel walked down the path. The cries of the wild peacocks, so startling and piercing, echoed from the darkened fields. *Help!* it seemed like they were yelling. *Help!* Marguerite's throat burned; she wondered how long it had been since she'd had anything to drink. She was thinking of this when she turned a corner on the path and saw—there, partly in the undergrowth—a human form.

And then she was running and then she was looking down at it—at the thing she couldn't have ever imagined. That body, that dear body. Adolfo lay next to the path. He'd been shot through the back. He was dead. There was—a few inches below his collarbone, just to the right of his spine—a hole about the size of an egg. The bleeding had stopped, but the blood was everywhere. It had soaked down through the back of his clothes;

it was clotted and thick and black around the woolen panel of his waistband. There was a lot of blood, more than Marguerite had ever seen.

I'll go with you, she thought. *My love, I'm coming.* She pawed at the air, looking for some benediction, some blessing that would relieve her of this, ease this. *Anything.*

She turned and was sick. She vomited on the path and fell to her hands and knees. She wanted to put her body with his body, she wanted to abandon her now inconsequential body and join him, wherever he was. Wherever he'd gone. "Come back!" she yelled. "Come back!"

Something flickered in her mind then. Something she'd witnessed just last month, in Father Soto's church, sitting on the stiff-backed wooden pew, watching Father Soto bless the Gospel, watching him raise his hands over the Holy Book, saying, *This is the Word, the word of God, our Savior and our King. Daughters of Jerusalem, weep not for me, but weep for yourselves, and for your children. For behold, the days are coming, in which they shall say: blessed are the barren, and the wombs that never bear, and the breasts which never gave milk. Then shall they begin to say to the mountains, follow us; and to the hills, cover us. For if they do these things in a green tree, what shall be done in the dry?*

And then—she sat up—and it began to rain.

Marguerite lay on the ground beside Adolfo's body.

"Where's safe?" Annabel asked. She was looking all around; she seemed menaced by the undergrowth—the lush and uncontrolled forestland—which obscured her ability to see into the distance. "We'll go back to your father's house," she said.

"No," Marguerite said. She never wanted to see that room again, see the stained carpet. It would be too terrible. "The church—the church or the road to Viñales. That might be safe. We could hide there, in the woods."

"Which is closer?"

The church, Marguerite told her. Annabel nodded.

Marguerite was saying Adolfo's name then—repeating it out loud—again and again, each time a new torment, each time more painful than the last. She stood and left him there, left him where he'd fallen, and then they were down the path, and then they were inside her home, she was stumbling from wall to wall within their house, almost as if she were being guided by the tips of her fingers, which reached out methodically for one surface after another: the sheer drape of the front curtains, the quiet pine surface of the bureau in their bedroom, the texture of the wall. Then she had a photograph in her hands: the picture her brother had arranged all those years ago. She took a small bag—one that hung on the coat-rack in the main room—and absentmindedly put the photograph inside. She clutched the bag to her chest as she walked out the door.

It was full daylight by the time they made it to the white-spired little church that sat between the plantation and the village. The building was a rectangular, single-story structure on a grassy slope. Its graveyard had been consecrated by Pedro Agustín Morell de Santa Cruz, the bishop of Havana, in 1756. Over the centuries, the church had been destroyed by fire—and then rebuilt—several times. But the graveyard had remained intact, the bones of the dead sanctified and still.

When they arrived at the church, they found that the door was locked. Annabel pounded on it with her first. There was no reply. "Hello?" she yelled. She knocked again. "Is anyone in there?"

Finally, they heard movement. Father Soto opened the door partway, just to see who it was. When he saw Marguerite and Annabel, he looked shocked. "You shouldn't be here," he said. "It's not safe."

"Adolfo—" Marguerite began.

Father Soto nodded. "I know. Your father-in-law's missing, too," he said. "I think he might have drowned in the river."

Marguerite breathed in. *Both sides*, she thought. Both sides lose.

"Come around to the side door," Father Soto said.

They went around the building and ducked through a door into the vestry. The priest's vestments hung in a long row here, all of them carefully arranged on hangers, spotlessly clean and orderly. Father Soto locked the door behind them—checking twice to make sure that it was secure. Even in the morning light the interior of this little room was dim; the only illumination came from the narrow tall windows on either side of the nave.

He looked at Marguerite, and then Annabel. "What is the condition," he said, "of your immortal soul?"

It was such an unexpected question that Marguerite almost laughed. But then Father Soto busied himself at a cabinet to the left of his vestments—reaching into it and removing two small inlaid silver containers. He was praying, and he removed three Communion wafers—with shaking hands—from their repository. He made the sign of the Cross and took one of them in his mouth. *Amen,* he said. Then, without asking, he turned to them. *"Cuerpo de Cristo,"* he said. Body of Christ.

Father Soto motioned for them to follow him into the

church, and they watched as he walked to the altar and stood on its top step. He reached behind the crucifix; momentarily, his arm looked like it was disappearing into the bloodied legs of Christ. And then he pulled out a long metal pole—one with a crude handle—and he walked over to the predella and pulled back the dusty red carpet that covered it. Then he put the pole in what appeared to be a lock, a lock that was hidden in the floor, concealed by the carpet. And—to Marguerite's amazement—the aisle, the aisle almost immediately beneath her feet, began to move. The stone floor itself was opening, and there was a pit beneath the church. It had a strange odor—not the scent of the ground exactly, but something different, something like the smell of oil, and something almost peppery. A ladder led into the darkness. Father Soto looked at Annabel and Marguerite and extended his hand.

"Careful," he said.

They each nodded. Marguerite nearly fell, her foot slipping on a rung. She caught herself, though, and when they were all down there, she saw that they were standing in a cavern; what was once the dim light of the interior of the church was now a blazing brightness, a grandly illuminated space above them. She was trying to peer through the dark at her surroundings, when she heard the ignition of a match—smelled the scent of phosphorous as it caught—and Father Soto lit a torch. And then she saw, stacked in piles, from floor to ceiling, weapons, rifles, guns of a quantity that she'd never, in her life, imagined.

"Well," Annabel said, "this isn't what I expected."

Father Soto nodded, but said nothing.

And then, looking around her, looking from place to place without respite, with only violent objects on which to rest her gaze—weapons meant to kill—Marguerite realized what was happening, what had been building throughout the country-side. She realized that war, which had stalked the margins of her life for years—to the northwest in Europe, to the south in Israel—had arrived in its center.

Batista had sent ten thousand soldiers out across the island, Father Soto was saying. What had been a slow-burning conflict had now become something different. Something new. And there was no battlefield. The villages, the countryside, houses like her father-in-law's, they would be the places this war was fought. They'd been caught, he said, between both sides last night. Adolfo had never imagined how quickly things would escalate; there'd been a firefight, people shooting at each other in the dark—nobody knowing who was who. Complete chaos. But this was how it would be now. Nothing would be safe anymore. Not while the country was at war. The best thing would be to get to Havana as quickly as possible. Annabel—he said—should leave the country while the borders were still open.

As for him, he couldn't stand by any longer. The church, officially, was neutral. But he was standing with the PSP. He'd seen the suffering of the rural poor for too long. And the best men of the country, men like Adolfo, were now dying for their ideals.

Marguerite saw Annabel put her hand on the wall to steady herself. "I'm having trouble," she said, "breathing."

And then the other woman sank down to the floor. Her skin glowed in the darkness—glowed with a luminosity that reflected the luminosity of the open church above them. She looked like living bones. Marguerite tried to help her to her feet. At first, she was unable to stand. *I'm so sorry,* she kept saying. *Desculpa me. I'm so sorry.* And then they got her to the ladder and she managed to negotiate it upward, into the church.

Bones, in a crypt, Marguerite thought. That was what she'd been expecting underneath the church. Not this.

Father Soto went back down the ladder and came up holding two hunting rifles and two small boxes of ammunition. Marguerite took an involuntary step back. "I've never shot a gun in my life," she said.

But Annabel had. She'd grown up hunting with her brothers. Although, shooting people was, Annabel said, different than shooting rabbits. *But what if those people thought of you as an animal?* Marguerite thought. What if they were willing to slaughter you, if they saw you as something to eliminate, an obstacle on their path to a larger goal? What then?

"We'll do what we can," Marguerite said. "But I don't want a rifle."

Father Soto pushed her to take it, but she wouldn't relent. He shook his head. "I love you, my dear," he said, and kissed Marguerite on each cheek. He shook Annabel's hand. Looking agonized and worried, he let them both out the side door.

A stunningly beautiful day, with a cool wind coming from the north and a layer of bright gray clouds in the sky. Marguerite told Annabel that they could hide in the curing barn, hide beneath the rows of drying tobacco leaves, the leaves that hung in pairs from eucalyptus poles. It was the off-season, and there'd be few workers there. Rough-hewn from pine, built over a hundred years ago, it was dark during the day, since it had no electricity, and many covered places they could hide. Once it was night, they could take two horses from the stables and leave; they could ride—if they were careful—through the open country, at least until they'd reached the outskirts of the city.

They never made it. They came around a turn in the road— a turn roughly five hundred meters from the barn—and saw three armed men, men with rifles strapped to their chests. They were walking in a loose triangular formation, with one man out ahead of the other two; they scanned the countryside as they walked along.

Marguerite and Annabel ran for cover, for the bright green countryside that grew wild for hundreds of acres to each side. They got as low as they could.

"Did they see us?" Annabel whispered.

"I don't think so."

The men came closer. They weren't men from the farm— not men Marguerite recognized. They weren't wearing formal uniforms, so they might not be Rural Guard—though Marguerite knew that the most brutal detachments, the ones responsible for extrajudicial killings—often wore civilian clothes. She happened to glance down. She still had Adolfo's blood on her dress. If she died now, she thought, had she done anything good and worthy with her life? Had she done anything except hurt and disappoint those who loved her? She whispered prayers for Adolfo, and felt he was nearby, that he was wrapping his arms around her.

Annabel had the gun sighted on the men, and as they got closer and closer, Marguerite realized that it would be a simple shot. But could Annabel do it? Could she choose to take a human life? And if she did—if Annabel chose to shoot the man walking point, the one she'd sighted as a target—would she be able to shoot the other men as well? Or would they react and kill them before Annabel could fire another shot? Would it be better to do nothing at all? To let the men simply walk past? But there was no way to discuss any of these things. Marguerite simply had to lie there, and watch, and wait.

The soldiers came closer. Twenty meters. Fifteen. Ten. Marguerite could clearly perceive Annabel's muscles getting more and more taut, contracting, tensing, her weight shifting in the dirt. *What if she misses?* But then—a catastrophe. The *santanillas*, the biting ants, had sensed these bodies, these intruders in their environment. And one, maybe more, maybe two or three, had crawled onto Annabel's bare arm. They were tiny. Half the size of a grain of rice. You would never feel them until they bit you. Until their fiery venom spread through your skin. And so Annabel suddenly seized. She rolled onto her side and let out an uncontrollable cry of pain.

The men scattered. They moved for defensive positions. Annabel tried to recover, to roll back onto her stomach, but the pain was too much, and she dropped the weapon next to her body, gasping. *Don't shoot!* Marguerite called out. She stood up. It was a reckless gesture. But, in fact, the soldiers didn't shoot. And so Marguerite grabbed Annabel's arm and pulled her to her feet as well. *Please don't shoot!* she said again. *Please!*

The soldiers pulled Annabel and Marguerite out of the forest and into the middle of the road. They didn't seem at first to know what to do. "Stay there," one of them said. Marguerite listened to their conversation—which they didn't bother to hide. They were debating what to do. The American Tobacco Company representative had escaped, one of them said; he'd somehow managed to get back to the city—no one was sure how.

One of the men felt they'd *already* sent a message. "Even

if the one we shot survives," he said, "the United States would think twice about investing their money here."

But a second man felt that it wasn't enough. "She's one of them, too," he said, looking over. "At least I think that's her."

"But which one?" the first man said.

"Don't say anything," Marguerite whispered to Annabel.

The men came over and—imperious, brusque—demanded to know the women's names. They hit Annabel hard, a sweeping brutal gesture, a backhand blow delivered at full force. The second soldier grabbed a handful of her hair and held her head back. He was vicious. But Annabel remained silent.

He turned to Marguerite. He started kicking her. And then the others joined in, all three of them. And she tried to fend off the blows, but she couldn't. She tried to make her body small, even smaller than it was, even more insignificant. She covered her ribs with her left hand, and she felt the steel tip of a boot crush her metacarpals. The bones seemed to splinter; it felt as if her hand was on fire. But she stayed silent, too.

The soldiers couldn't decide who was who, which one was the American.

"Let's shoot them both," the second soldier said.

Marguerite suddenly felt that maybe this was the most important moment of her life. The moment that she could do uncomplicated good. "I'm Annabel," she said, her voice strong and clear.

"No," Annabel said, looking frantically at her. "She's lying. I'm Annabel."

But both women had learned Spanish as adults; they both had accents. It was confusing. The men clustered together. *Look at her clothes,* Marguerite heard one of them say, pointing to her—and that was when she realized what the blue dress had been for. She could feel Adolfo so close to her at that moment—felt that he was almost with her, that the veil between life and death was getting perilously thin.

"Just kill them both, like I said. And then—let's go."

"No," the other man said, "we don't shoot innocent women." His voice had the power of command.

They searched the women's bags, emptying them out onto the dirt. And there, in *Annabel's* things—in her plain, serviceable traveling bag—was *Marguerite's* music, with the name, *Marguerite de Castillo*, printed at the top. The man turned to his commander and nodded. Then he reached down and grabbed Marguerite's arm.

"No!" Annabel screamed.

But it was definitive.

They started dragging Marguerite away. "You're free to go," they said to Annabel.

"No, no, no."

Marguerite put out her hand and her fingertips brushed the paper, touched her music for the last time. *Play it*, she said to Annabel—knowing it would never be mailed. There was no time to give her the address, and who knew where her family lived now anyway? They lived in her heart. And her last thought—as the soldiers carried her away—was that the music would spill out into the world, one way or another. It would find its mark. It would exist, unfettered. Pure. This was her child. This was her contribution.

Annabel Crandall watched as they carried Marguerite deeper into the woods. And as she stood up, she saw the photograph—the one that Marguerite had taken with her as they'd left her house that morning. Annabel picked it up. Then she ran. She ran, blindly. She didn't know where she was going—just away.

Then there was a single gunshot, clear and loud, and Annabel was clutching the photograph and the music, sprinting over the uneven woods toward the river, aware that every breath in her lungs—every jarring step—was a gift. Her life was a gift now—or maybe it always had been.

ANNABEL

Annabel ran without direction. Had Marguerite said that they'd take horses? She tried to find the stables, but she couldn't orient herself. For hours and hours and hours she walked, traveling along small gravel roads in an unfamiliar country, moving through terraced farmland, the road gradually gaining elevation, heading higher up along the spine of a mountain.

At first, she was just fleeing. She couldn't get her thoughts to organize themselves. Where was she, exactly? Who could she trust? She passed a few dozen farmhouses, scattered farther and farther apart as the elevation climbed. Where would it be safe to stop? She walked and walked. And then, at some point, a moment that she'd later be unable to remember, she folded downward and slept right there, right where she fell, her body unable to move, catatonic, immobile, spent.

She awoke to darkness. Darkness and the braying of a donkey. Her eyes popped open—disorientation, the world wouldn't focus. And thirst. Her throat burned. She hadn't eaten, hadn't had anything to drink—in at least a day and a half. She got to her knees and began walking again and then—in the middle of a wide field of newly planted sugarcane—she found it: an uncovered well, a well with a red iron mechanism for drawing out its water, drawing it out from deep within the earth. She reeled the bucket up, barely able to contain the pressure of her thirst. It came up full. She put her face in it and drank deeply, barely feeling the water as it went down her throat and filled her body.

Annabel continued walking through the increasingly rugged countryside. She kept walking even though it was dark.
She had to move, to keep her body in motion, make progress.
She couldn't think clearly. Struggling through a patch of especially dense forestland, Annabel took a step—and suddenly the
ground was gone. She tumbled and rolled down an embankment into a ravine. As she fell, all she could think about were
the things she'd been clutching, all this time, in her hands—the
photograph and the score to the song. Instead of letting go
of them and reaching out to protect herself, Annabel made a
quick calculation: if she tried to pivot onto her back, she might
protect them instead.

When she came to rest at the bottom of the embankment
she felt a furious stab of pain—pain comparable to the bite of
the ants when she'd been lying on the forest floor. She'd held
on to the papers. It was nearly dawn, and the sky was a pale
gray color. Annabel looked down at her ankle. Her foot hung
at a confusing, unnatural angle. She had to straighten it out,
she thought, and so reached out with one hand and pulled on
it, pulled on it and heard the rustling snap of the bones within
her leg.

The pain transported her. She rose and fled to some other
place, and then she was lying on her back and looking at the
sky. She heard the call of a bird—first one, then two, then three.
And then, rocketing across the space above her, she saw the
bodies of nightingales. Their heads were shaped like spears;
they surged through the forest, surged, and banked to the left,
and then disappeared.

Though she couldn't see the birds, Annabel could still hear
them. They were loud; they issued an alarm ahead of the sun-

rise. They called out to Annabel with a plaintive invitation: *Why won't you join us? Join us? Join us.*

She awoke to two worried-looking men—standing above her, talking. Everything felt like it was slow motion. *Quiet,* she thought—not forming the words exactly, but instead just impressions of words. *Careful. Don't move. Don't make noise. I'm nothing but another plant,* she thought. *A stalk rising out of the dirt. I am invisible.*

But then another thought: Perhaps they'd been guided here by Marguerite—by her spirit, which was still somehow tethered to this earth. Perhaps she was nearby. Leading them, somehow. Instructing them. The thought gave her comfort— the thought gave her comfort, *but* the pain had risen to her knee. It radiated upward through her leg. *Hail Mary, full of grace,* Annabel prayed for the first time in many years, *the Lord is with you. Holy Mary, I will pass by the gravedigger and tell him: Gather my beloved's hair from the dirt. Go and bring me a comb. I've been lying in the mud and my hair is dusty, too.*

Then Annabel felt the sensation of being lifted and then there was a doctor—again, looking down at her. *Again, worried.* He had a syringe in his hand. He flicked its tip with his finger. *This is a ten-milligram ampoule of morphine,* he said in Spanish. And then he—and the rest of the world—was gone.

She awoke in a hospital bed; the sheets were soft and surrounded her body. But—then—the pain of a headache, and her ankle throbbing with every heartbeat. It hurt to breathe. Only one of her eyes seemed to be opening—the world was flat, lacking its usual depth and perspective. She touched the other eye.

It was swollen and tender. Even the slightest pressure sent a puncture of suffering through her skull. Within moments, a nurse was there. She wore a starched white uniform and had clearly hurried to be at the side of Annabel's bed.

"Who are you?" Annabel said. "Where am I?"

Two weeks later—her leg in a cast—Annabel disembarked from Pan American World Airways Flight 28 to Washington, DC, and made her way through customs. *No*, she told them, *I have nothing to declare.*

As she passed the customs agent's desk and hobbled on her crutches into the arrivals' hall, she saw a man in a gray suit, holding a handwritten sign with her name on it. When she approached, he introduced himself.

"John McCone," he said. "US Central Intelligence. Before we get you home—we'd like to ask you a few questions."

Annabel looked at him, saying nothing.

"I've taken the liberty," he added, "of arranging a car."

The car was a brand-new DeVille sedan, a 1959. Onyx-colored, four-doored—seamed with narrow bands of chrome—it pulled smoothly away from the airport, merging into city traffic. The seats were soft and cushiony. The smell of leather permeated everything.

"You've been through quite an ordeal, Ms. Crandall," McCone said. "We're glad you've made it safely home."

"I'm not home yet," Annabel said.

They drove to Langley, and the intelligence complex—a sprawling set of office buildings in the suburb of McLean, Virginia. A cluster of people greeted Annabel at the door; they pushed her through the building's long linoleum hallways in a wheelchair. Even so, her body felt like it was full of needles. There were needles in her hips, needles along the backs of her legs, needles in her knees especially. And she couldn't, for some reason, relax her jaw. She found herself clenching it, grinding her teeth, and she would try to stop. Then, twenty minutes later, she'd notice that she'd started doing it again.

Now an official from the agency sat across from her, Dictaphone placed on the little rectangular table between the two of them. He had a notepad, and from time to time he'd scrawl something with a bright green pen.

"A farmer with morphine?" he said, clarifying.

Annabel shook her head. "A doctor," she said. "And I didn't say that they were farmers. They could have been schoolteachers or factory workers or ballerinas."

The tape rolled. It made a mechanical noise as it rotated through the cylinder.

"I see," the agent said.

And then the telephone rang. The man answered it. He'd introduced himself as Mr. Grant, and now Annabel listened as he began a terse, monosyllabic conversation with whoever was on the other end of the line. *Yes, sir,* he said. *No, sir,* he said. *Absolutely, sir.*

They'd been questioning her for two hours. Annabel leaned forward and got the agent's attention. He covered the receiver and looked at her, frowning. "Could you give me a moment?" she said. "I just want to step into the hall."

"I'd prefer," he started to say, "if you stayed in the—"

"Thank you," Annabel said, nodding. She stood up and maneuvered, on her awkward, ungainly crutches, out into the hallway. Though she was leaving the room, Grant made no attempt to turn off the tape recorder.

Annabel hobbled down one windowless hall to another windowless hall, and another, and another. There were no marked exits, and, in her condition, she didn't feel like opening random doors. Defeated, she slumped to the ground and closed her eyes. She closed her eyes, and she was sitting in that darkened house in Pinar del Rio, listening to a piece of music that was astonishing in its grace and beauty. It ended. She looked at the woman who'd written it, who'd brought it out into the world, from her own singular imagination. *Do you want me to play it again?* the woman asked.

"We'd like to continue the questioning now, Ms. Crandall."

Annabel opened her eyes.

"Terrific," she said without enthusiasm.

She hobbled back to the little room. The ritual began once more. Grant kept pushing her for details that, quite honestly, she couldn't remember. "And you're sure," he asked her, for the fifth or sixth time, "that prior to traveling to Cuba you had no contact with the Communist Party, or any of its affiliates?"

"What do you want me to say, Mr. Grant? That I'm a dear old friend of Nikita Khrushchev?"

"Aggressive demeanor noted," Grant said.

"Go to hell," Annabel said.

Grant scowled at her. "I just assume," he said, "that you'd want to do everything you could to help us out."

Annabel imagined taking one of her crutches and swinging it as hard as she could, hitting Agent Grant and knocking him to the floor.

"Sir," she said. She paused. *I'm carrying a dead woman with me, wherever I go,* she thought. "With all due respect: please don't tell me what I would or wouldn't want to do."

That night, Annabel slept in her bed for the first time in

weeks. Before she lay down, though, she tucked Marguerite's music—those handwritten pages—into a folder that she kept on the desk that she used as a nightstand. She couldn't believe the condition the score was in; it was barely smudged, barely dirty, as if someone had been protecting it the whole time.

But now Annabel needed the right frame, and the right place, to put the photograph of Marguerite's family. She still couldn't look at it directly, focus on it—or she would lose her composure and begin to cry. She looked around the room. There was nowhere that seemed appropriate. She placed it on her bedside table, aware that this was—at best—a provisional home for it. Maybe someday, in the future, Annabel thought, she'd find a place to tuck it away—to hide it, in safety, from the world.

West Falls
Church, Virginia

When Naïm returned home, his mother was lying down in her bedroom, resting. He boiled the noodles he'd taken from Ms. Crandall, warmed the sauce in the microwave. He combined the two in a bowl and carried it in to her. Fatima sat up as soon as he appeared.

"I thought I smelled cooking," she said. "But then I thought: it's not possible." He handed her the bowl. She frowned. "Where did you get it?"

"I went back to the grocery store," Naïm said. "I gave them my phone as collateral." He'd carefully planned this lie as he'd walked home from 815 Ridge Place. He'd needed something that seemed plausible—but also active—like he'd solved the problem himself, rather than asking for assistance. Otherwise, he'd known, his mother would have refused to eat. She'd have been too proud.

Fatima hesitated, but then devoured the food. It was a joy to watch her, huddling above the still-steaming pasta, shoveling the tube-shaped noodles into her mouth with a spoon, almost childlike in her ardor for them. She finished in a minute or two.

"Can we make more?" she asked.

When the new debit card arrived, Naïm walked down Arlington Boulevard to the little Asian grocery store. He bought several inexpensive chocolates—one shaped like a duck, the other like a baby chicken. He meant to give them to Annabel as a thank-you. He'd gone to her house three times now, coming back home each time with one or two more things, with food that he'd concealed in his room, hiding it under the laundry bag in his closet. They'd mostly just talked—in his mind, he was practicing English. But each day she also asked him to play something for her. Mostly, he'd just do right-handed scales, but then yesterday he'd constructed a few partial, simple chords.

On the walk home from the store, though, he looked at the chocolates more closely—and that was when he realized his mistake. They were cheap. Cute and novel, but cheap. And Annabel had been so careful to only eat a single piece of her chocolate. She'd want something good. And so he'd managed to make yet another mistake. It was just another in a long list, in the mistakes he made each day, time after time after time.

Al-Ghafūr. *The all-forgiving.* Forgives transgressions. Forgives errors. Does not punish. Naïm remembered the first birthday that his mother had celebrated in Za'atari. She'd had a single pair of earrings in the camp—the ones she'd worn on the day of the attack. They'd become something of a talisman to her, the only ornamentation, only possession—other than her clothes—that had survived, along with her body. They'd been small silver earrings in the shape of a laurel leaf, inlaid with tiny pieces of colored glass—milky green and pale yellow, a pale yellow color like the early-morning winter sun.

But one of the backings had fallen off and then, at some point, she'd lost the unanchored earring. When she'd gone to take them off that night, she'd felt her earlobe and found only empty space. It was gone. Her wail had startled him awake; he thought she'd somehow hurt herself, and he'd rushed to her side.

For her birthday, Naïm had decided to see if he could find

a replica. It had been a long shot, but he'd traded bread rations every day for tiny amounts of cash, and surreptitiously taken a photograph of the remaining earring, which Fatima kept in a little plastic bag, tucked among her clothes. *Never will you attain reward until you spend from what you love,* said the Sūrat āl Imrān. Naïm had found a vendor who promised him that he'd be able to find it—*Of course, of course, my friend, laurel leaves are very common jewelry*—and when the call had come in, Naïm had barely been able to contain his excitement. He'd restore this lost piece of his mother's past. He'd salve this wound.

But the earrings hadn't been right. They were close—shaped like a laurel leaf, yes—but not a match. He'd bought them anyway, but the colors had been wrong, too bright, too vibrant. Looking down at them, they'd filled him with despair. He'd spent many hours imagining this moment: handing his mother the earrings, taking in her shock and happy surprise. At the entrance to their street, he'd simply dropped them, realizing that giving them to her would only exacerbate the loss. They'd make things worse. He'd walked home disheartened, every step a disappointment. It had been a moment of profound emptiness. The emptiness was everywhere around him. Emptiness and the dry desert air. Emptiness and the distant reek—faint but noticeable—of sewage.

The ritual was the same all that week, and the next. Each day, after school—instead of going home—he'd go to Annabel's house. He'd find the spare key and open the door. *Hello!* he'd call, and enter. He'd invariably find her in the same place, sitting where the home health aide had installed her that morning—near the window, in her wheelchair.

Today, though, was a little different. She smiled when he arrived. She had a bag on her lap. "Good," she told him. "I need your help. Sit down."

She'd been knitting. It was something she'd always been good at, she said, but now, with her unsteady fingers, she could barely do the most basic stitch.

"You're not busy, are you?" she asked Naïm as he edged into the room. "Because this could take a little time."

"No," he said. "I'm here."

"Good. This is important," she said. "I'm making a very special sweater."

He nodded.

"You have to hold up your hands," she said, "like this." She spread her fingers out and flexed each one.

"Oh," Naïm said. He paused. "I can't. Can I just use one hand?"

"No," Annabel said.

"Maybe I should get somebody else. To help you."

"Who?" she said. "Just do it, please."

He held up his hands. As soon as they were in front of him, he had to glance away. He couldn't bear the sight of his left hand, under any circumstances. Purposefully holding it up—with its inarticulate, glossy stump, with its two missing digits—was almost more than he could bear. The joint they'd amputated above had started swelling; he'd taken to always hiding it, concealing it behind his body, or keeping the hand perpetually in a pocket.

Annabel began to slowly weave the yarn through several of the fingers on his good hand.

"Great," she said. "Can you stretch your hands a little wider?" She was counting on the boy not knowing anything

312

about knitting. She looped the wool around his eight good fingers. "Perfect," she said. "Actually," she added, "can you lift this one a little higher?" She pointed to the wounded hand. Its fingers trembled. Its wrist was weak, smaller than the other one.

"Now weave the yarn," she said. "Great. See? I couldn't do that myself." She made an elaborate display of pulling yarn from between his fingers—until his injured hand started to shake even more.

"What are you making again?" Naïm asked.

"A large sweater," she said. "Very large."

She didn't want to talk, not really. But she realized she might have to—in order to keep Naïm there—keep him working. She was grateful. And, ultimately, this gave her something to focus on. A way to be useful. So she cleared her throat and said: "Tell me something."

"Tell you?" Naïm said, confused. "Tell you what?"

Anything, she told him. She asked him to tell her about his life. A good memory.

"Do those exist?" Naïm asked.

"They do," she said.

"I don't think so," he said.

"Just try."

But the memories felt brittle to him. If he approached them, they might shatter. But then, deep in his childhood, there *was* something. And so, as he stretched out his hands to hold the yarn for Annabel's sweater, Naïm began to tell her about Survivors, the elaborate game of hide-and-seek that had been—in his childhood neighborhood—a matter of lore and legend.

It had been a great democracy, *Survivors*—a team-based game of hide-and-seek. When each game started, every child was assigned to one of two teams—and then someone would whistle and all the children would scatter. They'd hide everywhere in the neighborhood—underneath stoops, in trees, even under cars. They'd play for hours.

Naïm started to tell Annabel about one afternoon when he was eight, maybe nine years old. Most of his teammates had been captured. But Naïm was small. He was thin. And so he'd managed to fit himself into a tiny space—a gap between two buildings that was barely bigger than his body. No one could find him.

The game continued until every member of the hiding team had been rounded up and put in jail—which in this case was a rectangle drawn in white chalk on the sidewalk in front of 19 Tuhama. If a team lasted until sunset—then they'd be the winners. From his hiding place, Naïm could see them—all his teammates. Ten boys. They looked hopeless. Only *he* hadn't been caught. And yes, he was in a good position, a great hiding place—but their victory was by no means assured. If the other team found Naïm, which could certainly happen with just a single lucky glance, then the game was over.

But there was something else he could do. If he managed to sprint past the guards in front of the jail and tag even one of his team members—then everyone would be free. They'd have five minutes to scatter and hide again. They'd be unbeatable.

Risk and reward. Naïm waited and waited. And then a boy from the other team stopped in the one place on the street where he might have been able to see Naïm, but—as luck would have it—he happened to be looking in the other direction. He took a single step forward, and by the time his head had turned, he'd already moved beyond the point from which Naïm was visible.

THE REFUGEE OCEAN

But it had been close. And so Naïm had resolved to go for it; he would try to free his team from jail. He took one step—pulling himself out of the shadows, scraping his shoulder badly on the brick wall of one of the buildings. He inched forward. *How had he fit into this tiny space to begin with?* But finally, he did make it. He freed himself from his hiding place and he took the first step toward that chalk prison. Toward glory. *Did you hear about it? That skinny kid did it. That skinny kid from 19 Tuhama got us all free.* And then Naïm was running, and already in his imagination he'd become a neighborhood legend, and he was crossing traffic, but something nagged at him. He was in the middle of the street, but something didn't feel right, and he looked down, and with horror he saw what had happened: his pants had split at the waistband, torn open by the pressure of the two walls. His pants had come apart and they were sort of unraveling, flapping behind him as he ran. His underwear, bright white underwear, was visible—displayed for everyone to see.

In his shock, Naïm slowed down. And a taxi nearly clipped him, and the driver was cursing, and Naïm stumbled backward and sprawled into the gutter. And the boys from the other team loomed over him, and they roared with laughter, and they tagged him.

"So . . . I think," Naïm concluded, "that was not a happy memory."

"It's okay," Annabel said. "Just keep stretching your hands."

The next week, she had him do other tasks around the house. He was vacuuming, he was lifting heavy things—he was doing almost anything that would require both hands. Annabel would watch from her wheelchair—which she also made him push all around the main floor of the house—applying

315

equal pressure on each side, left and right. Annabel enjoyed it immensely. And every day, they'd conclude with work at the piano. Even using the one hand, he was surprisingly good. He reminded Annabel, inevitably, of a distant time, a distant place, a lost past. That moment braided with this one—varying strands of a single, fibrous rope—and the memory seemed, to Annabel, so clear that she could touch it.

For the next seven weeks, Naïm visited Annabel nearly every afternoon. He'd bring her candy of some kind, and then he'd hold the yarn in various ways—moving his hands in certain patterns that she told him shifted the fibers. Whatever she was making looked terrible. It was a formless, loosely stitched sweater—and an awful bright yellow color, the color of a bottle of mustard.

"And who is this for?"

"It's a secret," she said.

"You mean it's a gift?"

"Of course," she said. "*I* couldn't keep it."

He wasn't sure that he'd completely understood. "So, why do you do this?" he asked.

"Knit? Can you spread your palm a bit wider?"

He nodded. "No, no," he said. "I meant—why do you bring people to America?"

"Long story," Annabel said.

"Which means you don't want to tell me?"

She didn't answer right away. "And what do you think," she finally said, "of our country?"

Naïm shrugged. The country, right now, was incredibly confusing. At the end of January, Donald Trump had signed

Executive Order 13769, and Naïm had stayed up late at night reading the text of it, reading its title over and over, in both Arabic and English: EXECUTIVE ORDER 13769 OF JANUARY 27, 2017: PROTECTING THE NATION FROM FOREIGN TERRORIST ENTRY INTO THE UNITED STATES.

Foreign *terrorist* entry. At some point that night—he wasn't sure when—he'd started to weep. Anguish had filled his chest, his throat; anguish had pounded in his ears, a blood-borne anguish, a pressure that wouldn't ease or relent. It was this word that had stung the most: *terrorist*. And a full ban on all Syrian refugees—along with bans on immigrants from six other nations. Visas revoked, all around the world. Thousands of them. He'd stayed up all night, unable to sleep, reading and rereading the news articles with shock and confusion.

He told this to Annabel; she kept asking him questions. She'd been quiet in those first days; now she was curious about him, about the journey he'd taken to get here. In some ways, talking eased the pressure. The fractures that threatened to open on the margins of everything—that could spiral out of almost any moment, without warning—they lessened when he talked with Annabel. He told her this, too.

"Have you made any friends?" Annabel asked.

"Not that I know of," he said. He wanted to tell her that his family was coming and that it was only when they arrived that he'd begin his new life here. That he was incomplete. But somehow it was hard to tell her this, whereas it was easy to tell it to strangers. He told her instead about WhatsApp, and the group that had recently added him—a group of resettled Syrian teenagers on the East Coast. Naïm's phone automatically downloaded the photographs and images anyone sent to the Listserv. The images could be anything. They could be funny, or serious, or sad. He'd even posted an image of his Nike running shoes—donated by USAID—which felt like massive orange bubbles surrounding his feet. He'd also posted a photograph he'd taken of a robin—a robin with a bright red chest—perched on the railing of his apartment balcony. The hardest was when someone—usually someone who was struggling—posted an image from home. Those were the most difficult moments.

If a place changed in your absence, were you still a part of it? Or was it gone forever, receded into the departed past? And wouldn't it be better to uninstall WhatsApp? Wouldn't it be better to live here in West Falls Church, Virginia? Here in the Home of the Jaguars? He couldn't have his *phone* start to feel like his real life, like the life he actually cared about. Because then he'd become a ghost, too—a specter among embodied citizens—translucent, insubstantial.

Annabel listened. "You know," she said. "I've just made a decision."

"With the knitting?" Naïm said.

"Yes," she said, "with the knitting."

Naïm glanced over at the piano. Every day when he played, he'd see the same composition, a yellowed, handwritten score, sitting on the music rack. He could hear its beginning in his mind—just by glancing at the notes. And surely Annabel knew this. Gradually, he'd begun to understand what she was doing. He had questions about it—he wanted to ask her more about the piece—but he didn't want to give away his curiosity. It felt like an important secret to keep. It felt private. It was his own. "Did you ever play?" he asked.

"Me?" Annabel said, pausing in her stitch. "No. I always thought I would. But—somehow—it didn't come together."

Some other time, she said, she'd tell him about the composer of that song—the one that Annabel had hoped she'd someday learn to play. The composer had been a brilliant musician. And she'd once given an incredible gift to Annabel, an almost total stranger.

"She sounds kind."

It was funny. Naïm wondered if this was the way that his mother talked about him. He wondered what she said. *My poor son,* he imagined her telling someone at Sheetz. *I'm so worried about him.*

"I don't have," Naïm said, "that type of kindness in me."

"You don't?"

"I don't think so."

"But look at what you've helped me do," Annabel said, laying her knitting needles on her lap. "You've helped me knit this sweater."

Naïm realized that—in fact—she *had* finished. He looked at the garment that she was holding up in the air. He kept looking and looking—trying to control his laughter. But the more he tried to control it, the more it pushed to the surface. His body began to shake with the force of it. "Wow," he said. And then, again, laughing harder: "Wow."

Annabel took a moment to examine it at arm's length. She nodded. "It's really ugly, isn't it?"

"It's awful," Naïm agreed.

That afternoon, when Naïm closed the door and she was in her home, again—*alone*—she felt the finality of it, the finality of even the word itself. *Alone.* She'd never married, never had children, and that was easier now—thinking of the place she was going to. She'd felt herself falling toward it recently. She'd felt her mind plummet toward it—and the speed of the plunge would take her breath away. But she'd never quite made it. The tether to this world had always held.

That night, the home health aide assisted Annabel, as usual, helped her into the bathroom, where she washed her face and brushed her teeth. The aide was Eastern European; her name was Hasida Ribic; she'd emigrated from Bosnia as a teenager, fleeing that country's war with Serbia. She stood nearby, ready to catch Annabel if she fell—her hands out, her posture attentive.

Annabel put down her toothbrush and then—for some reason—paused to look in the mirror. It had been weeks since she'd really looked at herself, really paused to examine her appearance, to consider her image. Today, the look of her own face inspired tenderness within her. She'd inhabited this set of features for ninety years, her consciousness embedded within them, influenced by them, built out of them. *Ninety years*. In so many ways, that time was nothing. But in so many ways it was infinite.

Before she left, the home health aide helped Annabel change into a nightgown and get into bed. Annabel lay on top of the covers. The pillows cradled her head. She felt a deep, confusing drowsiness. Her dreams often started like this, with a sound or a picture. Then she'd follow that sound and the dreamworld would open around her. In her dreams she was almost never limited by an aging body; often she was young; often she possessed the vigor she'd had in her twenties and thirties and forties, when she'd never doubted her capacity, her ability, her power.

Tonight, as she fell asleep, Annabel was suddenly walking through an unfamiliar house, with rooms that seemed to shift in time as she moved through them. *What beauty*, she thought. *All these interiors of places that I've never been, things I've never seen.* She came through a set of double doors and stepped into a garden. It was night, but the flowers were illuminated, flowers of a kind—again—that Annabel had never encountered; lustrous and glowing from within, their corollas lit up the dark. Each flower was different; each flower was a separate light.

Now Annabel felt a surge of joy. Her troubles, her concerns, her worries—they all began to peel away. Stars had flooded the air above her. She looked up at them and imagined how she—how everyone—was hurtling toward them, away from them. *Intergalactic travelers*, she thought, *all of us*. Here we go. And what a lovely sky.

The next afternoon, Naïm let himself in with the spare key, as usual. "I brought a Kit Kat," he called out. Annabel loved Kit Kats—almost as much as he loved Skors. But he'd brought a Skor the day before, and he liked to provide her with some variety. "We can split it," he added.

But when he came around the corner, she wasn't in her customary place. The wheelchair was there, but it was empty. "Hello?" he called out. "Annabel?"

He worried immediately that she'd fallen, that she'd been unable to call for help. He hurried through the house, going into the kitchen, into the other rooms that he remembered from the previous year. Finally, he reached Annabel's bedroom. It, too, was empty. Had she been taken to the hospital overnight? There were footsteps in the hallway behind him. "Ah, good," he heard a woman's voice say. "I've got the paperwork right here."

Naïm turned around and saw a middle-aged woman; she wore pale blue jeans and had that same Inova badge, the badge from the hospital. She held a few folded sheets of paper in one hand and her cell phone in the other. "Where's Annabel?" Naïm said.

"I'm sorry," the woman said. "I assumed you were from the funeral home."

Naïm frowned. "Who are you?" he said.

The woman took a step back. She lifted her cell phone; she was clearly getting alarmed. Naïm raised his hands to indicate that he wasn't a threat. He told her his name. He said that he was Annabel's friend. Was everything okay? Where had she gone? Was there anything he could do?

She seemed startled, though, by his questions.

"I'm so sorry," she said, "didn't you know? Ms. Crandall passed away last night. The nurse found her this morning in her bed."

The days fell away with a kind of sameness. One after another, lacking differentiation. School was painful without the afternoon to look forward to; he couldn't concentrate on anything, couldn't focus, couldn't bring himself to care.

The funeral was on the following Saturday. Naïm attended by finding his way by himself to the big Episcopal church on Georgetown Pike. No matter how hard he'd tried, he'd been unable to convince Fatima to go with him. She'd been to enough funerals in her life, she told him. *Enough!* And she'd also have to ask for a day off from work—which she didn't yet feel comfortable doing. He couldn't say what he wanted to—to tell her that it was important to him that she be there, that she witness it, that she hear the service, and everything that would happen during it. His mother had simply decided not to go—and there was nothing he could do to make her relent. Her will was indomitable.

It was difficult to figure out how to get there; the church was in a part of the city that didn't have a nearby Metro station. He ended up walking down a series of sidewalk-free roads, with the traffic roaring by next to him, frightening him with every speeding vehicle. It wasn't just uncomfortable walking down these American roads, he'd decided, it was deeply hostile. They were designed to make sure he never wanted to do this again.

The nave of the building was dim, lit only by the natural light through the tall stained-glass window. Naïm took a funeral program and made his way to the seat that had been reserved for him in the front row. He greeted a few of Annabel's friends, shaking their hands, but not knowing what words to say. The coffin was already there, squat and soldierly on the altar, and Naïm felt himself staring at it, transfixed. How was it possible? How could Annabel be dead—there, in that small, glossy wooden box? The lifeless human body seemed like poor compensation for a lifetime of energetic thought.

The pastor took his place at the altar and began the funeral service. Naïm watched the other people for cues on when to stand, when to sit, when to kneel. Humility. That was the root of this all. Humility before the eternal mystery of death.

Naïm waited for his moment. Sitting there in the church, listening to the foreign vocabulary of the service, he felt awkward and out-of-place. Religious spaces, he thought, were similar throughout the world—but the religious spaces you belonged to felt different. They were a part of your personal relationship with God. Here, Naïm didn't feel that. He couldn't. He tried to relax, to mold his spine against the uncomfortable wooden back of the pew. But it was no use. Annabel's friends. Her cousins and nieces and nephews. He knew none of them. Where did he fit in? They all shared a sorrow; some of them seemed sadder than others; some seemed to be here almost as a formality. He could hear Annabel's voice, telling him about her childhood, asking him painful questions about his own. He felt her presence, in fact, all around him.

And then the pastor turned to the pew where Naïm was sitting. "I understand we have a young man here," the pastor said, "with whom Annabel spent a great deal of time as of late." Naïm felt his mouth go dry. He felt his hands begin to tremble. But the pastor continued. "And he would like to play an original composition—in Annabel's memory."

Naïm stood up. He walked the ten or fifteen feet to the piano that was positioned at the corner of the altar, conscious of the fact that everyone in the church was staring at him. He sat down.

Until a few days ago—when he'd arranged this all with Annabel's niece—Naïm hadn't considered how he might modify the song to fit his *new* body, how he might edit and change the chords to correspond to his diminished left hand. But he'd begun preparing for this moment, thinking through the finger placement. He'd have to stretch his middle finger so far—far beyond its natural reach—to play any three-fingered chord. The root note, the third, and then—*perhaps*—the fifth. But, still, it might be possible? he thought. *It might.* Why not play some of the chords without the fifth? he'd decided. It would be less dense, less secure in its harmonics, but it might still carry a similar emotional weight. There were a few other simple things he could do. Little changes. And so he'd penciled them in. And now, on this pale-lit afternoon, he began to play.

Marguerite's composition started with a few simple chords. Then there was a cluster of notes, notes that reminded Naïm of something he'd played before, at the International School on Salah al-Din—Erik Satie's *Gymnopédie No. 1*. He watched his hands moving across the keyboard, almost as if he were a spectator—an audience member and not a musician.

Naïm lost himself in the clear, echoing sound of the piano. The margins of his consciousness fell away, became permeable, porous. As he accumulated notes, as he built them slowly one on top of the next, something seemed to be happening at the sides of the room. At first it was just a shimmer, a smear, a place where the light caught and reflected back at him. But then Naïm was seeing shapes, luminous patches on the edge of his vision. Bright, streaky shapes shimmering in the doorway. Not even shapes, but sensations; something began to build in the air around him. And then he saw his father's face. His father's face and his body—wearing, of all things, his pajamas—solidifying in the corner of the room. His father was carrying a suitcase, which he set down. *My sweet boy*, he said. *I'm so glad to see you.* And then Omar was there, too, and he carried Aysha in his arms, cradling her just the way that he'd cradled her on that last morning on Tuhama Street. And Naïm's body was splitting into parts. He was playing the piano and he was also throwing his arms around his brother affectionately, feeling his brother's real, substantial flesh—and then looking down at his baby sister, who was asleep. Her fingers, he noticed, were like tiny drops of milky quartz.

You're here, he said. *I can't believe you made it.* And then his father nodded, and he told Naïm to go back to his playing—

325

they'd have time to catch up later. Omar sat on the floor in the aisle, cross-legged. He looked at his older brother with pride. It was *this* music, Naïm realized, that they'd been waiting to hear.

But even as Naïm felt this closeness, this sense of relief—*their long journey had finally ended*—his family began to flicker. They went slightly translucent; a wave passed through them. *No.* They couldn't have traveled this long, this far, just to disappear. That couldn't be it. One moment of connection—followed by a lifetime of remembered loss?

But then Naïm looked behind them and saw—slightly more shadowy—another group of people fading in. The far wall of the church was made of brick; it was unquestionably solid and substantial. The figures drifted in front of it, almost like a haze. And Naïm felt them soaring out and through him then as they lifted his playing up, pulled him skyward with the melody. They helped him shape the required structures of the song. His hand—his wounded hand—moved across the keyboard. Each note hurt. He struggled to keep up with the speed that the composition required.

Naïm glanced down, sight-reading, and glanced back up at the room. And then he recognized them, these other people—the family from the photograph that he'd found, all those months ago, in the Steinway. Here was the father—frustrated and impatient. Here was the mother—anxious and concerned. They all watched Naïm; they followed the movement of his hands across the ivory keys, the Schreger lines in the ivory catching with a kind of fire.

And there—in the middle of them all—was Marguerite. She nodded at Naïm and walked over to the piano. She sat on the bench. She reached out for a moment—only a moment—and brushed her fingertips against the paper of the score. Her expression was, Naïm thought, a little sad. She traced the notes with her fingertips, following along with the music, one hand opening and closing, marking time, a conductor's baton.

Naïm kept playing. He was surrounded by music—its rise and its fall. He was surrounded by ghosts.

EPILOGUE

The call from the Virginia number wasn't from someone Naïm's mother recognized, so she let it go to voicemail. When she listened to the message, though, she didn't understand it. So she brought it to Naïm. He listened. He didn't completely understand it, either. *The Law Offices of Kidwell and Kent are calling*, the message said, *for Fatima and Naïm Rahil.* They requested a call back at the earliest convenience.

It had been six weeks since the funeral. Naïm's days felt empty; he'd grown accustomed to Annabel's company and, quite honestly, to the piano. He'd continued doing exercises on his own, and now he'd begun thinking about how he might acquire a keyboard. He said nothing to his mother about it, though; she had enough to worry about on her own. She'd want to buy it for him, he knew, and he didn't trust her not to sacrifice something of her own in order to get something for him.

After discussing it, they decided that the next day, after school, Naïm would call the attorney's office on Fatima's behalf. They put the call on speakerphone. Was his mother in trouble? Naïm wondered. Had she done something wrong? It was difficult to imagine; she followed regulations at work to the smallest detail, arriving thirty minutes early for her shift, staying thirty minutes after she'd clocked out. Once the attorney got on the phone, she asked Naïm to confirm that he was a minor. He did. *We have a matter that we'd like to discuss in person*, she told him.

They came in the next day. Naïm skipped school; Fatima called in sick to work. They arrived at the offices and had to wait beyond the appointment time—there was an emergency matter that the firm had to take care of. Finally, the attorney came out of her office.

"I'm Sandra Kent," she said, reaching out to shake Fatima's hand. "So nice to meet you."

She ushered them into a conference room. She apologized for making them wait. She offered them coffee, or tea, or water. Both Naïm and Fatima declined. Sandra Kent arranged the folders on her desk, looked through one of them, and found the document she was looking for. "I just want to start by telling you," she said, "*congratulations!*"

Naïm and his mother looked at each other. Sensing their confusion, the attorney rushed to explain. She represented the estate of Annabel Crandall, she said. She was the executor of Annabel's will. And Annabel had—immediately before her death—modified that document. There had only been one change. The attorney looked at Naïm. He had been named as an heir, she told him. Specifically, Annabel had left Naïm—and his mother—the deed to her home.

"I'm sorry?" Naïm said. *Deed*, used in this context, was not a word he recognized. "Can you explain?"

She did. She said that the tax situation would be quite complex and, anticipating this, Annabel had instructed a small trust to be established to handle those details. They'd need representation, which Kidwell & Kent would be happy to provide at no cost. Both Fatima and Naïm were stunned. Later, in their apartment, they'd collapse wordlessly on the couch, nestled next to each other, Fatima holding her son in her arms, holding him close to her body, rocking him softly, back and forth, back and forth, like she had when he was a very small child. Naïm would tell her then about his afternoons with Annabel, and how she'd given them the food, helped sustain them through that crisis. He'd talk about his time in Annabel's house, walking from room to room in his imagination, trying to understand how that space could now be—in any way—their own.

But that day at Kidwell & Kent—after about an hour—Naïm and Fatima got up to leave. The attorney walked them to the door. As they were about to go, however, she grabbed Naïm's shoulder. "I almost forgot!" she said. She disappeared into the office. They waited. After a few minutes, Sandra Kent reemerged, holding a white plastic shopping bag. "She also left you this," the attorney said. And then—from the bag, bright as a second sunrise—she pulled out the yellow sweater.

Naïm took it. The garment was surprisingly light in his hands; its yarn had a gauzy, delicate feel. It was cotton, he knew—Annabel had told him that—but, even so, its lack of weight seemed implausible. How could it be so insubstantial—something they'd spent so many hours making? It had no heft, no bulk, no body. It barely weighed anything at all.

ACKNOWLEDGMENTS

My largest debt of gratitude—among so many—goes to Tim O'Connell, my editor at Simon & Schuster, who had the vision to see the *potential* book within the first draft, and the (seemingly) unending patience to coach me through seven years of work, enduring version after version, as we got sometimes closer and, unfortunately, sometimes farther away. Thank you for the steady hand at the wheel.

To Bill Clegg, my agent—I have no idea how you did it all—applying sober counsel, early editorial advice, and good-humored critique as needed. You are a unique talent and a bright light. Thank you so resoundingly.

To Will Aime, Rūta Toutonghi, Steve Toutonghi, Simon Toop, Maria Mendez, Cheston Knapp, and Peyton Marshall—my first readers—deep thanks as well.

And thanks to Hawthornden Castle, where in 2015 I began this novel.

And to Phineas and Beatrix—I'm so proud of you. I hope you read this someday and think of me, your father.

ABOUT THE TYPE

This book is set in New Aster, which was designed by Francesco Simoncini in 1958. As shown in its inclination toward Transitional characteristics, Aster is the result of designerss looking to old-fashioned values in the typographical world due to the effects of World War II.

ABOUT THE AUTHOR

Pauls Toutonghi's parents were both refugees to the United States. He has been awarded a Pushcart Prize, an Andrew W. Mellon research fellowship, a Fulbright Grant, and a residency at Hawthornden Castle. He has written for *The New Yorker*, *The New York Times Book Review*, *Outside* magazine, *Sports Illustrated*, *Granta*, *Tin House*, and other periodicals. He's married to the novelist Peyton Marshall. He lives in Oregon, where he teaches at Lewis & Clark College

2 1982 32419 6686